Praise for Michael Swanwick's
Nebula Award-winning masterwork

STATIONS OF THE TIDE

"Unusually effective . . .
Swanwick spins a solid tale and even manages
a truly transcendent finale."
Houston Post

"A sinuous narrative, worldly and very agreeably perverse."
William Gibson, author of *Virtual Light*

"Evocative and lushly inventive.
Hard-edged and exotic, full of terror and high technology,
mystery and magic, this is sure to be
one of the most prominent novels of the year."
Isaac Asimov's Science Fiction Magazine

"Intelligent, literate and compelling—high-quality
entertainment . . . a haunting story of changes and magic . . .
an expert orchestration of bizarrely beautiful images."
Pat Cadigan, author of *Patterns*

"A tour-de-force . . . a clever read, a wise book . . .
quite simply marvelous."
New York Review of Science Fiction

"A beautifully written, endlessly inventive book."
Paul Park, author of *Celestis*

"A magical book . . . wonderfully inventive,
exotic yet hauntingly familiar, important,
funny, intelligent, and visionary.
Michael Swanwick is a true seer,
in the best sense of that word."
David Zindell, author of *The Wild*

Other Avon Books by
Michael Swanwick

THE IRON DRAGON'S DAUGHTER
JACK FAUST

MICHAEL SWANWICK

STATIONS OF THE TIDE

AVON BOOKS ▰ NEW YORK

A leatherbound signed first edition of this book has been privately printed by The Easton Press.

AVON BOOKS
A division of
The Hearst Corporation
1350 Avenue of the Americas
New York, New York 10019

First Avon Books Trade Printing: September 1997
First Avon Books Mass Market Printing: March 1992

Printed in the U.S.A.

OPM 10 9 8 7 6 5 4 3 2 1

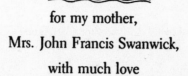

for my mother,
Mrs. John Francis Swanwick,
with much love

Acknowledgments

The author is indebted to David Hartwell for suggesting where to look, Stan Robinson for the gingerbread-maddrake trick, Tim Sullivan and Greg Frost for early comments and Greg Frost again for designing the briefcase's nanotechnics, Gardner Dozois for chains of the sea and for teaching the bureaucrat how to survive, Marianne for insights into bureaucracy, Bob Walters for dino parts, Alice Guerrant for whale wallows and other Tidewater features, Sean for the game of Suicide, Don Keller for nominal assistance, Jack and Jeanne Dann for the quote from Bruno, which I took from their hotel room when they weren't looking, and Giulio Camillo for his memory theater, here expanded to a palace; Camillo was one of the most famous men of his century, a thought which should give us all pause. Any book's influences are too numerous to mention, but riffs lifted from C. L. Moore, Dylan Thomas, Brian Aldiss, Ted Hughes, and Jamaica Kincaid are too blatant to pass unacknowledged. This novel was written under a Challenge Grant from the M. C. Porter Endowment for the Arts.

1

The Leviathan in Flight

The bureaucrat fell from the sky.

For an instant Miranda lay blue and white beneath him, the icecaps fat and ready to melt, and then he was down. He took a highspeed across the stony plains of the Piedmont to the heliostat terminus at Port Richmond, and caught the first flight out. The airship *Leviathan* lofted him across the fall line and over the forests and coral hills of the Tidewater. Specialized ecologies were astir there, preparing for the transforming magic of the jubilee tides. In ramshackle villages and hidden plantations people made their varied provisions for the evacuation.

The *Leviathan*'s lounge was deserted. Hands clasped behind him, the bureaucrat stared moodily out the stern windows. The Piedmont was dim and blue, a storm front on the horizon. He imagined the falls, where fish-hawks hovered on rising thermals and the river Noon cascaded down and lost its name. Below, the Tidewater swarmed with life, like blue-green mold growing magnified in a petri dish. The thought of all the mud and poverty down there depressed him. He yearned for the cool, sterile environments of deep space.

Bright specks of color floated on the brown water, coffles of houseboats being towed upriver as the haut-bourgeois prudently made for the Port Richmond incline while the rates were still low. He touched a window control and the jungle leaped up at him, misty trees resolving into individual leaves. The heliostat's shadow rippled along the north bank of the river, skimming lightly over mud flats, swaying phragmites, and gnarled water oaks. Startled, a clutch of acorn-mimetic octopi dropped from a low branch, brown circles of water fleeing as they jetted into the silt.

"Smell that air," Korda's surrogate said.

The bureaucrat sniffed. He smelled the faint odor of soil from the baskets of hanging vines, and a sweet whiff of droppings from the wicker birdcages. "Could use a cleansing, I suppose."

"You have no romance in your soul." The surrogate leaned against the windowsill, straight-armed, looking like a sentimental skeleton. The flickering image of Korda's face reflected palely in the glass. "I'd give anything to be down here in your place."

"Why don't you, then?" the bureaucrat asked sourly. "You have seniority."

"Don't be flippant. This is not just another smuggling case. The whole concept of technology control is at stake here. If we let just one self-replicating technology through—well, you know how fragile a planet is. If the Division has any justification for its existence at all, it's in exactly this sort of action. So I would appreciate it if just this once you would make the effort to curb your negativism."

"I have to say what I think. That's what I'm being paid for, after all."

"A very common delusion." Korda moved away from the window, bent to pick up an empty candy dish, and glanced at its underside. There was a fussy nervousness to his motions strange to one who had actually met him. Korda in person was heavy and lethargic. Surrogation seemed to bring out a submerged persona, an overfastidious little man normally kept drowned in flesh. "Native pottery always has an unglazed area on the bottom, have you noticed?"

"That's where it stands in the kiln." Korda looked blank. "This is a planet, it has a constant gravity. You can't fire things in zero gravity here."

With a baffled shake of his head Korda put down the dish. "Was there anything else you wanted to cover?" he asked.

"I put in a Request For—"

"—Authority. Yes, yes, I have it on my desk. I'm afraid it's right out of the question. Technology Transfer is in a very delicate position with the planetary authorities. Now don't look at me like that. I routed it through offworld ministry to the Stone House, and they said no. They're touchy about intrusions on their autonomy down here. They sent the Request straight back. With restrictions—you are specifically admonished not to carry weapons, perform arrests, or in any way represent yourself as having authority to coerce cooperation on your suspect's part." He reached up and tilted a basket of vines, so he could fossick about among them. When he let it go, it swung irritably back and forth.

"How am I going to do my job? I'm supposed to—what?— just walk up to Gregorian and say, Excuse me, I have no authority even to speak to you, but I have reason to suspect that you've taken something that doesn't belong to you, and wonder if you'd mind terribly returning it?"

There were several writing desks built into the paneling under the windows. Korda swung one out and made a careful inventory of its contents: paper, charcoal pens, blotters. "I don't see why you're being so difficult about this," he said at last. "Don't pout, I know you can do it. You're competent enough when you put your mind to it. Oh, and I almost forgot, the Stone House has agreed to assign you a liaison. Someone named Chu, out of internal security."

"Will he have authority to arrest Gregorian?"

"In theory, I'm sure he will. But you know planetary government—in practice I suspect he'll be more interested in keeping an eye on you."

"Terrific." Ahead, a pod of sounding clouds swept toward them, driven off of Ocean by winds born half a world away. The *Leviathan* lifted its snout a point, then plunged ahead. The light faded to gray, and rain drenched the heliostat. "We don't even know where to find the man."

Korda folded the desk back into the wall. "I'm sure you won't have any trouble finding someone who knows where he is."

The bureaucrat glared out into the storm. Raindrops drummed against the fabric of the gas bag, pounded the windows, and were driven down. Winds bunched the rain in great waves, alternating thick washes of water with spates of relative calm. The land dissolved, leaving the airship suspended in chaos. The din of rain and straining engines made it difficult to talk. It felt like the end of the world. "You realize that in a few months, all this will be under water? If we haven't settled Gregorian's case by then, it'll never be done."

"You'll be done long before then. I'm sure you'll be back at the Puzzle Palace in plenty of time to keep your sub from taking over your post." Korda's face smiled, to indicate that he was joking.

"You didn't tell me you'd given someone my duties. Just who do you have subbing for me anyway?"

"Philippe was gracious enough to agree to hold down the fort for the duration."

"Philippe!" There was a cold prickling at the back of his neck, as if sharks were circling overhead. "You gave my post to Philippe?"

"I thought you liked Philippe."

"I like him fine," the bureaucrat said. "But is he right for the job?"

"Don't take it so personally. There's work to be done, and Philippe is very good at this sort of thing. Should the Division grind to a halt just because you're away? Frankly that's not an attitude I want to encourage." The surrogate reopened the writing desk, removed a television set, and switched it on. The sound boomed, and he turned it down to the mumbling edge of inaudibility. He flipped through the channels, piling image upon image, dissatisfied with them all.

The *Leviathan* broke free of the clouds. Sunlight flooded the lounge, and the bureaucrat blinked, dazzled. The airship's shadow on the bright land below was wrapped in a diffuse rainbow. The ship lifted joyously, searching for the top of the sky.

"Are you looking for something on that thing, or just fidgeting with it because you know it's annoying?"

Korda looked hurt. He straightened, turning his back on the set. "I thought I might find one of Gregorian's commercials. It would give you some idea what you're up against. Never mind. I really do have to be getting back to work. Be a good lad, and see if you can't handle this thing in an exemplary fashion, hmm? I'm relying on you."

They shook hands, and Korda's face vanished from the surrogate. On automatic, the device returned itself to storage.

"Philippe!" the bureaucrat said. "Those bastards!" He felt sickly aware that he was losing ground rapidly. He had to wrap this thing up, and get back to the Puzzle Palace as quickly as possible. Philippe was the acquisitive type. He leaned forward and snapped off the television.

When the screen went dead, everything was subtly changed, as if a cloud had passed from the sun, or a window opened into a stuffy room.

He sat for a time, thinking. The lounge was all air and light, with sprays of orchids arranged in sconces between the windows and rainbirds singing in the wicker cages hung between the pots of vines. It was appointed for the tourist trade, but, ironically, planetary authority had closed down the resorts in the Tidewater to discourage those selfsame tourists, experience having shown offworlders to be less tractable to evacuation officers than were natives. Yet for all their obvious luxury, the fixtures had been designed with economy of weight foremost and built of the lightest materials available, cost be damned. They'd never recover the added expense with fuel savings; it had all been done to spite the offworld battery manufacturers.

The bureaucrat was sensitive to this kind of friction. It arose wherever the moving edge of technology control touched on local pride.

"Excuse me, sir." A young man entered, carrying a small table. He was wearing an extraordinary gown, all shimmering moons and stars, ogres and ibises, woven into a cloth that dopplered from deepest blue to profoundest red and back again as he moved. He set the table down, drew a cloth away from the top to reveal a fishbowl without any fish, and extended a white-gloved hand. "I'm Lieutenant Chu, your liaison officer."

They shook. "I thought I was to be assigned somebody from internal security," the bureaucrat said.

"We like to keep a low profile when we operate in the Tidewater, you understand." Chu opened the robe. Underneath he was dressed in airship-corps blues. "Currently, I'm posing as an entertainment officer." He spread his arms, tilted his head coquettishly, as if waiting for a compliment. The bureaucrat decided he did not like Chu.

"This is ludicrous. There's no need for all this hugger-mugger. I only want to talk with the man, that's all."

A disbelieving smile. Chu had cheeks like balls and a small star-shaped mark by his left eye that disappeared when his mouth turned up. "What will you do when you catch up with him then, sir?"

"I'll interview him to determine whether he's in possession of contraband technology. Then, if it develops that he is, it's my job to educate him as to his responsibilities and convince him to return it. That's all I'm authorized to do."

"Suppose he says no. What will you do then?"

"Well, I'm certainly not going to beat him up and drag him off to prison, if that's what you mean." The bureaucrat patted his stomach. "Just look at this paunch."

"Perhaps," Chu said judiciously, "you have some of the offplanet science powers one sees on television. Muscle implants and the like."

"Proscribed technology is proscribed technology. If we employed it, we'd be no better than criminals ourselves." The bureaucrat coughed, and with sudden energy said, "Where shall we start?"

The liaison officer straightened with a jerk, like a puppet seized by its strings, immediately all business. "If it's all the same to you, sir, I'd like to learn first how much you know about Gregorian, what leads you have, and so on. Then I can make my own report."

"He's a very charming man, to begin with," the bureaucrat said. "Everyone I've spoken with agrees on that. A native Mirandan, born somewhere in the Tidewater. His background is a bit murky. He worked for some years in the bioscience labs in the Outer Circle. Good work, as I understand it, but nothing exceptional. Then, about a month ago, he quit, and returned to Miranda. He's set himself up as some kind of bush wizard, I understand. A witch doctor or something, you doubtless have more information on that than I do. But shortly after he left, it was discovered that he may have misappropriated a substantial item of proscribed technology. That's when Technology Transfer got involved."

"That's not supposed to be possible." Chu smiled mockingly. "Tech Transfer's embargo is supposed to be absolute."

"It happens."

"What was stolen?"

"Sorry."

"That important, eh?" Chu made a thoughtful, clicking noise with his tongue. "Well, what do we know about the man himself?"

"Surprisingly little. His likeness, of course, geneprint, a scattering of standard clearance profiles. Interviews with a few acquaintances. He seems to have had no real friends, and he never discussed his past. In retrospect it seems clear he'd been keeping his record as uncluttered as possible. He must have been planning the theft for years."

"Do you have a dossier on him?"

"A copy of Gregorian's dossier," the bureaucrat said. He opened the briefcase, removed the item, gave it a little shake.

Chu craned curiously. "What else have you got in there?"

"Nothing," the bureaucrat said. He swiveled the briefcase to show it was empty, then handed over the dossier. It had been printed in the white lotus format currently popular in the high worlds, and folded into a handkerchief-sized square.

"Thank you." Chu held the dossier over his head and twisted his hand. The square of paper disappeared. He turned his hand back and forth to demonstrate that it was empty.

The bureaucrat smiled. "Do that again."

"Oh, the first rule of magic is never do the same trick twice in a row. The audience knows what to expect." His eyes glittered insolently. "But if I might show you one thing more?"

"Is it relevant?"

Chu shrugged. "It's instructive, anyway."

"Oh, go ahead," the bureaucrat said. "As long as it doesn't take too long."

Chu opened a cage and lifted out a rainbird. "Thank you." With a gesture, he dimmed the windows, suffusing the lounge with twilight. "I open my act with this illusion. Thusly:"

He bowed deeply and swept out a hand. His movements were all jerky, distinct, artificial. "Welcome, dear friends, countrymen, and offworlders. It is my duty and pleasure today to entertain and enlighten you with legerdemain and scientific patter." He cocked an eyebrow. "Then I go into a little rant about the mutability of life here, and its myriad forms of adaptation to the jubilee tides. Where Terran flora and fauna—most particularly including ourselves—cannot face the return of Ocean, to the native biota the tides are merely a passing and regular event. Evolution, endless eons of periodic flooding, blah blah blah. Sometimes I compare Nature to a magician—myself by implication—working changes on a handful of tricks. All of which leads in to the observation that much of the animal life here is dimorphic, which means simply that it has two distinct forms, depending on which season of the great year is in effect.

"Then I demonstrate." He held the rainbird perched on his forefinger, gently stroking its head. The long tailfeathers hung down like teardrops. "The rainbird is a typical shapeshifter. When the living change comes over the Tidewater, when Ocean rises to drown half of Continent, it adapts by transforming into a more appropriate configuration." Suddenly he plunged both hands deep into the bowl of water. The bird struggled wildly, and disappeared in a swirl of bubbles and sand.

The illusionist lifted his hands from the water. The bureaucrat noted that he had not so much as gotten his sleeves wet.

When the water cleared, a multicolored fish was swimming in great agitation in the water, long fins trailing behind. "Behold!" Chu cried. "The sparrowfish—in great summer morph an aviform, and a pisciform for the great winter. One of the marvelous tricks that Nature here plays."

The bureaucrat applauded. "Very neatly done," he said with only slight irony.

"I also do tricks with a jar of liquid helium. Shattering roses and the like."

"I doubt that will be necessary. You said there was a point to your demonstration?"

"Absolutely." The illusionist's eyes glittered. "It's this: Gregorian is going to be a very difficult man to catch. He's a magician, you see, and native to the Tidewater. He can change his own form, or that of his enemy, whichever he pleases. He can kill with a thought. More importantly, he understands the land here, and you don't. He can tap its power and use it against you."

"You don't actually believe that Gregorian is a magician? That he has supernatural powers, I mean."

"Implicitly."

In the face of that fanatical certainty, the bureaucrat did not know what to say. "Ahem. Yes. Thank you for your concern. Now, what say we get down to business?"

"Oh yes, sir, immediately, sir." The young man touched a pocket, and then another. His expression changed, grew pained. In an embarrassed voice he said, "Ah . . . I'm afraid I left my materials in the forward stowage. If you would wait?"

"Of course." The bureaucrat tried not to be pleased by the young man's obvious discomfort.

With Chu gone, the bureaucrat returned to his contemplation of the passing forest below. The airship soared and curved, dipped its nose and sank low in the air. The bureaucrat remembered his first sighting of it back in Port Richmond, angling in for a docking. Complex with flukes, elevators, and lifting planes, the great airship somehow transcended the antique awkwardness of its design. It descended slowly, gracefully, rotor blades thundering. Barnacles covered its underbelly, and mooring ropes hung from its jaws like strings of kelp.

A few minutes later the *Leviathan* docked at a heliostat tower at the edge of a dusty little river town. A lone figure in crisp white climbed the rope ladder, and then the heliostat cast off again. Nobody debarked.

The lounge door opened, and a slim woman in the uniform of internal security entered. She strode forward, hand extended, to offer her credentials. "Lieutenant-Liaison Emilie Chu," she said. Then, "Sir? Are you quite all right?"

2

Witch Cults of Whitemarsh

Gregorian kissed the old woman and threw her from the cliff. She fell toward the cold gray water headfirst, twisting. There was a small white splash as she hit, plunging deep beneath the chop. She did not surface. A little distance away, something dark and sleek as an otter broke water, dove, and disappeared.

"It's a trick," the real Lieutenant Chu said. On the screen Gregorian's face appeared: heavy, mature, confident. His lips moved soundlessly. Be all that you were meant to be. The bureaucrat had killed the sound after the fifth repetition, but he knew the words by heart. Give up your weaknesses. Dare to live forever. The commercial ended, skipped to the beginning, and began again.

"A trick? How so?"

"A bird cannot change into a fish in an instant. That kind of adaptation takes time." Lieutenant Chu rolled up her sleeve and reached into the fishbowl. The sparrowfish jerked away, bright fins swirling. Dark sand puffed up, obscuring the tank for an instant. "The sparrowfish is a burrower. It was in the sand

21

when he thrust the rainbird into the water. One quick movement, like this," she demonstrated, "and the bird is strangled. Plunge it into the dirt, and simultaneously the fish is startled into swimming."

She set the small corpse down on the table. "Simple, when you know how it's done."

Gregorian kissed the old woman and threw her from the cliff. She fell toward the cold gray water headfirst, twisting. There was a small white splash as she hit, plunging deep beneath the chop. She did not surface. A little distance away, something dark and sleek as an otter broke water, dove, and disappeared.

The bureaucrat snapped off the television.

The government liaison leaned straight-backed against a window, the creases of her uniform imperially crisp, smoking a thin black cigarillo. Emilie Chu was thin herself, a whippet of a woman, with cynical eyes and the perpetual hint of a sneer to her lips. "No word from Bergier. It appears my impersonator has escaped." She stroked her almost-invisible mustache with cool amusement.

"We don't know that he's gone yet," the bureaucrat reminded her. The windows were clear now, and in the fresh, bright air the encounter with the false Chu seemed unlikely, the stuff of travelers' tales. "Let's go see the commander."

The rear observatory was filled with uniformed schoolgirls on a day trip from the Laserfield Academy, who nudged each other and giggled as the bureaucrat followed Chu up an access ladder and through a hatch into the interior of the gas bag. The hatch closed, and the bureaucrat stood within the triangular strutting of the keel. It was dark between the looming gas cells, and a thin line of overhead lights provided more a sense of dimension than illumination. A crewman dropped to the walkway before them. "Passengers are not—" She saw Chu's uniform and stiffened.

"Commander-Pilot Bergier, please," the bureaucrat said.

"You want to see the commander?" She stared, as if he were a sphinx materialized from nothing to confront her with a particularly outrageous riddle.

"If it isn't too much trouble," Chu said with quiet menace.

The woman spun on her heel. She led them through the gullet of the airship to the prow, where stairs so steep they had to be climbed on all fours like a ladder rose to the pilothouse. On the dark wooden door was the faintest gleam of elfinbone inlay forming a large, pale rose-and-phallus design. The crewman gave three quick raps, and then seized a strut and swung up into the shadows, as agile as any monkey. A deep voice rumbled, "Enter."

They opened the door and stepped within.

The pilothouse was small. Its windshield was shuttered, leaving it lit only by a triad of navigation screens to the fore. It had a lived-in smell of body sweat and stale clothing. Commander Bergier stood hunched over the screens, looking like an aging eagle, his face a pale beak, suddenly noble when he raised his chin, a scrawny-bearded poet brooding over the bright terrain of his world. Turning, he raised eyes fixed on some distant tragedy more compelling than present danger could ever be. Two dark cuplines curved under each eye. "Yes?" he said.

Lieutenant Chu saluted crisply, and the bureaucrat, remembering in time that all airship commanders held parallel commissions in internal security, offered his credentials. Bergier glanced down at them, handed them back. "Not everyone welcomes your sort on our planet, sir," the commander said. "You keep us in poverty, you live off our labor, you exploit our resources, and you pay us with nothing but condescension."

The bureaucrat blinked, astonished. Before he could frame a response, the commander continued, "However, I am an officer, and I understand my duty." He popped a lozenge into his mouth and sucked noisily. A rotten-sweet smell filled the cabin. "Make your demands."

"I'm not making any demands," the bureaucrat began. "I only—"

"There speaks the voice of power. You maintain a stranglehold on the technology that could turn Miranda into an earthly paradise. You control manufacturing processes that allow you to undercut our economy at will. We exist at your whim and sufferance and in the form you think good. Then you walk in here carrying this whip and making demands you doubtless prefer to call requests and pretend it is for our own good. Let us not cap this performance with hypocrisy, sir."

"Technology didn't exactly make an 'earthly paradise' of Earth. Or don't they teach classical history here?"

"The perfect display of arrogance. You deny us our material heritage, and now you have as good as asked me to thank you for it. Well, sir, I will not. I have my pride. And I—" He paused. In the sudden silence it was observable how his head nodded slightly at irregular intervals, as if he fought off sleep. His mouth opened and shut, opened and shut again. His eyes slid slowly to the side in search of his lost thought. "And, ah. And, ah—"

"The illusionist," the bureaucrat insisted. "Lieutenant Chu's impersonator. Have you found him yet?"

Bergier straightened, his fire and granite restored. "No, sir, we have not. We have not found him, for he is not here to be found. He has left the ship."

"That's not possible. You docked once, and nobody debarked. I was watching."

"This is a seaward flight. It is all but empty. On the landward run, yes, perhaps an agile and determined man could evade me. But I have accounted for every passenger and had my crew open every stowage compartment and equipment niche in the *Leviathan*. I went so far as to send an engineer with an airpack up the gas vents. Your man is not here."

"It's only logical he'd've secured his escape beforehand. Maybe he had a collapsible glider hidden forward," Chu suggested. "It wouldn't have been difficult for an athletic man. He could have just opened a window and slipped away."

More likely, the bureaucrat thought, and the thought struck him with the force of inevitability, more likely he had simply bribed the captain to lie for him. That was how he himself would've arranged it. To cover his suspicion, he said, "What bothers me is why Gregorian went to all this trouble to find out how much we know about him. It hardly seems worth his effort."

Bergier scowled at his screens, said nothing. He touched a control, and the timbre of one engine changed, grew deeper. Slowly, slowly the ship began to turn.

"He was just baiting you," Chu said. "Nothing more complicated than that."

"Is that likely?" the bureaucrat said dubiously.

"Magicians are capable of anything. Their thinking isn't easy to follow. Hey! Maybe that was Gregorian himself? He was wearing gloves, after all."

"Pictures of Gregorian and of our impersonator," the bureaucrat said. "Front and side both." He removed them from his briefcase, shook off the moisture, laid them side by side beside the screens. "No, look at that—it's absurd to even contemplate. What does his wearing gloves have to do with anything?"

Chu carefully compared the tall, beefy figure of Gregorian with the slight figure of her impersonator. "No," she agreed. "Just look at those faces." Gregorian had a dark, animal power, even in the picture. He looked more minotaur than man, so strong-jawed and heavy-browed that he passed through mere homeliness into something profound. His was the sort of face that would seem ugly in repose, then waken to beauty at the twitch of a grin, the slow wink of one eye. It could never have been hidden in the pink roundness of the false Chu's face.

"Our intruder wore gloves because he was a magician." Lieutenant Chu wriggled her fingers. "Magicians tattoo their hands, one marking for each piece of lore they master, starting from the middle finger and moving up the wrist. A magus will have 'em up to the elbows. Snakes and moons and whatnot. If you'd seen his hands, you'd never have mistaken him for a Piedmont official."

Bergier cleared his throat and, when they both turned to him, said, "With the technology you deny us, a single man could operate this ship. Alone, he could manage all functions from baggage to public relations with nary a crewman under him."

"That same technology would make your job superfluous," the bureaucrat pointed out. "Do you think for an instant that your government would pay for an expensive luxury like this airship if they could have a fleet of fast, cheap, atmosphere-destroying shuttles?"

"Tyranny always has its rationale."

Before the bureaucrat could respond, Chu interjected, "We've located Gregorian's mother."

"Have we?"

"Yes." Chu grinned so cockily the bureaucrat realized this must be something she had dug up on her own initiative. "She lives in a river town just below Lightfoot. There's no heliostat station there, but if we can't find somebody to rent us a boat, it's not a long walk. That'll be the best place to start our investigation. After that we'll tackle the television spots, see if we can trace the money. All television is broadcast from the Piedmont, but if you want to follow up on the ads, there's a gate at the heliostat station, that's no problem."

"We'll visit the mother first thing tomorrow morning," the bureaucrat said. "But I've dealt with planetside banks before, and I very seriously doubt we'll be able to follow the money."

Bergier looked at him scornfully. "Money can always be traced. It leaves a trail of slime behind it wherever it goes."

The bureaucrat smiled, unconvinced. "That's very aphoristic."

"Don't you dare laugh at me! I had five wives in the Tidewater when I was younger." Bergier popped another lozenge, mouthed it liquidly. "I had them placed where they could do the most good, spaced out along my route distant enough that not one suspected the existence of the others." The bureaucrat saw that the commander did not observe how Chu rolled her eyes when he said this. "But then I discovered that my Ysolt was unfaithful. It drove me half mad with jealousy. That was not long after the witch cults were put down. I returned to her that day after an absence of weeks. Oh, she was hot. Her period had just begun. The whole house smelled of her." His nostrils flared. "You have no idea what she was like at such times. I walked in the door, and she slammed me to the floor and ripped open my uniform. She was naked. It was like being raped by a whirlwind. All I could think was that we must avoid scandalizing the neighbors.

"It would have made a fish laugh to see me struggling beneath that little hellcat, I should imagine. Red-faced, half-undressed, and flailing out with one arm to close the door.

"Well and good. I was a young man. But the things she did to me! From somewhere she had acquired skills I had not taught her, ideas that were not mine. Some of them things such as I had never experienced. We had been married for years. Now, all at once, she had acquired new tastes. Where had she learned them, hey? Where?"

"Maybe she read a book," Chu said dryly.

"Bah! She had a lover! It was obvious. She was not a subtle woman, Ysolt. She was like a child, showing off a new toy. Why don't we see what happens if, she said . . . Let's pretend you're the woman and I'm the man . . . This time I'm not going to move at all, and you can . . . It took her hours to demonstrate everything she had learned—'thought of,' she said—and I had a lot of time to mull over what I should do.

"It was dark when I left her. She was sleeping it off, her long black hair sticking to her sweaty little breasts. What an angelic smile she had! I went out to discover who had cuckolded me, and I brought along a gun. He would not be difficult to find, I determined. A man with such skill as Ysolt mirrored would be known in the right quarters.

"I went down to the riverbank, to the jugs and paintpots, and asked a few questions. They said yes, a man with the kind of skill I described had been through recently." A hidden speaker mumbled respectfully, and Bergier touched the controls. "Trim the port aerostat manually if you have to. Yes. No. You have your orders." He was silent for a long, forlorn moment, and the bureaucrat thought he had lost the thread of his tale. But then he began again.

"But I could not find the man. Everyone had heard of him— word had gone round like the latest dirty joke—and many hinted they had slept with him, but he was not to be found. There were a lot of odd types afoot in those days, after the suppression of Whitemarsh, and a sex-artist was the least of them. I learned that he was of moderate size, polite dress, wry humor. That he spoke little, lived off the largess of women, had dark eyes, rarely blinked. But the river lands swarmed with people who had something to hide. A cautious man could hide there forever, and he was the most evasive creature in the world. He moved unseen and un- noted through the night world, made no promises, had no friends, established no rhythms. It was like punching empty air! He was not to be found.

"After a few days, I changed my tactics. I decided Ysolt should find him for me. So I made myself impotent. You un- derstand how? With my fist. Old Mother Hand and her five daughters. By the time Ysolt got to me, there was nothing could make the old soldier stand erect for her. It drove her to distraction. And I, of course, feigned embarrassment, humiliation, distress. After a time I simply refused to try.

"Sure enough, she was driven back to her lover, to this man of extraordinary skill and knowledge. She returned to me with breathing exercises and relaxation techniques that ought to have worked, but did not. All this time, I acted cold and distant toward her. It was only natural she would assume that I was blaming her for my disability. By the time the corps called me back to duty, she was ready to do anything to effect my cure.

"When next I returned, she had 'discovered' a man who could aid me in my distress. She knew I didn't approve of the witch cultists. But he could prepare a potion for me. It would cost a great deal. She did not like that part. A man should not charge for such a thing. But a husband's happiness was so important to his wife. . . . She finally persuaded me.

"That night I filled a small, heavy box with silver and went as directed to a small garage just below the docks. There was a blue light over the side door. I went in.

"The minute the door closed, someone threw on every light in the place. My eyes crawled. Then the bright sting of vision resolved into automobiles, racks of grease guns, welding tanks. There were six waiting for me, two of them women. They sat in truck cabs and atop hoods, looking at me with unfriendly eyes, as unblinking as owls."

The speaker murmured again, and Bergier jerked his head to the side. "Why are you bothering me with this? I don't want to be disturbed with routine." Then, returning to his story, "One of the women asked to see my money. I opened my box, took out a moleskin bag containing eighty *fleur-de-vie* dollars, and threw it at her feet. She untied the bag, saw the flash of mint silver, and drew in her breath. This came from Whitemarsh, she said.

"I said nothing.

"The cultists traded glances. I slid a hand inside my coat and clutched my revolver. We need the money, a man said. The government dogs are slavering over our shoulders. I can smell their filthy breath.

"The woman held up a handful of silver, flashing like so

many mirrors. There was a coinmaker disappeared just before the rape of Whitemarsh, she said. They took his stock and gave it away to whoever wanted it. I was there, but felt I didn't need it. She shrugged. How quickly things change.

"I knew they thought I'd robbed a brother fugitive. I don't suppose you know much about the suppression of Whitemarsh?"

"No," the bureaucrat said.

"Only hearsay," Chu said. "It's not exactly the sort of history they teach in school."

"They should," the commander said. "Let the children know what government is all about. This was back when the Tidewater was young, and communes and utopian communities were as common as mushrooms. Harmless, most of them were, pallid things here and gone in a month. But the Whitemarsh cults were different; they spread like marsh-fire. Men and women went naked in public daylight. They would not eat meat. They participated in ritual orgies. They refused to serve in the militia. Factories closed for want of laborers. Crops went unharvested. Children were not properly schooled. Private citizens minted their own coinage. They had no leaders. They paid no taxes. No government would have tolerated it.

"We fell on them with fire and steel. In a single day we destroyed the cults, drove the survivors into hiding, and showed them such horror they would never dare rise again. So you understand that I was in great danger. But I did not show fear. I asked them, did they want the money or not?

"One of the men took the bag, weighed it in his hand. Then, as I had hoped, he slid a handful of coins into each of his trousers pockets. We will divide this evenly, he said. So long as the spirit is alive, Whitemarsh is not dead. He threw me a greasy bundle of herbs, and said sneeringly, This would make a corpse rise, much less your limp little self.

"I dropped the bundle in my lead box and left. At home I

beat Ysolt until she bled and threw her out in the street. I waited a week, and then reported to internal security that fugitive cultists were hiding in my area. They ran a scan and found the coins, and with the coins the cultists. I still did not know which specific one had defiled my Ysolt, but they all still held most of the coins, so he had been punished. Oh yes, he had been punished well."

After a moment's silence the bureaucrat said, "I'm afraid I don't follow you."

"I was sent into Whitemarsh just before it fell. I removed the coinmaker, and used a device my superiors had provided to irradiate his stock. Half of those who escaped our wrath carried their debased coinage with them. They never understood how we found them so easily. But it is observed that many of the men came down with radiation poisoning not long after, and where a man least wishes it. Disgusting sight. I still have the pictures." He stuck his hands in his trousers pockets and raised his eyebrows. "I fed the potion they gave me to Ysolt's dog, and it died. So much for the subtlety of wizards."

"The irradiator is illegal," the bureaucrat said. "Even planetary government is not allowed to use one. It can do a lot of damage."

"You see your duty, O hound of the people! Go to it. The trail is only sixty years cold." Bergier stared bitterly down at his screens. "I look down at the land, and I see my life mapped out beneath me. We're coming up on Ysolt's Betrayal, which is sometimes called Cuckold, and further on is Penelope's Lapse, then Feverdeath, and Abandonment. At the end of the run is Cape Disillusion, and that accounts for all my wives. I have retreated from the land, but I cannot yet completely leave it. I keep waiting. I keep waiting. For what? Perhaps for daybreak."

Bergier threw open the shutters. The bureaucrat winced as bright white light flooded in, drowning them all in glory, turning the commander pale and old, the flesh hanging loose on his cheeks. Down below they saw the roofs and towers, spires and one gold dome of Lightfoot rising toward them, bristling with antennae.

"I am the maggot in the skull," Bergier said deliberately, "writhing in darkness." The illogic of the remark, and its suddenness, jolted the bureaucrat, and in a shiver of insight he realized that those staring eyes were looking not back at horror but forward. There was a premonition of senility in that slow speech, as if the old commander were staring ahead into a protracted slide into toothless misery and a death no more distinct from life than that line dividing ocean from sky.

As they started from the cabin, the commander said, "Lieutenant Chu, I will expect you to keep me posted. I will be following your progress closely."

"Sir." Chu closed the door, and they descended the stairs. She laughed lightly. "Did you notice the lozenges?" The bureaucrat grunted. "Swamp-witch nostrums, supposed to be good for impotence. They're made out of roots and bull's jism and all sorts of nasty stuff. No fool like an old fool," she said. "He never leaves that little cabin, you know. He's famous for it. He even sleeps there."

The bureaucrat wasn't listening. "He's around here somewhere." He peered into the darkness, holding his breath, but heard nothing. "Hiding."

"Who?"

"Your impersonator. The young daredevil." To his briefcase he said, "Reconstruct his gene trace and build me a locater. That'll sniff him out."

"That's proscribed technology," the briefcase said. "I'm not allowed to manufacture it on a planetary surface."

"Damn!"

The air within the envelope was still, but filled with tension. It thrummed with the vibrations of the engines, as alive as a coiled snake. The bureaucrat could feel the false Chu peering at them from the shadows. Laughing.

Chu put a hand on his arm. "Don't." Her eyes were serious. "If you get emotionally involved with the opposition, they've got you by the balls. Cool off. Maintain your detachment."

"I don't—"

"—need to take advice from the likes of me. I know." She grinned cockily, the swaggering cynic again. "The planetary forces are all corrupt and ineffectual, we're famous for it. Even so, I'm worth listening to. This is my territory. I know the people we're up against."

"Watch yourself, buddy!"

The bureaucrat stepped back as four men hoisted a timber up out of the mud and wrestled it onto a flatbed truck. A chunky woman with red hair stood on the truckbed, working the hoist. The buildings here were as tumbledown a lot as he'd ever seen, unpainted, windows cracked, shingles missing. Crusted masses of barnacles covered their north sides.

The ground felt soft underfoot. The bureaucrat looked mournfully down at his shoes. He was standing in the mud. "What's going on?" he asked.

A withered old shopkeeper, all but lost in the folds of his clothes, as if he had shrunk or they grown, sat watching from his porch. A silver skull dangled from his left ear, marking him as a former space marine, and a ruby pierced through one nostril made him a veteran of the Third Unification. "Ripping out the sidewalks," he said glumly. "Genuine sea-oak, and it's been aging in the ground for most of a century. My granddaddy laid it down back when the Tidewater was young. Cheap as dirt then, but a year from now I can name my price."

"How do I go about renting a boat?"

"Well, I'll tell you plain, I don't see how you can. Not that many boats around now that the docks have been tore out." He smiled sourly at the bureaucrat's expression. "They were sea-oak too. Tore 'em out last month, when the railroad went away."

The bureaucrat glanced uneasily at the *Leviathan*, dwindling low in the eastern sky. A swarm of midges, either vampire gnats or else barnacle flies, hovered nearby threatening to attack, and then shrank to invisibility as they drew away. The flies, airship, railroad, docks, and walks, all of Lightfoot seemed to be receding from his touch, as if caught up by an all-encompassing ebb tide. Suddenly he felt dizzy, drawn into an airless space where his inner ear spun wildly, and there was no ground underfoot.

With a shout the timber was slammed onto the flatbed. The woman handling the crane joked and chatted with the men in the mud. "You gotta see my fantasia, though. You'll die when you see it. It's cut right down to here."

"Gonna show off the top of your tits, eh, Bea?" one of the men said.

She shook her head scornfully. "Halfway down the nipples. You're going to see parts of me you never suspected existed."

"Oh, I suspected something all right. I just never felt called on to do anything in particular about them."

"Well, you come to the jubilee in Rose Hall tomorrow night, and you can eat your heart out."

"Oh, is *that* what you want me to eat out?" He grinned wryly, then danced back as the beam slipped a few inches in its harness. "Watch that side there! A little remark like that don't deserve to get my toes crushed."

"Don't you worry. It's not your toes I'm thinking of crushing."

"Excuse me," the bureaucrat called up. "Is there any chance I can rent your truck? Are you the owner?"

The redheaded woman looked down at him. "Yeah, I'm the

owner," she said. "You don't want to rent this thing, though. See, I'm running it from a battery rated for a rig twice this size, so I gotta step down the voltage, okay? Only the transformer's going. I can get maybe a half hour out of it before it overheats and starts to melt the insulation. I been kind of nursing it along. Now Anatole's got a spare transformer, but he thinks he oughta be able to charge an arm and a leg for it. I been holding off. I figure it gets a little closer to jubilee, he'll take what he can get."

"Aniobe, I keep telling you," the shopkeeper said. "I could buy that sucker off him for half what—"

She tossed her head. "Oh, shut up, Pouffe. Don't you go spoiling my fun!"

The bureaucrat cleared his throat. "I don't want to go far. Just down the river a way and back again." A barnacle fly stung his arm, and he swatted it.

"Naw, the wheel bearings are starting to seize up too. Onliest place to get lubricant nowadays is Gireaux's, and old Gireaux has got a bad case of the touchy-feelies. Always trying to get a little kiss or something. If I wanted to get a tub of grease out of him on short notice, I'd probably have to get down on my knees and give him a sleeve job!"

The men grinned like hounds. Pouffe, however, shook his head and sighed. "I'm going to miss all this," he said heavily. The bureaucrat noticed for the first time the deep-interface jacks on his wrists, gray with corrosion; he'd served time on Caliban in his day. The man must have an interesting history behind him. "All your friends say they'll keep in touch after they move to the Piedmont, but it's just not going to happen. Who are they kidding?"

"Oh, come off it," Aniobe scoffed. "Any man as rich as you will have friends wherever he goes. It's not as if you needed to have a personality or nothing."

The last timber loaded, Aniobe shut down the truck and shipped the winch. The laborers waited to be dismissed. One, a roosterish young man with a comb of stiff black hair wandered onto the porch, and casually leaned over a tray of brightly bundled feathers—fetishes, perhaps, or fishing lures. Chu watched him carefully.

He was straightening from the tray when Chu stepped forward and seized his arm.

"I saw that!" Chu spun the man around and slammed him up against the doorpost. He stared at her, face blank with shock. "What have you got in that shirt?"

"I—nothing! W-what are—" he stammered. Aniobe stood up straight, putting hands on hips. The other laborers, the bureaucrat, the shopkeeper, all froze motionless and silent, watching the confrontation.

"Take it off!" Chu barked. "Now!"

Stunned and fearful, he obeyed. He held the shirt forward in one hand to show there was nothing hidden there.

Chu ignored it. She looked slowly up and down the young man's torso. It was lean and muscular, with a long silvery scar curving across his abdomen, and a dark cluster of curly hair on his chest. She smiled.

"Nice," she said.

The laborers, their boss, and the shopkeeper roared with laughter. Chu's victim reddened, lowered his head angrily, bunched his fists, and did nothing.

"You notice the way that redhead was teasing those men?" Chu remarked as they walked away. "Provocative little bitch." Far down the street was a weary-looking building, its ridgeline sagging, half its windows boarded over with old advertising placards cut to size. The wood was dark with rot, fragmented words and images opening small portals into a brighter world: ZAR, a fishtail, what was either a breast or a knee, KLE, and a nose pointed straight up as if its owner hoped to catch rain in the nostrils. A faded sign over the main door read TERMINAL HOTEL. The torn-up remains of the railbed ran beside it. "My husband's the same way."

"Why did you do that to him?" the bureaucrat asked. "That worker."

Chu didn't pretend not to understand. "Oh, I have plans for that young man. He's going to have a few beers now, and try to forget what happened, but of course his friends won't let him. By the time I've checked into my room, sent for my baggage, and freshened up, he'll be a little drunk. I'll go look him up then. He sees me, and he's going to feel a little hot and a little uncertain and a little embarrassed. He'll look at me, and he won't know what he feels.

"Then I'll give him the opportunity to sort his feelings out."

"Your method strikes me as being a little, um, uncertain. As far as effectiveness goes."

"Trust me," Chu said. "I've done this before."

"Aha," the bureaucrat said vaguely. Then, "Why don't you go ahead and book us rooms, while I see about Gregorian's mother?"

"I thought you weren't going to interview her until morning."

"Wasn't I?" The bureaucrat detoured around a rotting pile of truck tires. He had very deliberately dropped that scrap of information in front of Bergier. He didn't trust the man. He thought it all too possible that Bergier might arrange for a messenger sometime in the night to warn the mother against speaking to him.

It was part and parcel of a more serious puzzle, the question of where the false Chu had gotten his information. He'd known not only what name to give, but to leave the airship just before the real Chu boarded. More significantly, he knew that the bureaucrat hadn't been told his liaison was a woman.

Someone in his chain of command, either within the planetary government or Technology Transfer itself, was working with Gregorian. And while it need not be Bergier, the commander was as good a suspect as any.

"I changed my mind," he said.

3

The Dance of the Inheritors

Sunset. Bold Prospero was a pirate galleon sailing toward the night. It touched the horizon, flattening into an oval as it set continents of clouds afire. Under the trees the shadows were fading into blue air. The bureaucrat trudged down the river road, passing his briefcase from hand to hand as its weight made his palms and fingers ache.

At the edge of the village, three ragged men had built a fire in the road and were roasting yams in its coals. A dark giant sat soaking broadleaves in a bowl of water, and wrapping them about the tubers. A gray, lank man stuck them in the fire, and their aged companion raked the coals back. Two television sets were wedged in the sand, one with the sound off, and the other turned away, queasily imaging at empty trail. "Soft evening," the bureaucrat said.

"Same to you," the lank, colorless man said. Bony knees showed through holes in his trousers. "Have a sit-down." He hitched slightly to the side, and the bureaucrat hunkered down beside him, resting on the balls of his feet, careful not to soil his white trousers. On the pale screen, a young man stared moodily out a window at the crashing sea. A woman stood at his back, hands on his shoulders. "Old man doesn't believe he's seeing a mermaid," the lank man said.

"Well, that's the way fathers are." Soft blue smoke wisped into the darkening sky, smelling of driftwood and cedarbloom. "You lads out hunting?"

"In a manner of speaking," the lank one said. The giant snorted.

"We're scavengers," the old man said harshly. "If that's not good enough for you, then say so now and fuck off." They all stared at him, unblinking.

In the sudden silence, the bureaucrat could hear the show he'd interrupted. *Byron, come away from that window. There's nothing out there but cold and changing Ocean. Go into the air. Your father thinks—*

My father thinks of nothing but money.

"I've got a bottle of vacuum-distilled brandy in my brief-case." He fetched the bottle, took a swig, held it out. "If I could convince you . . ."

"Well, that is hospitable." The flask went around twice, and then Lank said, "You must be heading into the village."

"Yes, to see Mother Gregorian. Perhaps you know her house."

The three exchanged glances. "You won't get anything out of her," Lank said. "The villagers tell stories about her, you know. She's a type." He nodded toward the television. "Ought to be on the show."

"Tell me about her."

"Naw, I don't think so." He raised a sticklike arm, pointed. "The road dead-ends into the first street to the waterfront. Go down to the river, to the fifth—"

"Sixth," the old man said.

"Sixth street after that. Go up by the kirk and past the

boneyard to the end, right by the marshes. Can't miss it. Big fucking castle of a place."

"Thanks." He stood.

They were no longer looking at him. On the screen, an albino girlchild was standing alone in the middle of a raging argument. She was an island of serene calm, her eyes vacant and autistic. "That's Eden, she's the boy's sister. Hasn't spoken since it happened," Lank remarked.

"What happened?"

"She saw a unicorn," the giant said.

From the air the village had looked like a very simple antique printed circuit, of the sort Galileo might have used to build his first radio telescope, if he wasn't confusing two different eras, a comb of crooked lines leading inward from the water, too small for there to be any need of cross-streets. The houses were small and shabby, but warm light spilled from the windows, and voices murmured within. An occasional dog stridently warned him away from boat or yard. Other than an innkeeper who nodded lazily from the door of the watermen's hotel, he met no one by the riverfront. He turned onto the marsh road, the river cold and silver at his back. He went past a walled-in ground where skeletons hung from the trees, the bones bleached and painted and wired together so that they clacked gently in an almost unnoticeable breeze.

Beyond the boneyard the ground rose gently. He passed several large dark houses, still unscavenged, newly abandoned by their wealthy owners. Probably gone to the Piedmont to participate in the economic boom. Last on the road, just before the land wearily eased itself down into marsh, was his destination.

The house was blistered and barnacled, and it was meager light indeed that escaped the thickly curtained windows into the wider world. But under its mottling of chrysalids the wood planking was gracefully carved and fitted. He stood before the massive entranceway and touched the doorplate. Within, a voice gonged, "Callers, mistresses." Then, to him, the door said, " Please wait."

A moment later the door opened on a pale, thin face. On seeing him, it opened in startlement, revealing an instant's fear before tightening again into wariness. The woman lifted her chin defiantly, so that her eyes seemed simultaneously to flinch away from him. "I thought you were the appraiser."

The bureaucrat smiled. "Mother Gregorian?"

"Oh, her." She turned away. "I suppose you'd best come inside." He followed her down the gullet of a hallway flocked with a floral print gone dead brown into the crowded belly of a sitting room. She seated him in a dark lionfooted chair. It was a massy thing, shag-maned atop and fringed beneath, with padded armrests. He'd hate to have to move it.

A woman hurried into the room. "Is that the appraiser? Have him look at the crystal, I—" She stopped.

Tock. A metronome wedged between dusty specimen bells reached the end of its swing and began the long, slow return, ponderously counting out the slow seconds of mortality. Trophy beasts peered down at him from the tin ceiling with eyes of green and gray and orange glass. Now that he noticed, the room was full of faces. Heavy-lidded, openmouthed and disapproving, they were carved into the legs, sides and bases of the escritoires, tables, sideboards, and china cabinets that jostled one another, competing for space. Even the blond mahogany pieces had been extravagantly carved. He wondered where the shavings were now; they would not have been discarded. It was an enormously valuable room, and would have been twice as comfortable with half as much furniture. *Tock.* The metronome reasserted itself, and still the women studied him, as if they would never speak again.

"Honestly, Ambrym, must I wait forever for you to introduce your friend?"

"He's not mine, he's Mother's."

"All the more reason to show a little common courtesy."
She thrust forward a hand, and he stood so they could shake.
"I'm Linogre Gregorian," she said. "Esme! Where are you?"

A third woman, dressed in mousy brown, appeared, drying
her hands with a cloth towel. "If that's the appraiser, be sure he
knows that Ambrym broke the—" She stopped. "I'm sorry, I
didn't know you had a caller." She didn't leave, but stood there,
watching.

"Don't be stupid, Esme, this gentleman is here to see Mama.
Fetch him a glass of beer."

"You don't have to—"

"The Gregorians have always kept a decent house," she said
firmly. "Please, sit. The doctor is with Mother now. But if you'll
wait, I'm sure she'll want to see you, if only briefly. You must
take care, however, not to excite Mother, for she is extremely
ill."

"She's dying," Ambrym said. "She won't let us take her to
the Piedmont, where the good hospitals are. She's taken a notion
into her head to stay in this decaying hovel to the bitter end. I
think she's expecting to be washed away with the tides. Not that
the evacuation authorities would allow that." A faraway look
came into her eyes. "That will be the final indignity, to be
removed as paupers."

"If you don't mind, Ambrym, I'm sure our visitor is not
interested in our private sorrows." The bureaucrat did not miss
the way Ambrym stepped back from her sister, nor the defiance
with which she did so. "May I ask your business with our
mother?"

"Yes, certainly." Esme placed a delicate crystal beerglass in
his hand. "Thank you." She set a saucer by his elbow, lacy
porcelain that was faintly translucent even in the evening light.
It was a fairy mist of crockery, delicate beyond belief. "I'm from
the Division of Technology Transfer within the System government. We'd like to talk with your brother, but unfortunately

when he left our employ, he didn't leave his forwarding address. Perhaps you . . . ?" He let his voice trail off, and took a sip from his glass. It was lager, thin and almost tasteless.

"I'm sure we wouldn't know," Linogre began coolly.

But Ambrym snapped, "Are you his agent? He left home when he was a child. He's not entitled! We've worked all our lives, we've slaved—"

"Ambrym," her sister said meaningfully.

"I don't care. When I think of the years of work, the suffering, the shit she's put me through . . . !" She appealed directly to the bureaucrat. "Every morning I polish her riding boots, every morning for the last five years! I have to kneel on the floor before her, while she tells me she's thinking of leaving the best things to Linogre. It's not as if she were ever getting out of that bed again."

"Ambrym!"

They fell silent, eyeing one another. The metronome doled out six heavy ticks, and the bureaucrat thought, surely Hell must be like this. Finally Linogre prevailed, and her sister looked away. From the shadows Esme said timidly, "Would you like another glass of beer?"

The bureaucrat held up his glass, all but untasted. "No, thank you." Esme reminded him of a mouse, small and nervous, hovering at the edges of light in hopes of some small crumb. And yet on Miranda the mice were dimorphic, like everything else. At the end of the great year they would swim out into the ocean and drown in great numbers, and the few survivors would transform into—he tried to remember—little amphibious creatures, like vest-pocket seals. He wondered would she change too, come the tides?

"Don't think I can't see how you suck up to her," Ambrym snapped angrily. "Miss Meek-and-Harmless. I saw you hiding away the silver gravy boat."

"I was cleaning it!"

"In your room, uh-huh, sure."

Panicky little eyes. "Anyway, she said it was mine."

"*When?*" both sisters cried in outraged unison.

"Just yesterday. You can ask her."

"You remember—" Linogre glanced at the bureaucrat and lowered her voice, half-turning her back to him. "You remember that Mother said we were to divide the silver evenly, share and share alike. She's always said that."

"Is that why you took the sugar tongs?" Ambrym asked innocently.

"I never!"

"You did."

Listening intently, the bureaucrat put his glass down beside him. It landed a trifle harder than he'd intended, and he heard a faint *crack* of breaking china.

Sharp-eared Esme was the only sister to notice. With a quick warning shake of her head, she whisked away the broken fragments of saucer, and replaced them with another before anyone else had realized what had happened.

"The moment Mother's estate is settled," Ambrym was saying, "I intend to leave the house and never return. As far as I'm concerned, without Mother there is no family, and I am not related to either of you."

"Ambrym!" Esme squeaked, horrified.

"This is a shameful way to talk, with Mother dying just above us!" her elder sister cried.

"She won't die, not when she knows how happy that would make us. Spite will keep her alive," Ambrym said. Her siblings turned disapproving frowns on her, but did not disagree.

They came to an abrupt halt then, and there was about the group a satisfied air of fulfillment, as if they had just enacted a private drama for his benefit and were awaiting applause so they could link hands and take their bows. There, their collective attitude seemed to be saying, now you know all about us. It was a well-rehearsed scene, and he could tell that no one who entered the house would be allowed to escape without witnessing some variant of it.

At that moment the doctor descended the stairs, and all three looked up expectantly. He solemnly shook his head at the sisters, and departed. It was an ambiguous gesture at best.

"Come." Linogre started up the stairs.

In a somber mood, he followed.

She led him into a chamber so dimly lit he was not sure of its exact dimensions. An enormous bed dominated the room. Bed-curtains hung from brass hooks set into the ceiling, a tapestry of some bright land where satyrs and astronauts, nymphs and goats, frolicked. The edges were bordered with the constellations of old earth, wands and orchids, and other symbols of generative magic. Age had faded the colors, and the browned fabric was torn by its own weary weight.

Within the bed, propped up on a billowing throne of pillows, lay a grotesquely fat woman. He was reminded inevitably of a termite queen, she was so vast and passively immobile. Her face was doughy white, her mouth a tiny gasp of pain. A ringed hand hovered over a board floating atop her swollen belly, on which was arranged a circle of solitaire cards: stars, cups, queens, and knaves in solemn procession. A silent television flickered at her feet.

The bureaucrat introduced himself, and she nodded without looking up from her slow telling out of cards. "I am playing a game called Futility," she said. "Are you familiar with it?"

"How does one win?"

"You don't. You can only postpone losing. I've managed to keep this particular game going for years." She looked up at her daughter.

"Don't think I don't understand what you're talking about."

"All is pattern," she said. She had to pause ever so slightly between sentences to take in air. "Relationships between things shift and change constantly; there is no such thing as objective truth. There is only pattern, and the greater pattern within which the lesser patterns occur. I understand the greater pattern, and so I've learned to make the cards dance. But inevitably the game must someday end. There is a lot of life in how one tells the cards."

"Everyone knows. You're not very subtle about it. Even this gentleman beside you understands."

"Do you?" The mother looked directly at him for the first time, both she and her daughter awaiting his answer with interest.

The bureaucrat coughed into his hand. "I must have a few words in private with you, if I may, Mother Gregorian."

She favored Linogre with a cold look. "Leave."

As the daughter closed the door, her mother said loudly, "They want to put me away. They conspire against me, and think I don't notice. But I notice. I notice everything."

In the hallway Linogre made an exasperated noise. Her footsteps descended the stairs.

"It's the only way to keep her from listening at the door," the old woman whispered. Then, louder, almost shouting, "But I'll stay here, I'll die here. In this bed." Quieter, conversationally, "This was my bridebed, you know. I had my first man here." On the ghostcandling television, he could see Byron staring out his window again. "It's a good bed. I've taken each of my husbands to it. Sometimes more than one at once. Three times it's been my childbed—four, if you count the miscarriage. I intend to die in it. That's little enough to ask." She sighed, and pushed the tray of cards away. It swiveled into the wall. "What do you want of me?"

"Something very simple, I hope. I wish to speak with your son but don't have his address, and I was hoping you'd know where he is now."

"I haven't heard from him since he ran away from me." A crafty look came on her face. "What's he done to you? Taken off with your money, I expect. He tried to run off with mine, but I was too clever for him. That's all that's worth anything in life, all that gives you any control."

"So far as I know, he hadn't done anything. I'm only going to ask him a few questions."

"A few questions," she said disbelievingly.

He did nothing to break their shared silence, but let it flower and bloom, content to discover when she would finally speak again. Finally Mother Gregorian frowned with annoyance and said, "What kind of questions?"

"There's a possibility, nothing more, that some controlled technology may be missing. My agency wants me to ask your son whether he knows anything about it."

"What'll you do to him when you catch him?"

"I am not going to catch him at anything," the bureaucrat said testily. "If he has the technology, I'll ask him to return it. That's all I can do. I don't have the authority to take any serious action." She smiled meanly, as if she'd just caught him out in a falsehood. "But if you don't mind telling me just a little about him? What he was like as a child?"

The old woman shrugged painfully. "He was a normal enough boy. Full of the devil. He used to love stories, I remember. Ghosts and haunts and knights and space pirates. The priest would tell little Aldebaran stories of the martyrs. I remember how he'd sit listening, eyes big, and tremble when they died. Now he's on the television, I saw one of his commercials just the other day." She fiddled with the control, fanning through the spectrum of stations without finding the ad, and put it down again. It was an expensive set, sealed in orbit and guaranteed by his own department as unconvertible. "I was a virgin when he was born."

"I beg your pardon?" he said, startled.

"Ah, I *thought* that would draw your attention. It has the

stench of offworld technology to it, doesn't it? Yes, but it was an ancient crime, when I was young and very, very beautiful. His father was an offworlder like yourself, very wealthy, and I was just a backwoods witch—a pharmacienne, what you'd call an herbalist."

Her pale, spotted eyelids half closed; she lay her head further back, gazing into the past. "He came down from the sky in a red-enameled flying machine, on a dark night when Caliban and Ariel were both newborn—that's an important time for gathering the roots, your mandragon, epipopsy, and kiss-a-clown especially. He was an important man, he had that glitter about him, but after all these years I somehow cannot remember his face—only his boots, he had wonderful boots of fine red leather he told me came from stars away, nothing you could buy on Miranda even if you had the money." She sighed. "He wanted a motherless child, of his own genes and no others. I have no idea why. I could never wheedle that from him, for all the months we stayed together.

"We haggled up a price. He gave me money enough to buy all this"—she gestured with her chin to indicate all her cluttered domain—"and later, several husbands more to my liking than he. Then he carried me away in his batwinged machine to Ararat, far deep in the forests. That's the first city was ever built on Miranda. From the air it looked like a mountain, built up in terraces like a ziggurat, and all overgrown. I stayed there for all my pregnancy. Don't believe those who say that haunts live there. I had it to my own, all those stone buildings larger than anything this side of the Piedmont, nobody there but myself and the beasts. The father stayed with me when he could, but it was usually just me and my thoughts, wandering among those overgrown walls. They were green with mosses, trees growing out of windows, fields of wildflowers on every roof. Nobody to talk to! I tell you, I earned that money. Sometimes I cried."

Her eyes were soft and distant. "He spoke very fondly to me, as if I were his house pet, his soft cat, but he never once thought of me as a woman, I could tell. I was only a convenient womb to him, when you come down to it, there was that reserve to him.

"I broke my hymen with these two thumbs. I'd been trained as a midwife, of course, and knew my diet and exercises. When he brought me offworld food and medicines, I threw them away. It amused him when he found out, for by then he could see that I was healthy and his bastard safe. But I made my plans. He was away the week of the birth—I'd told him the wrong date—and I gave him the slip. I was young then, I took two days' rest, and then I left Ararat. He thought I'd be lost, you see, that I could never find my way out. But I was born in the Tidewater, and he on some floating metal world, what did he know? I'd saved up supplies in secret, and I knew what plants I could eat, so food was never a problem. I followed the flow of streams, took the easy way around marshes, and eventually I ended up at Ocean. There was nowhere else I could have ended up at, given I was consistent. It wasn't a month before I had come here, and set workmen to building this house."

She laughed lightly, and the laugh caught in her throat, causing her to choke. Her face twisted and reddened, until the bureaucrat feared she might be in serious distress. Then she calmed somewhat, and he poured her a glass of water from a nearby carafe. She took it without thanking him. "I fooled the bugger, all right. I bested him. I had his money safe in Piedmont banks, and his bastard with me, he never knew where to look, and he couldn't inquire openly. Probably never bothered. Probably thought I died out there. It's marshy around Ararat."

"That's a remarkable story," the bureaucrat said.

"You think I was in love with him. It's what anyone would think, but it's not so. He'd come and bought me with his offplanet money. He thought himself important, and me nothing compared to him, a convenience he could pick up and put down as he wished. And he was right, damn him, that's what made me mad. So I took his son from him, to teach him otherwise." She cackled. "Ah, the pranks I used to play!"

"Do you have any pictures of him?"

She lifted a hand, pointed to a wall where petty portraits and ancient photomechanicals vied for space. "That picture there, in the tortoiseshell frame, bring it here." He obeyed. "The woman, that tall goddess, was me, believe it or not. The child is young Aldebaran."

He looked carefully. The woman was heavy and slatternly, but clearly proud of her solidity, her flesh: She'd've had her admirers. The child was a spooky thing, staring straight at him with eyes that were two dark circles. "This is a picture of a girl."

"No, that's Aldebaran. I dressed him like that, in skirts and flounces, for the first several years to hide him from his father, in case he came looking. Until he was seven. He turned willful then, nasty creature, and wouldn't wear his proper clothes. I had to give in, he walked out in the street buck naked. But I didn't give in easy. Three days he went bare before the priest came and said this could not be."

"How did Aldebaran come to have an offworld education?"

She ignored the question. "I wanted a daughter, of course. Girls are so much more tractable. A girl would not have run off to find her father, the way he did." Abruptly she commanded, "Put your hand under my bed. Pull out what you find there."

He reached into the vaginal shadows under the bedskirts, drew out a shallow trunk carved with half-human figures. Mother Gregorian rolled over, grunting with effort, to look. "Under that green silk—there ought to be a brown package. Yes. That. Unwrap it."

It was alarmingly easy to obey this monster, she was so sure of her commands. He held a battered notebook in his hand, a faded scrawl of sigils running across its cover.

"That belonged to Aldebaran. He lost it just before he ran away." Her smile hinted at stories untold. "Take it with you, perhaps it'll tell you something." She closed her eyes, let her face relax into a flaccid mask of pain. She was panting now, steadily as a dog in summer, but quieter.

"You've been very helpful," the bureaucrat said cautiously. He could sense the old woman about to name a price for information given.

"He thought he was so clever. He thought that if he went far away enough, he could escape me. He thought he could escape me!" Her eyes flickered open, glittered venomously. "When you find him, give him a message for me. Tell him that no matter how far you go, in miles or learning or time, you cannot escape your mother."

He could think of nothing to say. So instead, he bowed politely and turned to leave.

"Oh, and you needn't bother about the broken saucer. We have more, and it was an incomplete set anyway."

He smiled. "That's a good trick. How did you know that?"

She reached a hand up in the air, a gesture that managed to be both languid and laborious, like a drowning woman reaching for the water's surface, and tripped a switch beam. The lights went out, and the room was plunged in darkness, save for a snowflake of light on the ceiling. It was a rosette of small circles, like a festival cookie. He looked down, and there was a smaller rosette on the floor, and brighter.

Her voice came out of the darkness, gloating. "The hot-air register. When it's open, I can hear every word in the room below. I heard the saucer crack, and Esme scuttling out into the pantry and back." She laughed at him. "Too straightforward for you, eh? You offworlders think yourselves so sophisticated. Something as simple as our ventilation system is beyond you."

In the room below, he met a dignified-looking man with a dark mustache, holding a glass of the daughters' thin beer. His hair was slicked down, Piedmont style. "You must be the appraiser," the bureaucrat said.

They shook hands. "Yes, I come here every few weeks, to draw up another schedule of prices. A year ago, these pieces were worth a fortune; now, shipping costs have gone up and they're not so valuable. Most will have to be left behind." The appraiser held up a battered sheaf of papers and sighed piously. "These are the figures, anyone can check them. There's no profit in it for me. The only reason I agree to come back so often is that there are so many beautiful things here, it would be a pity if they were lost to the tides."

Linogre and Ambrym stood nearby, and Esme out of sight. Yet he could feel her watchful from some dim recess, all tiny black beadglass eyes and quivering whiskers.

"Esme," Linogre said. "Please show mother's visitor to the door. We must see to her wardrobe."

The elder two sisters swept away in the wake of the appraiser. As soon as they were gone, Esme emerged from shadow. The bureaucrat glanced up at the air register and impulsively took her hand. He felt the sudden, urgent need to get her out of this poisonous atmosphere. To save something from disaster. "Listen to me: Your mother has told me she's cut you out of her will," he said. "She's not willing you a thing. Leave this house tonight, child. Right now. I'll help carry your things. There's nothing here for you."

The girl's dusty-glass eyes took on a dull sheen of malice. "I want to see her die!" she spat. "She can keep her money, I just want to see her dead and never coming back!"

It was night when he left the house, but Caliban was high in the sky and full, Ariel low but gibbous and bright, so the river road was well-lit, and the trees had ghostly pairs of shadows arcing away from each other. The tree stars had come down from their high perches and, faintly luminous, were rooting for mites in the humus. The walk was peaceful, and the bureaucrat used it to sort out his impressions. It seemed to him that the house he'd just left was frozen in time. When the tides come, everything will change. Only some have rendered themselves beyond change, and caught by the sun, will be revealed as lifeless stone.

It wouldn't hurt to find out who the magician's father was. Even given that he'd doubtless broken tariff when he brought his money planetside, he must've been a rich and quite likely influential man. He thought again of the three sisters, unaged and unsexed by greed and inertia.

I could almost like Gregorian, he said to himself, just for escaping that woman.

At last he asked his briefcase, "Well—what is it?"

"Judging by the sketches and diagrams scattered within, it's a magical diary—the account book an aspiring sorcerer maintains to keep track of his spiritual progress. It's written in a floating cypher, using obsolete alchemical symbols, the sort of thing an extremely bright adolescent might invent."

"Decode it, then."

"Very well." The briefcase thought for a moment, and then said, "The first entry begins: *I killed a dog today.*"

4

Sibyls in Stone

The famous witch Madame Campaspe, who claimed she had transcended humanity and thus had no need to die and who always carried with her a tame water rat, was nowhere to be found. Some said she had retired to the Piedmont, where she owned a walled estate in the Iron Lake district under an assumed name, others that she had been drowned by a horrified lover, that her clothes had been discovered by the river and taken to the local church to be burned. Nobody expected her back.

Hammers sang. Workmen were tearing walls from houses and stringing waxflowers over the streets of Rose Hall. The little river community was half-dismantled, the houses at its core reduced to roofs and floors so that they might serve as dance pavilions. They looked like so many skeletons, flanked by sad piles of rubble.

The bureaucrat and Chu stood before what was once Madame Campaspe's house. The high roof, ironically like a squared-off version of a witch's peaked cap, and the corner posts were all that remained intact. The interior had been filled with scrap lumber and other inflammables. "What a mess," the bureaucrat said disgustedly of the heaped and broken wardrobes and divans, stained blankets, clotted masses of paper, and filthy brown rugs, the flotsam and jetsam of a hastily abandoned life. A broken-backed stuffed angel shark leered from the bottom. The house reeked of white kerosene.

"It'll make a nice bonfire, anyway," Chu said. She stepped back as a canvas-gloved woman threw in more planks. "Hey— lady! Yeah, you. You from around here?"

The woman brushed back her short black hair with her wrist, not bothering to doff her work glove. "I was born here." Her eyes were green, cool, skeptical. "What do you want to know?"

"The woman who used to live here, the witch. Did you know her?"

"I know of her, of course. Madame Campaspe was the richest woman in Rose Hall. Tough old bird. There was plenty of gossip. But I live on the other side of town. I never actually' met her."

Chu smiled dryly. "Of course not. A big place like this, how could you meet her?"

"Actually," the bureaucrat said, "we're more interested in a student of hers. A man named Gregorian. Did you know him?"

"I'm sorry, I—"

"This is the man who made all the commercials," Chu said. Then, when the woman continued to look blank, "On television. Television! Have you ever heard of television?"

Quickly the bureaucrat said, "Excuse me. I couldn't help but notice that lovely pendant you're wearing. Is it haunt work?"

Startled in the first flush of anger, the woman glanced down at the stone hanging between her breasts. It was smoothly polished, the length of a human thumb, straightedged on one side, curved on the other, rounded atop and tapering below to a blunt point. It was too big for a fishing weight and too edgeless and asymmetrical to be a spear point. "It's a shell knife," she said.

Then, brusquely, she seized her barrow and trundled it away.

The bureaucrat stared after her. "Have you noticed how evasive the locals get when we start asking questions?"

"Yes, it does seem they've got something to hide, doesn't it?" Chu said thoughtfully. "There's a local trade smuggling haunt artifacts. Stone projectile points, bits of pottery, and so on. Things that properly belong to the government. It would be easy enough for a witch to get involved in that sort of thing. They're always poking around in odd places, nosing about boneyards, mucking about ravines. Digging holes."

"Is there much money in haunt artifacts?"

"Well, they aren't exactly making any more of them."

Chu smiled at the bureaucrat, and he realized guiltily that his face must bear that exact same expression, sharp little grins with an unclean edge to them, as if they were predators that had caught scent of blood. "I wonder what they're hiding."

"It'll be interesting to find out."

They headed back to the hotel. In the weeds by the edge of town some children had caught a nautilus. Shrieking blissfully, they rode its shell, two and three at a time, while it slowly pulled itself forward with long, fluid arms. The bureaucrat commiserated silently with the wretched creature. It was hard to imagine it as it would be within the year, soaring and swooping in Ocean's waters, a creature of preternatural speed, of uncanny grace.

In the center of town, they passed through a loose congeries of trucks belonging to entertainers and concessionaires brought in by the local businesses as a farewell gesture. A proud-bellied man was cranking out the canopy for a puppet theater. Others were raising a Wheel into the sky. It all looked tawdry, cheap, immeasurably sad.

The bureaucrat led the way through the lobby and into the hotel bar. It was cool and dark here, cluttered with neon signs advertising discontinued brands of alcohol and behemoth tusks gone chalky with age, and redolent with a lifetime's spillage of cheap ale. Strings of paper flowers gone gray as dust hung over adhesive-backed holos of fighters trapped in greasy rainbow smears while they threw the same famous punches over and over.

A sloppily fat bartender leaned back against a narrow counter, watching television. Their reflections swam up from the depths of a corroded mirror, rising from behind a ragged line of bottles, pale and popeyed, exotics from Ocean's trenches. The bureaucrat put his briefcase up on the bar, and Chu with a nod slipped away to the toilets.

The bureaucrat coughed. With a lurch, the bartender straightened, turned, laughed. "Whoah! You want to know something, I didn't see you there." His head was bald as a toadstool and speckled with thumbprint-sized brown spots. Splaying his hands on the bar, he leaned forward leeringly. "So what the fuck can I do for—" He stopped. "That thing for sale?"

The bureaucrat looked down at the briefcase, up at the barkeep. He was the most physically repulsive man the bureaucrat had ever seen. Fleshy growths sprouted from his eyelids like small tentacles; they jiggled as he talked. His over-sly smile was a caricature of cunning.

"Why do you ask?"

"Well." The man's teeth were bruised and cracked, his gums purple, his breath sweet with corruption. "I know a man who might be interested in buying such a thing." He winked. "Let's not mention any names."

"I could get in a lot of trouble if I went back up without this."

"Not if it fell in the river." The old troll touched the bureaucrat's arm ingratiatingly, as if to draw him into a shared fantasy universe of conspiracy, treachery, and sleazy profit. "What the fuck. Accidents happen. A smart fucker could arrange for them to happen in front of witnesses."

Suddenly the man's face paled, and he sucked in air between

his teeth. Lieutenant Chu's reflection rose up in the mirror. The bartender turned away quickly.

"Where to next?" Chu asked. She glanced curiously at the fat man, now gazing fixedly into the television.

"I still have some things to see to upcountry." The bureaucrat rapped the bar. "Excuse me! Do you have a gate here?"

"Back room," the old man muttered. He didn't look up.

More bodies were discovered today in the Plymouth Hundreds in Estuary Province, a newswoman said. *Shown here are just a few of the dozens of corpses removed from shallow graves this morning. Authorities say the hands, feet, and heads had been removed to slow identification.*

"I'd hate to be working homicide hereabouts," Chu commented. "Lots of old scores are being settled nowadays."

In the back room the bureaucrat related his conversation with the bartender to Chu. She whistled softly. "You really do have a way of stumbling into things! Well, now I know where to begin looking. Let me go poke around and see what I can turn up."

"Do you need any help?"

"You'd only be in the way. See to your business. I'll give you a nudge when I find something." She left.

The surrogation device was an antique, ungainly as an armored squid, and too battered to be worth the cost of hauling away. The bureaucrat lay down on a cracked vinyl sofa. Tentacular sensors jointed delicately to touch his forehead. Colors swam behind closed eyelids, resolving into squares, triangles, rectangles. He touched one with his thought.

A satellite picked up the signal and handed it down to the Piedmont. A surrogate body came alive, and he walked it out into the streets of Port Richmond.

*   *   *

The House of Retention was a neolithic granite peak, one of the range of government buildings known locally as the Mountains of Madness. Its stone halls were infested by small turquoise lizards that skittered away at the surrogate's approach and reappeared behind him. Its walls were damp to the touch. The bureaucrat had never been anywhere, the Puzzle Palace of course excepted, where there was so little green. He was directed to its moist interior, where sibyls operated data synthesizers under special license from the Department of Technology Transfer.

It was a long, gloomy walk, and the bureaucrat felt the weight of the building on him every step of the way. The passage took on allegorical dimensions for him, as if he were trapped inside a labyrinth, one he had entered innocently enough in his search for Gregorian, but which he now found himself too far into for retreat but not far enough for any certainty of reaching whatever truth might lie at its center.

When he came to the hall of sibyls, he chose a door at random and stepped inside. A thin, sharp-featured woman sat in the center of a workdesk. Dozens of black cables as thick as her little finger looped out of darkness to plug into her skull. They shook when she looked up to see who had entered the room. It was a clumsy setup, typical of the primitive systems his department enforced when onplanet use of higher-level technologies was unavoidable. "Hello," the bureaucrat said, "I'm—"

"I know who you are. What do you want?"

Somewhere, water slowly dripped.

"I'm looking for a woman named Theodora Campaspe."

"The one with the rat?" The sibyl stared at him unblinkingly. "We have a great deal on the notorious Madame Campaspe. But whether she's alive or dead, and in either case where, is not known."

"There's a rumor that she drowned."

The sibyl pursed her lips, squinted judiciously. "Perhaps. She hasn't been seen for a month or so. It's well documented that her clothes were burned on the altar of Saint Jones's outside of Rose Hall. But all that is circumstantial at best. She may simply not want to be found. And of course half our data are corrupt; she may be minding her own business without any intent to deceive anyone."

"But you don't think so."

"No."

"Just what is her business, anyway? What exactly does a witch do?"

"She would never have used that word," the sibyl said. "It has unfortunate political overtones. She always referred to herself as a spiritualist." Her eyes grew dreamy as she drew in widely scattered snippets of information. "Most people did not make that distinction, of course. They came to her back door at night with money and requests. They wanted aphrodisiacs, contraceptives, body chrisms, stillbirth powders to sprinkle before their enemies, potions to swell breasts and change genitalia from male to female, candles to conjure up wealth, charms to win back lost love and to ease the pain of hemorrhoids. We have sworn testimony that she could shed her skin like a haunt and turn into a bird or a fish, suck the blood of her enemies, frighten children with masks, ride faithless husbands across the hills where it would take them days to return, ring bells from the tops of trees, send dreams to steal the mind or seduce the soul, emerge from swimming in the river and leave no footprints behind, kill animals by breathing in their faces, reveal the location of Ararat and disclose the existence of a gland inside the brain whose secretions are addictive on first taste, walk shadowless at noon, foresee death, prophesy war, spit thorns, avert persecution. If you want specifics, I could spend the rest of the day on them."

"What of the magician Aldebaran Gregorian? What do you have on him?"

She bowed her head to concentrate on the search. "We have the text of his commercials, the data presentation your department made to the Stone House, a recent internal security report bylined Lieutenant-Liaison Chu, and the usual anecdotia: consorts with demons, blasphemes, hosts orgies, climbs mountains, couples with goats, eats rocks, plays chess, seduces virgins of both sexes, walks on water, fears rain, tortures innocents, defies offplanet authority, washes with milk, consults mystics on Cordelia, employs drugs on himself and others, travels in disguise, drinks urine, writes books in no known language, and so on. None of it reliable."

"And of course you don't know where I can find him."

"No."

The bureaucrat sighed. "Well, one more thing. I want to know the provenance of an artifact I saw recently."

"Do you have a picture?"

"No, but I can visualize it quite clearly."

"I'll have to patch you into the system. Open a splice line, please."

He called up the proper images, and a face appeared before him, twice human size, a gold mask afloat in midair between himself and the sibyl.

It was the face of a god.

Warmly handsome, inhumanly calm, the system tutelar said, "Welcome. My name is Trinculo. Please allow me to help you." His expression was as grave and serene as the reflection of the moon on night waters.

In the back of his head the bureaucrat felt the buzzing encephalic presence of all twenty sibyls hooked into the system. But Trinculo's presence was all-pervasive, riveting, a charismatic aura he could almost touch. Even knowing, as he did, that it was an artifact of the primitive technology, that his attention was artificially focused so rigidly on Trinculo that the hindbrain registered it as awe, the bureaucrat felt humbled before this glowing being. "What do you have on this object?"

He visualized the shell knife. A sibyl picked up the image

and hung it in the air over the desk. Another opened a window into a museum catalog. She scanned through bright galleries that looked as if they'd been carved from ice and lifted the knife's twin from a glass shelf. The bureaucrat wondered what the actual museum looked like; he had known collections with perfect catalogs and empty, looted source buildings.

"It's a haunt artifact," one sibyl said.

"A shell knife, used to unhinge the muscle of midden clams," added another. In the air beside the knife she opened a window onto a primitive scene depicting a fish-headed haunt squatting by the river demonstrating the tool's use, then closed it again.

"Quite useless now. Humans do not find midden clams digestible."

"This particular knife is about three-hundred-fifty years old. It was used by a river clan of the Shellfish alliance. It is a particularly fine example of its class, and unlike most such was not gathered by the original settlers on Miranda, but is a product of the Cobbs Creek dig."

"Documentation is available on the Cobbs Creek dig."

"It is presently on display in the Dryhaven Museum of Prehuman Anthropology."

"Is that sufficient, or do you wish to know more?"

Trinculo smiled benignly. The tutelar had spoken not a word since his original greeting. "I saw this knife not half an hour ago in the Tidewater," the bureaucrat said.

"Impossible!"

"It must be a reproduction."

"The museum has offplanet security."

"Trinculo," the bureaucrat said, "Tell me something."

In a friendly, competent voice the gold mask said, "I am here to assist you."

"You have the text of Gregorian's commercials on file."

"Of course we do!" a sibyl snapped.

"Why hasn't he been arrested?"

"Arrested!"

"There's no reason to."

"Whatever for?"

"Gregorian claims he can transform people so that they can live in the sea. That's false representation. He's taking money for doing so. That's fraud. And it looks likely that he's drowning his victims in the course of his fraud. That's murder."

There was a brief silence. Then the sibyl sharing the room with his surrogate, head still down as she sifted through her data, said, "It must first be determined that he can't actually fulfill his claims."

"Don't be ridiculous. Human beings cannot live in Ocean."

"Perhaps they could be adapted."

"No."

"Why not?"

"To take the very simplest matter first, there's hypothermy. If you've ever been swimming, you know how rapidly you grow cold. Your body can afford to lose heat at that rate for only a relatively short time. After a few hours, you've used up your resources and you lose isothermy. You go into shock. And you die."

"Haunts managed to live in the water quite comfortably."

"Human beings are not haunts. We're mammals. We need to maintain a high blood temperature."

"There are mammals too that live in the water. Otters and seals and the like."

"Because they've evolved to. They're protected by a layer of fat. We're not insulated that way."

"Perhaps that's part of the change that Gregorian makes, an insulating layer of fat."

"I refuse to believe that I'm having such a puerile argument when I'm within an information system!" The bureaucrat addressed the tutelar directly. "Trinculo, tell your people whether such an extreme rearrangement of human physical structure is possible."

Trinculo turned slightly to one side and then to the other in confusion, and stammered, "I'm . . . No, I'm sorry, I . . . can't answer that question."

"It's just a simple correlation of available science!"

"I don't . . . have the . . ." Trinculo's eyes were pained. His glance darted back and forth frantically.

Suddenly the tutelar and the buzzing presence of his attendants were gone. The office was empty save for the sibyl. She had yanked the patch.

The bureaucrat frowned. "Your tutelar seems woefully inadequate for your needs."

The sibyl looked up sharply, making the cables rustle and rattle. "And whose fault is that? It was your own department that sent in the ravishers and berserkers when they decided the Quiet Revolution had gone too far. We had a completely integrated system before your creatures ate holes in it."

"That was a long time ago," the bureaucrat said. He knew of the incident, of course, the quixotic attempt to regear an entire planet to a technological level so low they could afford to cut off all offplanet commerce, but he was surprised to hear her speak of it so emotionally. "Back when the Tidewater was still underwater, just before the Resettlement. Long before either of us was born. Surely there's no need to go into old grievances now."

"That's easy for you to say. You don't have to live with the consequences. You don't have to operate a senile information system. Your people condemned Trinculo as a traitor and burned out all his higher functions. But he's still remembered here as a patriot. Children light candles to him in the churches."

"He was your leader?" The bureaucrat was not surprised, then, that Trinculo's higher functions had been pithed. After what had happened to Earth, there was no creature more feared than an independent artificial entity.

The sibyl shook her cables wrathfully. Drops of condensate went flying. "Yes, he was our leader! Yes, he masterminded the rebellion, if that's what you want to call it. We wanted nothing more than freedom from your interference, your economics, your technology. When Trinculo showed us how we could disentangle ourselves from your control, we didn't stop to ask if he came from a factory or a womb. We'd have dealt with the devil for a chance to slip our necks from your noose, but Trinculo was nothing of the kind. He was an ally, a friend."

"You can't disengage from the outside universe, no matter how—" the bureaucrat began. But the woman's skin was white now, her lips thin, her eyes hard. Her face had closed and turned to stone. It was hopeless trying to reason with her. "Well, thank you for your help."

The sibyl glared him out of the room.

The bureaucrat backed outside, turned, and realized he was lost.

As he stood there, hesitating, a door opened down the hall. Out stepped a man who shone as bright as an angel. He looked as if he had swallowed the sun and could not contain its light within his flesh. The bureaucrat turned down external gain, and saw within the dimming figure the steel ribs and telescreen face of a fellow surrogate. It was a face he knew.

"Philippe?" he said.

"Actually I'm just an agent." Philippe had recovered from amazement first; now he grinned in a comradely fashion. "I'm afraid I'm under such pressure at work, I haven't been able to gate here in person." He took the bureaucrat's arm and steered him down the hall. "If that was your first encounter with Trinculo's widows, you need a drink. Surely you have time for a drink."

"You spend a lot of time on Miranda, do you?"

"More than some, less than others." Philippe's teeth were

perfect, and his face, even though he was old enough to be the bureaucrat's father, was unlined and pink. He was the living avatar of the eternal schoolboy. "Does it matter?"

"I suppose not. How's my desk doing?"

"Oh, I'm sure Philippe has it well in hand. He's very good at that sort of thing, you know."

"So everyone tells me," the bureaucrat said glumly.

They stepped onto a sudden balcony overlooking a city street. Philippe called a moving bridge, and they rode it over the hot river of moving metal to the next wing of the building. "Where is Philippe nowadays?"

"Diligently at work in the Puzzle Palace, I presume. Down this way." They came to a deserted refreshment niche and plugged in. Philippe called up a menu, hooked a metal elbow over the bar. "The apple juice looks good."

The bureaucrat had meant where Philippe was physically. Agenting in realspace was so much more expensive than surrogation—the ministries responsible for the conservation of virtual reality made sure of that—that normally agents were only employed when the primary was so far away the lag time made surrogation impractical. It was clear, though, that the agent wasn't going to answer that particular question.

Back in the hotel, somebody nudged the bureaucrat's shoulder. "I'll be done in a minute," he said without opening his eyes. A drink materialized in his hand, as chill and slippery with moisture as a real glass would be.

"Tell me," the agent said after a moment. "Does Korda have anything against you?"

"Korda! Why would Korda have anything against me?"

"Well, that's exactly what I was wondering, you see. He's said some odd things lately. About possibly eliminating your position and reassigning your responsibilities to Philippe."

"That's ridiculous. My workload could never be—"

Philippe threw up his hands. "This isn't my doing—I don't

want your job. I'm overburdened with responsibility as it is."

"Okay," the bureaucrat said disbelievingly. "All right. Tell me exactly what Korda said to you."

"I don't know. Don't look at me like that! Honestly I don't. Philippe only gave me the broadest outline. You know how cautious he is. He'd keep what he knew from himself, if that were possible. But, listen—I'll be merging back into him in a couple of hours. Do you want to give him a message? He could gate down to talk with you."

"That won't be necessary." The bureaucrat swallowed back his anger, hid it away from the agent. "I ought to have this case wrapped up in a day or two. I can talk with him in person then."

"You're that close, are you?"

"Oh yes. Gregorian's mother gave me a great deal of information. Including an old notebook of Gregorian's. It's full of names and addresses." Actually the book was largely taken up with occult diagrams and instructions for ceremonies—full of serpents, cups, and daggers—that the bureaucrat found both obscure and tedious. Other than the insights it gave into the young Gregorian's character and youthful megalomania, its only solid lead had been the references to Madame Campaspe. But the bureaucrat wanted to give Philippe something to think about.

"Good, good," the agent said vaguely. He stared down at his hand, swirling the liquid only he could see in its imaginary glass. "Why is it that line-fed fruit juice never tastes as good as what you get in person?"

"That's because when you're just being line-fed the flavor, you don't get the body rush from the sugars and so on." Philippe looked blank. "It's like getting a line-fed beer—all flavor and no alcohol. Only the physical component of apple juice isn't so pronounced, so while your body feels the difference, you're not consciously aware of what the lack is."

"You know a little bit of everything," Philippe said amiably.

*   *   *

When the bureaucrat opened his eyes, Chu was waiting for him.

"I've found it," she said. That small, feral smile again, conspiratorial flash of teeth and gone. "Come on out back."

On the blind side of the hotel was a long storage shed with a single narrow door. Chu had smashed the lock. "I need a light," the bureaucrat said. He took one from his briefcase and entered.

Amid a litter of tools, lumber, and scrapwood, were a dozen new-made crates. "They were all set to close up shop," Chu said. Setting a sawhorse aside, she reached into a crate she'd already ripped open, and handed the bureaucrat a shell knife just like the one he'd seen earlier.

"So they're smuggling artifacts, just as we thought, eh?"

Chu took a second shell knife from the crate, a third, a fourth.

They were all identical.

"There's other stuff too. Pottery, digging sticks, fishnet weights. All in multiplicate." She reached into the shadows. "Look what else I found."

It was a briefcase, the perfect twin of the one the bureaucrat held. He could tell by its markings that it had been issued by his own department.

"You see the scam, don't you? They got hold of some genuine haunt artifacts, fed them to the briefcase, and had it make them copies. Then they returned the originals to the source. Or maybe copies, I don't imagine it would make any difference."

"Only to an archeologist. Maybe not even then."

"Did you find out where the knife came from?"

"The original was from Cobbs Creek," the bureaucrat said. "It's on display in Dryhaven."

"Cobbs Creek is just down the river. Not far from Clay Bank."

"I'm less interested in where the artifacts came from than in how the counterfeiters got hold of one of our briefcases. Have you questioned it yet?"

"Don't waste your breath." Chu held it open to the light so that he could see the interior, blackened and blistered. "It's dead."

"Idiots." The bureaucrat took patch lines from his own briefcase and wired the two together. "They must've overloaded it. It's a delicate piece of equipment; if you order it to keep making copies of something and don't take care to keep it supplied with the elements it needs, it'll dismantle itself trying to follow instructions. I need a full readout of this thing's memory."

His briefcase was silent for a second, then said, "There's nothing left but the identification number. It managed to disassemble all its insulation before it died, and the protected memory rotted out."

"Shit."

"Give me a hand with this crate," Chu said.

Grunting and puffing, they wrestled the crate outside, and let it fall to the ground with a crash. The bureaucrat went back in for his briefcase, took out a handkerchief and mopped his brow. "Won't all this noise alert the counterfeiters?"

"I'm counting on it."

"Hah?"

Chu took out a cheroot, lit it. "You think the nationals are going to arrest anybody over this? With the jubilee tides so close? A petty little counterfeiting ring that's probably not even cheating Mirandans? Face it, these things are being sold to offplanet tourists. Hereabouts that amounts to a victimless crime. The briefcase might have been a bigger noise, but it's *dead*. Anyway, the hot rumor is that the Stone House is going to announce a general amnesty on crimes committed in the Tidewater, a few days before the tides. To make things easier for the evacuation authority. So the national police aren't going to be very excited about this. I figure there's only two things we can do. The first is to throw this crap in the river, so they can't make any more profit off it."

"And the second?"

"That's to make so much noise hauling it out that anyone involved will know we're on to them. *They* don't know about the amnesty. I figure that barkeep must be a mile away by now, and running fast. Wait here, and I'll go requisition a wheelbarrow."

When they came back from the river, the bar was empty and the bartender gone. He had left without even turning off the television. Chu went behind the bar, found a bottle of remscela and poured them both a shot. "To crime," she said.

"I still hate to see them get away."

"Enforcement is a dirty business, sonny," Chu said scornfully. "And there's a lot more dirt down here than you have up in Cloud-wonderland. Buck up, and enjoy your drink like a grown-up."

On the television a man was arguing with old Ahab about the man's twin brother, long ago lost at sea. *Murderer!* Ahab shouted. *He was your twin, and your responsibility!*

Since when am I my brother's keeper?

Unseen by either, a mermaid peered in at them through a window, her face open with wonder, and with pain.

5

Dogs Among the Roses

The strings of waxflowers were all lit now, red-blue-yellow-white fuzzglobes of light swaying overhead, and the music was hot and urgent, a magnetic field in which the revelers swirled and eddied, caught in its invisible lines of force and sent spinning away in a rush of laughter. Among the fantasias were lesser costumes, representational rather than interpretive, angels with carnal smiles, clowns, and sentimental devils with goatees and pitchforks. A satyr stumbled drunkenly by on short stilts, hairy and near-naked, waving panpipes to keep from falling.

The bureaucrat found Chu behind the bandstand, hustling a red-faced young roisterer. She leaned against him, one palm casually resting on his rump, and teased a paper cup from his hand. "No, you don't need any more of that," she said patiently. "We can find better uses for—" The bureaucrat backed away unnoticed.

He let the crowds sweep him down the main street of a transformed Rose Hall, past dance stands, rides, and peepshows. Pushing through a cluster of surrogates—kept to the fringes since they weren't physically present—he watched the fantasia presentations for a time, shoved up against the stage with a rowdy group of soldiers with central evac armbands who hooted, whistled, and cheered on their favorites. The event was too esoteric for his offworld tastes, and he drifted on, through the odors of roast boar, fermented cider, and a dozen fairy foods.

Children materialized underfoot and, laughing, were gone.

Somebody hailed him by name, and the bureaucrat turned to face Death. Flickering blue light showed through the sockets of the skull mask, and the bureaucrat could see between metal ribs through to the cape. Death handed him a cup of beer.

"And who are you?" he said, smiling.

Death took his elbow, strolled him away from the bright center of the celebration. "Oh, do let me have my mysteries. It's jubilee, after all." The tattered black cape Death wore smelled musty; the costumier had taken advantage of his distant customer's limited senses. "I'm a friend, anyway."

They came to a footbridge over the little stream marking the end of town. The light here faded to gloom, and the clustered buildings were silent and oppressively dark. "Have you located Gregorian yet?" the surrogate asked.

"Just who *are* you?" the bureaucrat asked, not smiling.

"No, of course you haven't." Death looked to the side distractedly. "Excuse me, somebody's just . . . No, I don't have time to . . . Okay, just leave it right there." Then, directly again. "I'm sorry about that. Listen, I don't have the time, I'm afraid. Just tell Gregorian, when you find him, that someone he knows—his sponsor, tell him that his old sponsor will take him in again, if he gives up this folly. Do you understand? That's what you want too, isn't it?"

"Maybe it isn't. Why don't you tell me who you are and what you actually want, and maybe we can work together on this."

"No, no." Death shook his head. "It's a long shot, anyway,

probably won't work. But if you have trouble dealing with him, it's an argument you can use. I mean it, he'll know that my word is good." He turned away.

"Wait," the bureaucrat said. "Who are you?"

"I'm sorry."

"Are you his father?"

Death turned to look at him. For a long moment it said nothing; then, "I'm sorry. I have to leave now." The surrogate swayed as if about to fall, and then locking gyros froze into place and it stood there, a statue.

He touched the metal skull. It was inert, lacking the almost subliminal hum of an active unit. Slowly he walked away, turning now and again to look back, but it remained dead.

In the thick of things again, he drained off his spiced beer and picked up a powdered fairy cruller from a drunken teenager who waved away his money: "It's been paid for!" There was a banner on the stand reading TIDEWATER PRODUCE AND ANIMAL BY-PRODUCTS COLLECTIVE. He raised the pastry in toast, and wandered into the fairway again, feeling distant and a trifle wistful. All these happy people.

The crowd swirled about him, as changing-unchanging as waves crashing on the beach, endlessly fascinating even as the eye grabs and fails to comprehend. Faces contorted with laughter that was too shrill, too manic, skin too flushed, beaded with sweat. What am I doing here? the bureaucrat asked himself. I'm not going to accomplish anything tonight. The forced gaiety depressed him.

The evening was growing late. The children had evaporated, and the adults remaining were louder and drunker. Sucking powdered sugar from his fingers, the bureaucrat almost stumbled into a brawl. Two drunks were pushing a surrogate around, flattening its ribs and ripping off its arms and legs one by one. The thing struggled on the ground, protesting loudly as they tore off its last remaining limb, then went dead as the operator gave up on the evening as a bad cause. The bureaucrat skirted the laughing spectators and continued down the road.

A woman in a green-and-blue fantasia, Spirit of the Waters perhaps, or Sky and Ocean, emerald plumes flying up from her headdress, came toward him. Her costume was cut low, and she had to hold up the spangled skirt with one hand to keep it from brushing the ground. The crowd parted like water before her, cleaved by an almost tangible aura of beauty. She looked straight at him, her eyes blazing green as the soul of the forest. Nearby, a chanteuse sang that the heart was like a little bird, looking for a nest. She set the crowds swirling like brightly painted metal bobbins. The green woman was swept to him, a mermaid cast up by the sea.

Automatically the bureaucrat took a step backward to let this vision by. But she stopped him with a touch of one green leather glove. "You," she said, and those green eyes and crisp white teeth seemed about to tear into him, "I want you."

She put an arm about his waist and led him away.

By the edge of the jubilee the woman paused to pluck a waxflower from one sagging string. She cupped it in both hands, and bent at stream's edge to place it in the water. Other flowers bobbed and whirled on the stream, spinning slowly, a stately ballroom dance.

As she crouched over the sphere of light, he saw that her arms above the gloves were covered with stars and triangles, snakes and eyes, gnostic tattoos of uncertain meaning.

Her name, she said, was Undine. They strolled down Cheesefactory Road beyond the ruck of houses, deep into a forest of roses. Thorny vines were everywhere; they climbed pillars formed by trees that had been choked by their profusion, sprawled along the ground, exploded into bloodspeckled bushes large as hills. The air was heavy with their scent, almost cloying. "I should have trimmed these back some," the woman said as they ducked under a looping arch of the small pink flowers. "But so close to the jubilee tides, who'd bother?"

"Are these native?" asked the bureaucrat, amazed at their extent. The flowers were everywhere he looked.

"Oh, no, these are feral Earth stock. The original industrielle had them planted along the roadside; she liked their look. But without any natural enemies, they just exploded. This extends, oh, kilometers around. On the Piedmont they'd be a problem; here, the tides will just wash them away."

They walked some way in silence. "You're a witch," the bureaucrat said suddenly.

"Oh, you've noticed?" He could feel her amused smile burning in the night air beside his face. The tip of her tongue touched the edge of his ear, gently traced the swirls down into its dark center, withdrew. "When I heard you were looking for Gregorian, I decided to have a look at you. I studied with Gregorian when we were children. Ask me anything you want." They came to a clearing in the rosebushes, and a small unpainted hut. "Here we are."

"Will you tell me where Gregorian is?"

"That's not what you want." That smile again, those unblinking green eyes. "Not at the moment."

"This must have a thousand eyelets," he said, clumsily unhooking the back of the fantasia. A slice of flesh appeared just below the downy nape of Undine's neck, widened, reached downward. The tips of his fingers brushed pale skin, and she shivered slightly. A single waxflower burned on a nightstand beneath a sentimental holo of Krishna dancing. The flame leaped and fell, throwing warm shadows through the room. "There. That's the last of them."

The witch turned, reached hands to shoulders, lowered the

gown. Large breasts, the faintest trifle overripe, floated into view, tipped with apricot nipples. Slowly she let the cloth slip down, over a full, soft belly, its deep navel aswim in shadow. A tuft of hair appeared, and, laughing, she held the dress so that only the very topmost hint of her vagina showed.

"Oh, the heart is like a little bird," she sang softly, swaying in time to the music, "that perches in your hand."

This woman was a trap. The bureaucrat could feel it. Gregorian had his hooks set in her just below the skin. If he were to kiss her, the barbs would pierce his own flesh, too deep and painful to rip out, and the magician would be able to play him like a fish, wearing him down, tiring him out, until he lost the will to fight and sank to the bottom of his life and died.

"And if you do not seize it . . ." She was waiting.

He should leave now. He should turn and flee.

Instead, he reached for her face, touched it lightly, wonderingly. Her lips turned to his, and they kissed deeply. The costume rustled as it fell to the floor. Her hands reached inside his jacket to undo his shirt. "Don't be so gentle," she said.

They tumbled to the bed, and she slid him within her. She was wet and open already, slippery and warm and fine. Her soft, wide belly touched him, then her breasts. She was just past her prime, poised on the instant before the long slide into age, and especially arousing to him for that. She'll never be so beautiful again, he thought, so ripe and full of juices. She clasped her legs about his waist and rocked him like a ship on the water, gently at first, then faster, as if a storm were building.

Undine, he thought for no reason. Ysolt, Esme, Theodora—the women here have names like dried flowers or autumn leaves.

A gust of wind sent the flowerlight scurrying for the corners, hurrying back again. Undine kissed him furiously on the face, the neck, the eyes. The bed creaking beneath them, they rolled over and over one another, now on the bottom, now on top, and over again, until he lost track of who was on top and who on the bottom, of where his body ended and hers began, of exactly which body belonged to whom. And then at last she was Ocean herself, and he lost all sense of self, and drowned.

"Again," she said.

"I'm afraid you've mistaken me for someone else," the bureaucrat said amiably. "Someone considerably younger. But if you're willing to wait twenty minutes or so, I'll be more than happy to try again."

She sat up, her magnificent breasts swaying slightly. Faint daggers of Caliban's light slanted through the window to touch them both. The candle had long since guttered out. "You mean to say you don't know the method by which men can have orgasm after orgasm without ejaculating?"

He laughed. "No."

"The girls won't like you if you have to stop a half hour every time you come," she said teasingly. Then, seriously, "I'll teach you." She took his cock in her hand, waggled it back and forth, amused by its limpness. "After your vaunted twenty minutes. In the meantime I can show you something of interest."

She threw the blanket lengthwise over her shoulders, as if it were a shawl. It made a strange costume in the dim light, with sleeves that touched the ground and a back that didn't quite reach her legs, so that two pale slivers of moon peeped out at him. Naked, he padded after her into the clearing behind the hut. "Look," she said.

Light was bursting from the ground in pale sheets of pink and blue and white. The rosebushes shimmered with pastel light as if already drowned in Ocean's shallows. The ground here had been dug up recently, churned and spaded, and was now suffused with pale fire. "What is it?" he asked wonderingly.

"Iridobacterium. They're naturally biophosphorescent.

You'll find them everywhere in the soil in the Tidewater, but usually only in trace amounts. They're useful in the spiritual arts. Pay attention now, because I'm going to explain a very minor mystery to you."

"I'm listening," he said, not comprehending.

"The only way to force a bloom is to bury an animal in the soil. When it decomposes, the iridobacteria feed on the products of decay. I've spent the last week poisoning dogs and burying them here."

"You killed dogs?" he said, horrified.

"It was quick. What do you think is going to happen to them, when the tides come? They're like the roses, they can't adapt. So the humane-society people organized Dog Control Week, and paid me by the corpse. Nobody's about to haul a bunch of mutts to the Piedmont." She gestured. "There's a shovel leaning against my hut."

He fetched the shovel. In a month this land would be under water. He imagined fishes swimming through the buildings while drowned dogs floated mouths open, caught head down in tangles of drowning rosebushes. They would rot before the hungry kings of the tides would accept their carcasses. At the witch's direction, he shoveled the brightest patches of dirt into a rusty steel drum almost filled with rainwater. The dirt sank, and bright swirls of phosphorescence rose in the water. Undine skimmed the top with a wooden scraper, slopping the scum into a wide pan. "When the water evaporates, the powder that remains is rich in iridobacteria," she said. "There's several more steps necessary to process it, but now it's in concentrated form, that can wait until I reach the Piedmont. It's common as sin now, but it won't grow up there."

"Tell me about Gregorian," the bureaucrat said.

"Gregorian is the only perfectly evil man I've ever met," Undine said. Her face was suddenly cold, as harsh and stern as Caliban's rocky plains. "He is smarter than you, stronger than you, more handsome than you, and far more determined. He has received an offplanet education that's at least the equal of yours, and he's a master of occult arts in which you do not believe. You are insane to challenge him. You are a dead man, and you do not know it."

"He'd certainly like me to believe that."

"All men are fools," Undine said. Her tone was light again, her look disdainful. "Have you noticed that? Were I in your position, I'd arrange to contract an illness or develop a moral qualm about the nature of my assignment. It might be a black mark on my record, but I would outlive the embarrassment."

"When did you meet Gregorian?" The bureaucrat dumped more dirt in the drum, raising mad swirls of phosphorescence.

"That was the year I spent as a ghost. I was a foundling. Madame Campaspe bought me the year I first bled—she'd seen promise in me. I was a shy, spooky little thing to begin with, and as part of my training, she imposed the discipline of invisibility. I kept to the shadows, never speaking. I slept at odd times and in odd places. When I was hungry, I crept into the homes of strangers and stole my food from their cupboards and plates. If I was seen, Madame beat me—but after the first month, I was never seen."

"That sounds horribly cruel."

"You are in no position to judge. I was watching from the heart of an ornamental umbrella bush the morning that Madame tripped over Gregorian. Literally tripped—he was sleeping on her doorstep. I learned later that he'd walked two days solid without food, he was so anxious to become her apprentice, and then collapsed on arrival. What a squawk! She kicked him into the road, and I think he broke a rib. I climbed to the roof of her potting shed and saw her harass him out of sight. Quick as a thought, I slid to the ground, stole a turnip for my breakfast from the garden, and was gone. Thinking that was the last of that ragged young man.

"But the next day he was back.

"She chased him away. He came back. Every morning it was the same. He scrounged for food during the day—I do not know if he stole, worked, or sold his body, for I was not quite interested enough to follow him, though by now I could walk down the center of Rose Hall in broad daylight without being noticed. But every morning he was back on the stoop.

"After a week, she changed tactics. When she found him on the doorsill, she would throw him some small change. The little ceramic coins that were current then, the orange and green and blue chips—they've gone back to silver since. She treated him as a beggar. Because, you see, he held himself very proudly, and there was a dirty gray trace of lace on the cuffs of his rags; she could tell he was haut-bourgeois. She thought to shame him away. But he'd snatch the coins from the air, pop them into his mouth, and very ostentatiously swallow. Madame pretended not to notice. From the attic window of the beautician's shop across the street, I watched this duel between her stiff back and his nasty grin.

"A few days later I noticed a horrible smell by the stoop, and discovered that he'd been shitting behind the topiary bushes. There was a foul heap of his leavings studded with the ceramic coins she had been throwing him. So that finally Madame had no choice but to take him in."

"Why?"

"Because he had the spirit of a magician. He had that unswerving, unbreakable will that the spiritual arts require, and the sudden instinct for the unexpected. Madame could no more ignore him than a painter could ignore a child with perfect visualization. Such a gift only comes along once in a generation.

"She tested him. You are familiar with the device used to give the experience of food to surrogates?"

"The line-feed. Yes, very familiar."

"She had one mounted in a box. An offworld lover had

wired it up for her. It was stripped down so that she could feed raw current into the nerve inductor. Do you know how it would feel to hold your hand within its field?"

"It would hurt like hell."

"Like hell indeed." She smiled sadly, and he could see the ghost of the schoolgirl behind her smile. "I remember that box so well. A plain thing with a hole in one side and a rheostat on top calibrated from one to seven. If I close my eyes, I can see it, and her long fingers atop it, and that damned water rat of hers perched on her shoulder. She warned me that if I took my hand out of the box before she told me to, she would kill me. It was the most terrifying moment of my life. Even Gregorian, ingenious though he was, could never top that."

Undine skimmed more slop off the water. Her voice was soft and reminiscent. "When she moved the dial off zero, it felt like an animal had bitten right through my flesh. Then slowly, oh, excruciatingly slowly, she moved it up to one, and that was an order of magnitude worse. What agonies I suffered! I was crying aloud by three, and blind with pain by four. At five I yanked out my hand, determined to die.

"She gave me a hug then, and told me she had never seen anyone do as well, that I would someday be more famous than she."

For a long moment the witch was silent.

"I slipped through an open window and into the next room when Madame led Gregorian in. More silent than a wraith, I drifted from shadow to shadow, leaving not the echo of a footfall behind. I left the door open one fingerspan, so I could peer from darkness into light. Then I retreated to a closet within the second room. Through the crack of the door I could see their distant reflections in the mantel mirror. Gregorian was skinny, barefoot, and dirty. I remember thinking how insignificant he looked alongside Madame Campaspe's aristocratic figure.

"Madame sat him down by the hearth. A murmur of voices

as she explained the rules. She drew away the fringed cloth that covered the box. Cocky as a crow, he placed his hand within.

"I saw his face jump—that involuntary hop of the muscles—when she first touched the dial. I saw how pale he grew, how he trembled as she increased the pain. He did not take his eyes off of her.

"She took him all the way up to seven. His body was rigid, his fingers spasming, but his head held straight and unforgiving, and he had not blinked. I think even Madame feared him then. Sitting there in his ragged clothes, his eyes burning like lanterns.

"I was so still my heart did not beat. My immobility was perfect. But somehow Gregorian knew. His head rose, and he looked in the mirror. He saw me, and he grinned. A horrible grin, a skull's grin, but a grin nonetheless. And I knew then that try though she might, she would never break him."

"I'm done now." She set a piece of cheesecloth over the tray, and the bureaucrat followed her back inside, slim crescent moons winking at him one after the other from beneath the blanket.

"What's it good for?" he asked when they were both seated on the bed again, facing each other cross-legged, her vagina a sweet dark shadow within the protective circle of her legs. "The powder you make from dogs."

"We mix it with ink and inject it beneath the skin." She rotated a hand before his face; in the shadows it was colorless, unmarked. "Each design represents a ritual the woman of power is entitled to perform, and every ritual represents knowledge, and all knowledge properly applied is control." Suddenly a marking on her hand flared into light. It was a small fish, visible through the skin. "Turning the markings on and off at will is a reminder of that control." One by one the tattoos flickered on: a pyramid, a vulture, a wreath of cocks. Stars flared into subdermal novae and struck fire to serpents, to moons, to alchemical elementals.

"Mirandan microflora is all but incompatible with Terran biology. Injected beneath the skin, they can get enough nourishment to stay alive but not enough to grow. There they stay, starving and comatose until I awaken them." Now all the tattoos were aglow. They climbed her arms almost to her shoulders.

"How do you do that?"

"Oh, that's one of the very first things you learn, how to raise the temperature of your body. Here." She lifted one of his hands. "It takes next to nothing. Concentrate on your fingertips, will them to be warmer. Think of hot things. Try to make them hot." She waited, then said, "Well?"

His fingertips tingled. "I'm not sure."

"You think it's just power of suggestion." A tiny starburst appeared at the tip of her finger, floated before his eye. "This is the first marking I received. Turn your finger hot, the goddess said, and it burst into light. I was so amazed. I felt then that my life had taken a great turn, that nothing would ever be the same again." She was touching his leg gently, sliding fingers slowly up, rapidly down, stroke stroke stroke.

"What goddess said?"

"When someone teaches you that which is of spiritual value, you do not learn such things from a human: The person partakes of divinity, becomes as one with the godhead. Thus, when Madame Campaspe taught Gregorian and me, she was to us the goddess." Her hand reached up, to stroke his penis, which almost without his noticing it had grown hard and aroused again. "Well! It's time for me to be your goddess now." She lay back, legs wide, and drew him atop her.

"I want to talk about Gregorian," the bureaucrat said uncertainly. She had him by both hands now, and was sliding him into her warm depths.

"No reason we can't do both." She clasped him tight and rolled him over, so that she sat on top. "The ritual you are about to learn from the goddess, the way of controlling ejaculation, is known as the worm ouroboros, after the great serpent of Earth which eats its own tail forever and is replenished thereby: a perfect closed system, such as does not exist on the mundane realm, not even your floating metal cities." She moved up and down on him slowly, graceful as a swan in moonglimmer, and he reached up to caress her breasts. "It has physical benefits that extend beyond the obvious, and is an excellent introduction to the Tantric mysteries. What specifically do you want to know about Gregorian?"

His hands slid down the front of her body, touched gently the tip of her pinkness, moved to clasp her as she eased herself down on him: nipples, breasts, belly, chin. "I want to know where I can find him."

"Somewhere downriver, I'd guess. People say he has a permanent place in Ararat, but who can say? He doesn't really need a permanent address, because he never allows people to find him."

"What about the people who pay to be changed into sea-dwellers?"

"They don't find him—he finds them. He's looking for a special sort of person, isn't he? Anxious to stay in the Tidewater, willing to change into a nonhuman shape to do so, ready to be convinced by Gregorian's commercials, and rich enough to pay his prices. I'm sure he had a sucker list drawn up long ago."

"When did you see him last?"

"Oh, it was years and years ago." Her teeth played with his earlobe; her breath was warm on his cheek. "He was headed for Ocean when he finally left Madame, but he got no further than heliostat station seventeen. He met somebody there, and the next anybody heard, he was offplanet. Do you like this?" Her nails ran lightly up his sides.

"Yes."

"Good." She put her hands at the base of his spine and abruptly raked them up his back. He arced involuntarily, sucking in air. She'd left stinging tracks up his skin. "You like that too, and it surprises you, doesn't it? I learned that with Gregorian; he became a god and taught me how close pleasure and pain lie to each other." She laughed at him. "But one lesson per evening— pull out of me and lie down, I have something to show you."

She guided him over on his side, gently lifted one of his knees, and lowered her head between his legs. Playfully she kissed the tip of his penis, slid her tongue down its stalk, teased his balls with her lips. "Down here, this soft spot midway between your scrotum and your anus." She tickled it with her tongue. "Can you feel it?"

"Yes."

"Good. Ease your left hand down here—no, from behind, that's good. Now push at the spot I just showed you with the tips of your forefinger and middle finger. A little harder. Just so." She reared up on her knees. "Now I want you to breathe in deeply the way I do, not from the lungs but from the abdomen." She demonstrated, and the bureaucrat smiled at the solemn beauty of her breasts in the pale moonlight. Gently but firmly she moved his hand away. "It's your turn now. Sit up for this. Draw in deeply and slowly."

He obeyed.

"From the stomach."

He tried again.

"That's the way." She leaned back on her hands, put her legs about his waist, and drew him close. "This time I want you to pay attention to your body. When you feel ready to ejaculate— not when it's already begun, but just before—reach back and push down on yourself as I showed you. At the same time breathe in deeply, slowly. It should take about four seconds." She waved a hand back and forth slowly four times, counting out the beats. "Like that. You can slow down while you're doing that, but don't stop entirely, okay?"

"If you say so," the bureaucrat said dubiously.

The tip of his cock was touching her. Undine steadied it, and slid forward, atop it. "Ahhh," she said. Then, "You think it's too easy, that if something so simple were as effective as I say, your mommy would have told you about it, eh? Well, whether you believe me or not is of no importance. As long as you do as I say, you can postpone ejaculation indefinitely."

He clasped her tightly, lay back beneath her. "I think—"

"Don't."

He followed the exercise faithfully, listening to his body and stopping the ejaculation whenever it threatened. The moon rocked crazily through the window. Then an astonishing thing happened. Shortly after one of the near-ejaculations, he had an orgasm. The sensation took him, and he cried out, seizing Undine with all his strength, and felt the small taste of God wash through him. Then the orgasm was through, and he hadn't come yet. He was still erect, and strangely clearheaded, preternaturally aware and alert.

"What was that?" he asked in amazement.

"Now you understand," Undine said. "Orgasm is more than just a squirt of salt fluid." She was moving atop him, like a ship in the swell before the storm, her eyes half-lidded, her mouth open slightly. She licked her lips, smiled almost jeeringly. Her hair and breasts were sweaty. "You haven't mentioned Gregorian recently. Have you run out of questions?"

"Just the opposite, I'm afraid." He played with one breast, tracing circles about the aureole, lightly tugging at the nipple with thumb and forefinger. "My questions multiply with each answer. I don't understand why your mistress mistreated Gregorian so, why she tried to break him with pain. Surely that was counterproductive."

"With Gregorian it was," she agreed. "But had it worked . . . There's really no way to make you understand this without undergoing a similar experience. You'll have to take my word for it. But when the goddess claims your life, the first thing she has to do is to shatter your old world, in order to force you into the larger universe. The mind is lazy. It's comfortable where it is, and can only be driven into reality with pain or fear.

"But this is never done with malice, but with love. At the end of her test, Madame hugged me. I thought she despised me, I believed I was about to die, and then she hugged me. I can't tell you how good that hug felt. Better than anything we've done tonight. Better than anything I'd ever felt before. I cried. I felt wrapped in love, and I knew that I would do anything to be worthy of it. I would have died for that woman in that instant."

"But this didn't happen with Gregorian."

"No." She rocked slightly from side to side, moving him within her. "She never broke Gregorian. She tried many times, and each failed attempt made him stronger and more savage. And that's why he's going to kill you." Abruptly she rolled him atop her. For a second he was afraid he'd hurt her with his weight. "Well, in the meantime," she said, "I have my own uses for you."

He had four more orgasms before he finally came, and that final time was of an order of magnitude more intense than anything he'd ever felt before.

He did not so much fall asleep as pass out.

When he awoke, Undine was gone. Groggily he looked about the room: The furniture remained and a few discarded oddments. The fantasia lay on the floor, sad and a little tattered, several of the long rainbird plumes already broken. But there was an emptiness, a sense of abandonment, about the room; all personal touches were gone. He dressed and left.

It was late in the morning. Prospero was already high in the sky, and the town was empty. Doors hung open. Bedthings lay where they'd been flung in the grass. The husks of last night's fantasias littered the streets, like abandoned cicada shells. The bureaucrat strolled back to the center of Rose Hall, head clearing slowly, and felt like singing. His body ached, but pleasantly; his cock felt pink and raw. All he needed was a good breakfast to put him right with the world.

Chu stood by a truck with THE NEW BORN KING painted on the fender, and ARSHAG MINTOUCHIAN'S STRING THEATER AND ILLUSARIUM OF HEAVEN AND HELL, THE TEN MILLION CITIES AND THE ELEVEN WORLDS in seven garish colors on the van's sidewall. The bureaucrat remembered seeing it last night, shutters open and a puppet play in progress. Chu was talking to a fat, sweaty man with a fastidious little mustache. Arshag Mintouchian himself, evidently. "Have a good night?" she asked, and abruptly burst into laughter.

The bureaucrat stared at her in astonishment. Then Mintouchian too began laughing.

"What the hell's so funny?" the bureaucrat demanded, offended.

"Your hand," Chu said. "Oh, I see you've had a night to remember!" Then they were off again, the two of them, soared aloft on gusts of laughter like kites.

The bureaucrat looked at his hand. There was a fresh new tattoo there, a serpent that circled the middle finger of his left hand three times and then took its tail in its mouth.

6

Lost in the Mushroom Rain

"I'm the biggest thing you've ever seen," Mintouchian's thumb said. "Hey, I don't want to brag, babe, but you're gonna be sore in the morning." It paraded back and forth, proud as a rooster.

"Mmmm, I can see that," said Mintouchian's other hand, the one held closed with a long vulval slit between thumb and forefingers slightly ajar. "Come here, big boy!" He gaped it suddenly wide.

Everybody laughed.

"Modeste!" Le Marie called. "Arsène! Come and look at this."

"This isn't really the sort of thing children should witness," the bureaucrat demurred softly. Two pig farmers and one of the evac planners looked at him, and he reddened.

But none of the youngsters came in from the next room. They were watching television, engrossed in a fantasy world in which people traveled between stars not in lifetimes but in hours, where energies sufficient to level cities were wielded by lone altruists, where men and women changed sex four and five times a night, where everything was possible and nothing was forbidden. It was a scream straight from the toad buried at the base of the brain, that ancient reptile that wants everything at once, delivered to its feet and set ablaze.

The children sat in the darkness, saucer-eyed and unblinking.

"I'm so good. I'm gonna stretch you all out of shape."

"So you keep *saying*."

It was raining outside, but the kitchen was an island of warmth and light. Chu leaned against a wall, drink in one hand, careful to laugh no more than anyone else. The room smelled of fried pork brains and old linoleum. Under the table Anubis noisily thumped his tail. Le Marie's wife bustled about clearing away the dishes.

The landlord himself brought out two more pitchers of blood mixed half and half with fermented mare's milk. "Have another glass! I can't give it away!" The skinny old man set a glass before Mintouchian. With a small, tipsy smile and a nod, the puppeteer interrupted his performance to accept it. He drank deep, leaving a thin transient line of foam on the bottom edge of his mustache. Other roomers held forth their glasses as he returned his thumb and fist to combat.

"Don't you want any?"

"No, no, I'm stuffed."

"Try some! Do you have any idea how much this costs down North?"

Smiling, the bureaucrat held up his hands and shook his head. When the old man shrugged and turned away, he slipped backwards out onto the porch. As the door was closing, Mintouchian's fist spat out a limp and subdued thumb.

It giggled. "Next!"

Raindrops fell like small hammers, so hard they stung when they struck flesh. The bureaucrat stood on the lightless porch, staring through the screens. The world was all one color, neither gray nor brown but something that partook of both and neither. A sudden gust of wind parted the rain like curtains, and gave him a glimpse of the barges anchored on the river, then hid them away again. A house and a half down the street, all of Cobbs Creek faded to nonexistence.

Cobbs Creek was all hogs and lumber. The last of the pigs had already been butchered and hung in the smokehouses, but logs still floated down the creek to the mills, in a final fevered slashing of timber before the tides turned the trees to kelp. The bureaucrat watched the rain splash mud knee-high on the clapboard walls. It forced up the stale smell of earth from ground and road, tempered by the rising odors from the tomato bush by the herb garden and the red brick walkway around to the back.

He felt sad and lost, and he could not stop thinking of Undine. When he closed his eyes, he could taste her tongue, feel the touch of her breasts. The nail tracks lingering on his back stung at the memory of her. He felt utterly ridiculous and more than a little angry at himself. He was not a schoolboy to be haunted so by the vision of her eyes, her cheeks, the warm amusement in her smile.

He sighed, took Gregorian's notebook from his briefcase, flipped idly through its pages. *A new age of magic interpretation of the world is coming, of interpretation in terms of the will and not of the intelligence. There is no such thing as truth, either in the moral or the scientific sense.* Impatiently he skipped ahead.

What is good? Whatever increases the feeling of power, the will to power, and above all else, power itself. Rereading the words, he could see the young Gregorian in his mind, the doubtless gaunt magician-apprentice, filled with that sourceless teenage hunger for importance and recognition. *Men are my slaves.*

He put the book back, irritated by the naive posturing tone of its aphorisms. He knew this type of young man all too well; there had been a time when he was one of them. Then something tugged at his mind, and he took the notebook out again. There was an early exercise captioned *The Worm Ouroboros*. He read through the instructions carefully: *The magician places his wand in the chalice of the goddess. The handmaid herself* . . . Yes, under the newly transparent allegory was the same technique Undine had taught him the other day.

The people in the kitchen laughed again.

The bureaucrat found himself wishing the day were over, that the roads were safe to travel again, and he could be off and away. This town had been nothing but disappointing. The archeologists who had worked here were gone, the dig covered over and ground-stabilized, all trace of Gregorian lost in the outmigration of citizens to the Piedmont.

He squinted into the rain. There was a faint smudge of light in the gloom to the east, indistinct, almost nonexistent, and for a second he thought the storm was ending. Then it moved slightly. Not a natural light, then.

Who would be out on a day like this? he wondered.

The light brightened slowly, intensifying, drawing in on itself, picking up a touch of blue coloration. Now he could see it for what it was: the glowing videoscreen face of a surrogate trudging through the rain. Slowly the body took shape beneath that spark of blue—a scarecrow caricature of human form, with a rain slicker tied about the body and a wide-brimmed hat lashed to the headpiece to help keep water out of the mechanism.

Raincoat flapping in the wind, the surrogate approached.

It came straight for the hotel. The bureaucrat saw now that it carried something under one arm, a long, skinny box, exactly the right length to hold a dozen roses or perhaps a short rifle.

The bureaucrat stepped to the edge of the doorway, down onto the top step. Rain spattered his shoes, but an overhanging eave sheltered the rest of him. The surrogate came to the foot of the stoop, and looked up at him, grinning.

It was the false Chu.

* * *

"Who are you?" the bureaucrat said coldly.

"My name is Veilleur. If it matters." Veilleur smiled with sweet indifference. "I have a message for you from Gregorian. And a gift."

He frowned down at that arrogant adolescent smirk. This must surely be what Gregorian had been like in his youth. "Tell Gregorian I wish to speak with him in person, on a matter of interest to us both."

Veilleur pursed his lips with mock regret. "I'm afraid that the master is terribly busy these days. There are so many who desire his help. But if you care to share your matter of concern with me, I'd be happy to do whatever I can."

"It's of a confidential nature."

"Alas. Well, my business is brief. Master Gregorian understands that you have come into possession of a certain item which has some sentimental value to him."

"His notebook."

"Just so. A valuable learning tool, I might point out, that you lack the training to take advantage of."

"Still, it is not exactly devoid of interest."

"Even so, my master must beg its return. He trusts you will prove cooperative, particularly considering that the book is not, properly speaking, yours."

"Tell Gregorian he can pick up his book from me any time he wishes. In person."

"I am in the master's confidence. What can be said to him can be said to me, what can be given him can be given me. In a sense one might say that where I am he is indeed present."

"I won't play this game," the bureaucrat said. "If he wants his book, he knows where I am."

"Well, what can't be arranged one way must be arranged another," Veilleur said philosophically. "I was also instructed to give you this." The surrogate laid its box at the bureaucrat's feet. "The master directed me to tell you that a man bold enough to fuck a witch deserves something to remember her by."

Briefly his electronic grin burned on the telescreen, bright as madness. Then the surrogate turned away.

"I've spoken to Gregorian's father!" the bureaucrat shouted. "Tell him that too!"

The surrogate strode away without a backward glance. The wind lifted and swirled its raincoat, and then it was gone.

Suddenly fearful, the bureaucrat crouched down and lifted the box. It held something heavy. He stepped back onto the porch, unwrapping the wet oilskin, then removed the lid.

Stars, snakes, and comets burned wildly in the box's dim interior. Putrefaction had just begun, and the iridobacteria were feasting.

The laughter in the kitchen died when he entered. "Lord of ghouls, man," Le Marie said, "what happened to you?" Chu seized his arm, steadied him.

"I'm afraid something unfortunate has occurred," a voice said. His own. The bureaucrat laid down the box on the kitchen table. A little girl wearing a red jeunes évacuées kerchief with tiny black stars about her neck craned up on tiptoe to reach for the box, and had her hand slapped. Mintouchian, who stood close enough to see within, hastily slapped the lid back on and rewrapped the cloth. "Something untoward." He sounded dreadful, like a recording played at the wrong speed, false and subtly inhuman.

A scurry of activity. Two men ran outside. A chair was scraped forward, and Le Marie folded him down into it. "I'll call the nationals," Chu said. "They can lift in a laboratory as soon as the rain ends." Somebody gave the bureaucrat a drink, and he gulped it down. "My God," he said. "My God." Anubis emerged from beneath the table and licked his hand.

The men who had run outside returned, wet to the skin. The door slammed to behind them. "Nobody out there," one said.

More children came crowding in. Mother Le Marie hastily set the box up atop the pie cabinet, out of reach. "What's in there?" one of the locals asked from the far side of the kitchen.

"Undine," the bureaucrat said. "It's Undine's arm." To his utter and complete embarrassment, he burst into tears.

They led him protesting feebly to his room, eased him down on the bed, took off his shoes. His briefcase was laid by his side. Then, with consoling murmurs, they left him alone. I shall never be able to sleep, he thought. The room smelled of mildew and old paint. Barnacles speckled the walls and encrusted the mirror, from flies blown in at night by the fever wind, over the top of a window that would not quite close. Wind through that same, narrow slot stirred the curtains now. Doubtless it would never be repaired.

The dim thunder of water on the roof slowly faded as the storm abated. The rain died away to a drizzle and finally a mist.

A voice separated from the kitchen conversation and floated up the stairs. "Mushroom rain," it said gently.

The bureaucrat could not sleep. The pillow was hard and buzzed with fatigue. His skull was stuffed with gray cotton. After some time he arose, picked up his briefcase, and went outside, shoeless and unnoticed.

The rain was so fine that the droplets seemed to hang in the air, muting and silvering a changed world. Sprays of translucent blue tubes arched over the street. Little violet mandolins sprouted from doorways, and the rooftops were hidden under delicate fantasy architectures of tan and rose and palest yellow latticework. Mushroom rain. The frothy structures were growing even as he watched.

Houses had mutated into nightmare castles caught midway in transition from stone to organic life. Like a crab, he scuttled by their swaying spires, brushing back dainty lace fans that crumbled at his touch. There was a warm orange glow in the street ahead of him, and he made for it.

The rectangle of light was the open back doorway to the New Born King's van. He entered.

Mintouchian sat behind a small folddown table. A circle of yellow light rested on its center, and within it danced a small metal woman.

Mintouchian's fingers were studded with radio remotes. He wove his hands back and forth, warping and interpenetrating the fields. "Ah, it's you. Couldn't sleep, eh?" he said. "Me neither." He nodded toward the woman. "Lovely little thing, isn't she?"

Looking closer, the bureaucrat could see that the woman's figure was made up of thousands of gold rings of varying sizes, so that the arms and legs and torso tapered naturally. Her head was smooth and featureless, but angled to suggest high cheekbones and a narrow chin. She wore a simple cloth poncho tied at the waist and long enough to suggest a dress. It flew up in the air when Mintouchian spun his hands.

"Yes." The golden woman rippled her arms with impossible, thousand-jointed fluidity. "What are you doing?"

"Thinking." Mintouchian stared blindly down into the light. "I loved a witch once, a long time ago. She—well, you don't want to hear the story. Very much like yours. Very much. She was drowned when I . . . Well. There's no such thing as a new story, is there? As who should know better than me?"

Without interrupting the dancer, he half-closed his eyes and leaned back against the wall. The wall was covered with puppets, bagged in plastic membranes and bound so tightly escape was unimaginable. It was a museum of puppetry. There were Mr. Punch and his wife, Judy, his cousin Pulchinello, moon-pale Pierrot, famed Harlequin and sweet Columbine, Tricky Dick, Till Eulenspiegel, Good Kosmonaut Minsk, all the ancient archetypes of roguery and heroism awaiting their next breath of borrowed life. "You realize that puppetry is the purest form of theater?"

"The simplest, you mean?"

"Simple! You give it a try, if you think it's so simple! No, I mean the purest. Here I sit, the creator, and you there, the viewer. Our minds are distinct, they cannot touch. But there, between us, I place our little poppet." The lady glided forward, swooned into a curtsy that swept the ground, drew up lightly as a leaf caught by the wind. "She exists partly in my mind, and partly in yours. For the instant they overlap." His hands were dancing, and the metal figure with them. The bureaucrat's attention shifted from one to the other, unable to focus entirely on either.

"Look," Mintouchian marveled. The doll froze motionless. "She has no face, no sex. Yet look at this." The puppet raised her head coquettishly, and glanced sidelong at the bureaucrat. Her body shifted weight on distinctly feminine hips. The bureaucrat looked up from her and saw Mintouchian staring intently into his eyes. "Do you know how television works? The screen is divided into horizontal lines, and the scanner draws a picture on the screen two lines at a time, skips two lines, then draws two more, down to the bottom. Then it goes back to the beginning and fills in those spaces it skipped the first time around. So that you don't actually see the whole picture at any time. You assemble it within your mind. Holistic screens have been tried from time to time, but people didn't take to them. They lacked the compulsive element of real television. Because they only provided pictures. They did not seduce the brain into cooperating with the violation of reality." The puppet danced lightly, gracefully.

The bureaucrat's lips were dry, and there was a strange, vivid taste in his mouth. He had a hard time focusing on the puppeteer's argument. "I'm not sure I'm following this."

The golden woman threw the bureaucrat a scornful look over an upraised shoulder. Mintouchian smiled. "Where does this illusion before you exist? In my mind or yours? Or does it exist within the space in which our two minds intermesh?"

He raised his hands, and the woman dissolved in a shower of golden rings.

The bureaucrat looked up at Mintouchian, and the rings continued to spin and fall within his mind. He closed his eyes and saw them in the blackness, still falling. Opening his eyes did not rid him of them. The van seemed oppressively close and then as if it were not there at all. It seemed to pulse open and shut about him. He felt queasy. Carefully he said, "There is something wrong with me."

But Mintouchian was not listening. In a musing, drunken voice he said, "Sometimes people ask why I got into this business. I don't know. Usually I just say, Why would anyone want to play God? Make a face and shrug. But sometimes I think it's because I wanted to prove to myself that other people exist." He looked straight at and through the bureaucrat, as if he were alone and talking to himself. "But we can't know that, can we? We can never really know."

The bureaucrat left without saying a word.

He wandered down to the river. The docks were transformed. He looked over a sudden forest of gold mushrooms that had swallowed up a line of electric lights, and now burned with borrowed light, fairy peninsulas out into the water. He looked again and saw naked women wading in the river. With slow grace the moon-white women glided by the anchored boats, stirring them with gentle wake, their eyes level with the tips of the masts.

The bureaucrat stared up at them wonderingly, these silent phantoms, and thought, There are no such creatures, though for the life of him he could not imagine why not. Thigh-deep, they moved silent as dreams and large as dinosaurs, somnambulant yet bold as a wish. Something black turned and tumbled in the water, bumped against one rounded belly and sank away, and for one horrible instant he feared it was Undine herself, drowned in the river and gone to feed the hungry kings of the tides.

Then, with an electric thrill of terror, he saw one of the women turn to look directly at him, eyes as green as the sea and merciless as a northern squall. She smiled down on him over perfect breasts, and he stumbled back from her. Drugged, he thought, I have been drugged. And the thought made wonderful sense, struck him with the force of revelation even, though he did not know what to do with it.

With no sense of transition whatsoever he found himself walking through the woods. The trail was hedged around with mushrooms, bristling with soft-tipped spears that brushed their fleshy heads lightly against his face and arms as he passed. I must find help, he thought. If only he knew which way the trail went, toward town or away.

"What did you do then?"

"Hah?" The bureaucrat shook himself, looked around, and realized that he was sitting on the forest floor, staring at the blue screen of a television set. The sound was off and the image inverted, so that the people hung down from above like bats. "What did you say?"

"I said, what did you do then? Is there some problem with your hearing?"

"I've been having a little trouble preserving continuity lately."

"Ah." The fox-faced man opposite him gestured at the set. "Let us watch some more television, then."

"It's upside down," the bureaucrat protested.

"Is it?" The fox man stood, flipped the television over effortlessly, squatted again. He was not wearing any clothing, but there was a folded pair of dungarees where he had been sitting. The bureaucrat had likewise made a pad of his jacket to protect himself from the damp. "Is that better?"

"Yes."

"Tell me what you see."

"There are two women fighting. One has a knife. They are rolling over and over in the dirt. Now one is standing. She brushes her hair back from her forehead. She's all sweaty, and she holds up the knife and looks at it. There's blood on the blade."

The fox sighed. "I have fasted and bled for six days without results. Sometimes I doubt I will ever be holy enough to see the pictures."

"You cannot see any images on television?"

A sly smile, a twitch of whiskers. "None of my kind can. It is ironic. We few survivors hide among you, attend your schools, work in your field, and yet we do not know you at all. We cannot even see your dreams."

"It's just a machine."

"Then why can we see nothing on it but a bright and shifting light?"

"I remember—" he began, almost dropped the thought, then caught the wind and sailed effortlessly forward—"I remember talking with a man who said that the picture does not exist. That the images are made in two parts and woven together within the brain."

"If that is so, then our brains must lack the loom, and we will never see your dreams." The creature licked its lips with a long black tongue. The bureaucrat felt a sudden shiver of dread.

"This is madness," he said. "I cannot be talking with you."

"Why is that?"

"The last haunt died centuries ago."

"There are not many of us left, true. We were very near

extinction before we learned how to survive in the interstices of your society. Physically altering our appearance was easy, of course. But passing as human, earning your money without attracting your interest, is more of a challenge. We are forced to hide among the poor, in shanties at the edge of farmlands and shotgun flats in the worst parts of the Fan.

"Well, enough of that." Fox stood, offered his hand, raised the bureaucrat to his feet. He helped him into his jacket, and handed him his briefcase. "You must leave now. I really ought to kill you. But your conversation was so interesting, the early parts especially, that I will give you a short head start." He opened his mouth to show row upon row of sharp teeth.

"Run!" he said.

He had been running through the forest so long, crashing through tunnels of feathery arches, stumbling into towers of spiked and antlered tentacles that collapsed noiselessly about him, that it had become a steady state of existence, as natural and unquestionable as any other. Then it all melted about him, and he was in a boneyard, among skeletons grown together and refleshed, rib cages growing fungal breasts, pelvises sprouting pale phalluses, and incurvate vaginas. The dead were reborn as monsters, twins and triplets joined at hip and head, whole families overwhelmed by yeasting masses, a single skull peering up from the top, red-painted teeth agape as if it were either laughing or screaming.

Then that was gone too, and he was stumbling across flat, empty ground. Gasping, he stopped. The earth here was hard as stone. Nothing grew on it. To one side he could hear the excited water music of Cobbs Creek, in full flood and eager to merge with the river. This would be the dig site, he realized, a full eighth-mile square injected down to the bedrock with stabilizers after burying no fewer than three sealed navigation beacons in its heart, against the return of the land in a new age. He breathed convulsively, lungs afire. Was I running? he wondered, and felt the sudden dead weight of futility as he remembered that Undine was dead.

"I found him!" someone cried.

A hand touched his shoulder, spun him around. Slowly he turned, and a fist struck his jaw.

He fell, legs sprawling out beneath him. His head smashed to the ground, and his arms flew wide. With a vague, all-encompassing amazement he felt a booted foot crash into his ribs. "Whoof!" His breath fled out of him, and he knew the grinding darkness of granite-boned earth turning under impact. Something loose and giving.

Three dark figures floated above him, shifting in planes of depth, movement defining and redefining their spatial relationship with each other and himself. One of them might have been a woman. He was too alert to possibilities, his attention too quick and darting, to be sure. They danced about him, images multiplying and leaving dark trails, until he was woven into a cage of enemies. "What," he croaked. "What do you want?"

His voice gonged and reverberated, coming deep and from a distance, like a vast drowned bell tolling from the bottom of the sea. The bureaucrat tried to raise his arms, but they responded oh so slowly. It was as if he were consciousness alone, seated within the head of a carved granite giant.

They beat him with a thousand fists, blows that rippled and overlapped, leaving pain in their wake. Then, abruptly, it was over. A round face, limned with witch-fire, floated into view.

Veilleur smiled down on him mockingly. "I told you there were ways and ways," he said. "Nobody ever takes me seriously, that's my problem."

He took up the briefcase.

"Come on," Veilleur said to the others. "I've got what we were after."

Then gone.

*   *   *

Time was a flickering gray fire constantly consuming all things, so that what appeared to be motion was actually the oxidation and reduction of possibility, the collapse of potential matter from grace to nothingness. The bureaucrat lay watching the total destruction of the universe for a long time. Perhaps he was unconscious, perhaps not. Whatever he was, it was a state of awareness he had never experienced before. He had nothing to compare it to. Could one be drugged-conscious and drugged-asleep? How would you know? The ground was hard, cold, damp, under him. His coat was torn. He suspected that some of the dampness was his own blood. There were too many facts to deal with. Still, he knew he should be concerned about the blood. He clung to that island scrap of surety even as his thoughts spun dizzily around and around, lofting him high to show him the world and then slamming him down to begin the voyage again.

He dreamed that a creature came walking down the road. It had the body of a man and the head of a fox. It wore a tattered pair of dungarees.

Fox, if Fox it was, halted when he came to where the bureaucrat lay, and crouched beside him. That sharp-nosed face sniffed at his crotch, his chest, his head. "I'm bleeding," the bureaucrat said helpfully. Fox frowned down at him. Then that head swung away again, dissolving into the air.

He was whirled up into the ancient sky, thrown high as planets into old night and the void.

7

Who Is the Black Beast?

The common room was dark and stuffy. Thick brocade curtains with tinsel-thread whales and roses choked out the afternoon sun. Floral pomanders sewn into the furniture failed to mask the smell of mildew; rots and growths were so quietly pervasive here that they seemed not decay but a natural progression, as if the hotel were slowly transforming itself from the realm of the artificial to that of the living.

"I won't see him," the bureaucrat insisted. "Send him away. Where are my clothes?"

Mother Le Marie placed soft, cool brown-spotted hands on his chest and forced him back down on the divan, more by embarrassment than actual force. "He'll be here any minute now. There's nothing you can do about it. Be still."

"I won't pay him." The bureaucrat felt weak and irritable, and strangely guilty, as if he had done something shameful the night before. The water-stained plaster ceiling liquefied and flowed in his vision, its cracks and imperfections undulating like strands of seaweed. He squeezed his eyes shut for an instant. Nausea came and went in long, slow waves. His bowels felt loose.

"You don't have to." Le Marie tightened her jaw, a turtle trying to smile. "Dr. Orphelin will do the work as a favor to me."

In the hallway, the coffin-shaped coroner hummed gently to itself. One corner caught the light and glowed a pure and holy white. The bureaucrat forced himself to look away, found his gaze returning anyway. Two bored national police officers lounged against the wall, arms folded, staring into the television room. *Who was the father?* old Ahab roared. *I think I'm entitled to know.*

"I trust I have not grown so gullible as to consult a doctor," the bureaucrat said with dignity. "If I want medical attention, I shall employ the qualified machinery or, in extremis, a human with proper biomedical augmentation. But I will not swill down fermented swamp guzzle at the behest of some quasi-literate, uneducated charlatan."

"Be sensible. The nearest diagnostician is in Green Hill, while Dr. Orphelin is—"

"I am here."

He paused in the doorway, as if posing for a commemorative hologram: a lean man in a blue jacket of military cut with two rows of gold buttons. Then the worn white path down the middle of the carpet carried him past a rotting vacuum suit propped ornamentally against the bookcase, and he dumped his black bag alongside the divan. His hands were heavily tattooed.

"You have been drugged," the doctor said briskly, "and a diagnostician cannot help you. The medicinal properties of our native plants are not in its data base. Why should they be? Synthetics can do anything that natural drugs can, and they can be manufactured on the spot. But if you wish to understand what has happened to you, you must go not to one of your loathsome machines but to one such as I who has spent years studying such plants." He had a lean, ascetic face with high cheekbones and cold eyes. "I am going to examine you now. You are not required to heed a word of what I have to say. However, I insist on your cooperation in the examination."

The bureaucrat felt foolish. "Oh, very well."

"Thank you." Orphelin nodded to Mother Le Marie. "You may leave now."

The old woman looked startled, then offended. She raised her chin and walked stiffly out. *Why won't you tell your uncle who the father is?* someone said, and a young woman's agonized voice cried, *Because there is no father!* before it was muffled by the closing door.

Orphelin peeled back the bureaucrat's eyelids, shone a small light in his ears, took a scraping from inside his mouth, and fed it to a diagnostick. "You should lose some weight," he remarked. "If you want, I can show you how to balance real and fairy foods in a diet." The bureaucrat stared stoically at a spray of pink silk roses, brittle and browning at the edges, and said nothing.

At last the examination ended. "Hum. Well, you shan't be surprised to learn that you've taken in some variety of neurotoxin. Could be any of a number of suspects. Did you experience hallucinations or illusions?"

"What's the difference?"

"An illusion is a misreading of actual sensory data, while a hallucination is seeing something that isn't there. Tell me what you saw last night. Just"—he held up a hand—"the high points, please. I have neither the time nor the patience for the extended story."

The bureaucrat told him about the giant women wading in the river.

"Hallucinations. Did you believe in their reality?"

He thought. "No. But they frightened me."

Orphelin smiled thinly. "You wouldn't be the first man with a fear of women. Oh be still, that was a joke. What else did you see?"

"I had a long talk with a fox-headed haunt. But that was real."

The doctor looked at him oddly. "Was it?"

"Oh yes. I'm quite sure of it. He carried me back to the hotel, later."

Nausea welled up again, and the room took on a heightened clarity and vividness. He could see every thread of fiber on the rug, every frayed fabric end on the divan crawling in his vision. He felt flushed, and the finger that Undine had tattooed burned.

There was a rap on the door.

"Yes?" the bureaucrat said.

Chu stuck her head in and said, "Excuse me, but the autopsy is complete, and we need you to accept the report."

"Come in here, please," Orphelin said. "And I'll need somebody else as well." Chu glanced at the bureaucrat, and then, when he shrugged, ducked into the hall. She spoke to the guards. The taller one shook his head. "Hold on," she said. A minute later she returned with Mintouchian in tow. He looked more hound than man, his face puffy and pink, his eyes sad and bloodshot.

"There's more to this than I had originally thought." The doctor held out his arms. "Grasp me by the wrists and hold on as tightly as possible." Chu took one arm, Mintouchian the other. "Pull! We're not here to hold hands."

They obeyed, and he slowly leaned forward, letting his head loll on his chest. The two had to struggle to hold him upright.

Orphelin's head whipped up, face transformed. His eyes were wide open, startlingly white. They quivered slightly. He parted his lips, and a third eye glared out from his mouth.

"Krishna!" Mintouchian gasped. All three eyes glanced toward him, then dismissively away. Horrified, the bureaucrat stared into that cold third eye.

Orphelin stared unblinkingly back. That eerie triple gaze

drove like a spike deep into the bureaucrat's skull. For a long moment nobody breathed.

Then the doctor's head collapsed on his chest again.

"All right," he said calmly. "You can let go now." They obeyed. "Have you ever considered spiritual training?" he asked.

The bureaucrat felt as if he'd just emerged from a dream. It seemed impossible now, what he had just seen. "I beg your pardon?"

"First off, the entity you spoke with was not a haunt, attractive though that notion might seem to you. The last haunt died in captivity in lesser year 143 of the first great year after the landing. What you saw was an avatar of one of their spirits. The one we call the Fox. It is an important natural power, though unreliable in certain aspects, and is generally taken as being an auspicious omen."

"I spoke with a solid, living being. He was neither ghost nor hallucination." The room was alive now, each strand of carpeting undulating in unseen currents, mottled light dancing on the ceiling.

"Perhaps," Mintouchian offered, "you spoke with a man in a mask."

Nausea made the bureaucrat snappish. "Nonsense. What would a man in a fox mask be doing out in the woods in the middle of the night?"

Chu stroked her mustache. "He could have been waiting for you. I really think we should consider the possibility that he was part of this elaborate game that Gregorian is playing with us."

The doctor looked startled. "Gregorian?"

"I studied offplanet," Orphelin said when the others had been dismissed. "Many years ago. I had a Midworlds scholarship." His back was to the bureaucrat; he had not spoken until the door was well and fully closed. "Six of the most miserable years of my life were spent in the Laputa Extension. The people who hand out the grants never consider what it's like to go from an artificially suppressed level of technology to one of the floating worlds."

"What does this have to do with Gregorian?"

Orphelin looked around for a seat, settled wearily down. His face was stiff and gray. "That was how I met Gregorian."

"You were friends, then?" Whenever the bureaucrat looked at Orphelin's face too long, the flesh melted away layer by layer, and the skull rose grinning to the surface. Only by regularly glancing away could he banish the vision.

"No, of course not." The doctor gazed sightlessly at a dusty crucifix ringed by a small collection of sepia flats. His clasped hands rested upon his knees. "I despised him on sight.

"We met in the dueling halls of the Puzzle Palace. Suicide was nominally illegal, but the authorities winked at it—training grounds for leadership and so on. He had a coterie of admirers listening to him talk about control theory and the biological effects of projective chaos weapons. A striking young man, charismatically self-assured. He had a bad reputation. His skin was pale, and he wore the offworld jewelry that was popular back then: bloodstones embedded in the fingers, bands of silver around the wrists with the veins routed through crystal channels."

"Yes, I remember that style," the bureaucrat said. "Expensive, as I recall."

Orphelin shrugged. "It was his popularity that most offended me. I was a material phenomenologist. So while Gregorian could freely discuss what *he* was learning, my education was very strictly controlled, and I wasn't allowed to take any of it out of class. What status I had in student circles came from my having studied under a pharmacienne before I came to Laputa. Oh, I was their trained ape all right! Dressed all in black with saltmouse skulls and feather fetishes hung on the fringes. I played suicide not so much for the prestige of winning, but to brush fingertips against death—morbid shock was much more common than anyone ever let on. I made dark hints that I won because I had occult powers. And Gregorian burst out laughing at the sight of me! Did you ever play suicide?"

The bureaucrat hesitated. "Once . . . I was young."

"Then I don't have to tell you that it's a rigged game. Anyone foolish enough to play by the rules is going to lose. I had mastered the standard means of cheating—tapping in extra data sources, relaying your opponent's signal through a millisecond-delay circuit, all the usual—and enjoyed a local reputation as a mind warrior. But Gregorian beat me three times running. I had a mistress, an Inner Circle bitch with those aristocratic near-abstract features that take three generations of intensive gene reworking to achieve. He humiliated me in front of her and his father and what few friends I had."

"You met his father? What was he like?"

"I have no idea. It was edited out before we left the halls. His father was somebody important who couldn't afford to be connected with the games. All I remember of him was that he was there.

"A year later I returned home to the Tidewater with Gregorian beside me. We shared a room at my parents' hotel as if we were close friends. By then, antipathy had blossomed into hatred. We'd agreed to have a wizard's duel—three questions each, winner take all.

"The night we went in search of the maddrake root was wet and starless. We dug by the paupers' boneyard, where we would not be disturbed. Gregorian straightened first, hands all mud. I have it, he said. He snapped the root in two and held it to my nose. Maddrake has a distinctive odor. It was only after I had swallowed my half that—that smile of his!—it occurred to me that he might have rubbed his hands with maddrake sap and offered instead the halfaman root, which is a close cousin but can be counteracted with a simple antidote. Too late. I had to trust him. We waited until the trees burned green to their cores and the wind spoke. Let us begin, I said.

"Gregorian leaped up and walked through the bones with his arms out, making the skeletons rattle. They were not well maintained, of course. The paint was faded, and half the bones had fallen to the ground so that we trod them underfoot. The death-forces flowed up from them and crawled under my skin, and that made me bold. I felt strong with death. Turn and face me, I commanded. Or are you afraid?

"He turned, and to my horror I saw that he had taken on the aspect of Crow. His head was huge and black: black beak, black feathers, bright obsidian eyes. There was that little bristle of hairlike feathers at the base of the beak, the narrow nostril slits halfway to its point. I had never seen a spirit invoked before. That's one question, he said in Crow's harsh voice. No, I am not.

"I assumed this was all illusion, an effect of the maddrake. Angrily I strode forward and seized his arms. The little deaths flowed into him and fought beneath his skin, so that his muscles writhed and spasmed. I squeezed. I was strong then, you must know. My grip should have choked off the blood and left his arms paralyzed. The death-forces should have killed him. But he shook my hands away effortlessly, and laughed.

"You cannot overpower Crow with your little tricks.

"How did you know I was seeing Crow? I asked. Feeling that horror that comes on realizing that one is completely out of his depth.

"That's two questions. Crow stropped his beak against a nearby skull, setting the whole skeleton aswing. I know all about you. I have an informant who tells me everything. The Black Beast.

"Who is the Black Beast? I cried.

"That's three questions. Crow poked his beak into a skull socket, teased out some small sweetmeat. I have answered two of them, and now it is my turn. First tell me: What does it mean when I say Miranda is black?

"I was angry at how he'd tricked the questions from me, but the duel's purpose is to test will against will; it had been fairly done. An inch down, I said, all the world-globe is an egg of blackness. Starlight does not touch it; only Prospero, Ariel, and Caliban contend for influence. Mystery is that close. This was all catechism, you see, baby stuff, and so I regained much of my confidence. As beneath the skull the brain is black. The magician understands this and contends for influence.

"Crow ruffled his feathers, then parted his beak as he threw back some dark gristly bit. That black tongue! What are the black constellations?

"They are the shapes formed by the starless spaces between the bright constellations. The uninitiated cannot see them and believe they do not exist, but once pointed out they cannot be forgotten. They are emblematic of the mysteries anyone can master but few realize exist.

"Crow poked about among the teeth with the tip of his beak. I'd offer you a maggot, he said, but there are barely enough here for me. One last question. Who is the Black Beast?

"What do you mean? I said angrily. I asked you that same question, and you wouldn't answer me. I don't believe in your Black Beast at all.

"Crow threw his head back then and screamed in triumph. Those beady little eyes were dark novae of malice. He spread out thumb and forefinger and said, you are that long erect. Your mistress was once involved in the Committee for the Liberation of Information, and only her mother's money hushed up the scandal. You suspect she is unfaithful to you because she says nothing of your own infidelities. You wet the bed long into your adolescence—you wound up apprenticed to your pharmacienne after she cured your bladder problem. The Black Beast has told me all about you. The Black Beast is someone very near to you. You trust the Black Beast, but you should not. The Beast is not your friend but mine.

"And he walked away. I shouted after him that our duel was not over, that there had been no clear winner. But he was gone. I told my parents he had been called away."

Dr. Orphelin sighed. "Gregorian disappeared from my life. Perhaps he transferred to another extension. But I could not get his question out of my mind. Who was the Black Beast? What false friend had told Gregorian my secrets? One morning I woke to find a drawing of a crow in flight tacked up on the wall. I awoke my mistress, pointed to it. What is that? I demanded.

"A picture of a bird, she said.

"What does it mean?

"It's just a picture, she said. You never objected to it before. She put a hand on my arm. I knocked it away. It wasn't there yesterday. I said. She was baffled and began to cry. Are you the Black Beast? I asked her. Are you?

"I could not read that sleek face of hers. That complex and all but noseless plane whose geometries I would trace by the hour with finger, tongue, and eye, now seemed a mask to me. What could lie behind it? I set her various traps. I asked her sudden questions. I accused her of impossibilities.

"She left me.

"But the Black Beast did not. I was expelled from Laputa for dueling. I came home to find a stuffed crow on the center of the dinner table. A big, jeering thing, with wings outspread. Nobody in his right mind would put such a thing where people ate. What does this mean? I asked. My mother thought I was joking. Who put this here? I demanded. She stammered guiltily. I overturned the table, screaming, How could you do this to me?

"My father said I was raving and should apologize. I called him a senile old fool. We had a fight, and I split open his head.

He had to go all the way to Port Deposit for treatment. My parents disowned me, and sued to remove my patronymic. I had to take on a new name.

"Who was the Black Beast? I was obsessed. I had lost my family; now I gave up my friends. Better to live alone than with a traitor at my back. Still, the Black Beast taunted me. I would wake up to find my chest covered with black feathers. Or I would receive a letter from Gregorian telling me things no one could know. I had dreams. Strangers passing through told painful stories from my childhood, secrets from my affairs.

"It was maddening.

"There came a day when my isolation was complete, my life shattered, my ambition gone. I lived alone in a hut by the salt marshes. Still the Black Beast left his sign. I would return from gathering herbs to find the word 'crow' scrawled above my bed. I would hear the cries of crows in the middle of the night. Mocking laughter followed me down the street. Finally I was driven to contemplate killing myself, just to get it over with. I held the knife to my heart and carefully judged the angle of thrust.

"Then the door opened—it should have been locked, but it opened anyway—and Gregorian stood before me. He grinned down at my fear, all teeth and malice, and said, Surrender.

"So I bowed down to him. He took me to a star-shaped room in the Puzzle Palace with a vaulted ceiling where five great wooden beams came together, and between them was blue plaster with gilt stars. There, he copied from me what herb lore I held—it was all he valued of what I knew—and cut away the bulk of my emotions, leaving me little more than the gray capacity for regret. And when I was no conceivable rival to him anymore, I asked the question, the one that had ruined my life: Who was the Black Beast?

"He leaned forward and whispered in my ear.

"You are, he said."

*   *   *

With sudden energy Orphelin stood and snapped shut his bag. "My diagnosis is that you were given three drops of tincture of angelroot. It is an intensive hallucinogen that leaves the user open to spiritual influences at the height of its action, but has no serious aftereffects. You're experiencing a touch of vitamin depletion. Have Mother Le Marie cook up a plate of yams and you'll be fine."

"Wait! Are you saying that Gregorian tapped your agent in the Puzzle Palace?" It was rare, but it happened, the bureaucrat knew. "Was that the forfeit when you lost to him in suicide?"

"You would believe that, of course," Orphelin said. "I know your type. Your eyes were closed long ago." He opened the door, unmuffling screams from the room across the hall.

Mother Le Marie stood just outside, back to them, staring through the door at a badly bruised woman lying unconscious on the floor. On the screen a door opened, and a figure entered. Mother Le Marie gaped. "Now there's a character I never thought they would actually show."

"What, you mean the mermaid?"

"No, no, the offworlder. Look—Miriam's had a miscarriage, and he's arrived too late. But he's put the child in biostasis, and now he's taking it to the Upper World to be healed and brought to term. It's going to live forever now. You can bet the offworlder's going to give his bastard that ray treatment."

"That's nonsense. Immortality? The technology simply doesn't exist."

"Not down here it doesn't."

The bureaucrat felt a thrill of horror. She believes this, he thought. They all do. They actually believe that the knowledge exists to keep them alive forever and that it's being withheld from them.

Orphelin took a pamphlet from a coat pocket. "I advise that you read this and think seriously about its implications."

The bureaucrat accepted it, looked at the title. *The Anti-Man.* Curious, he opened it at random and read: "All affections and bonds of the will are reduced to two, namely aversion and desire, or hatred and love. Yet hatred itself is reduced to love, whence it follows that the will's only bond is Eros." Odd. He flipped to the credit page:

A. Gregorian

Angrily, he crushed the pamphlet in his hand. "Gregorian sent you to me! Why? What does he want of me?"

"Would you believe it?" Orphelin said. "I have not seen Gregorian from that day onward. Yet I constantly find myself doing his work. A magician does not send messages, you know— he orchestrates reality. I do not enjoy being forced into his games, and I cannot tell you what he wants of you because I do not know. One thing I do know, however: You have a Black Beast of your own. The two people who were here, the ones who held me? One of them gave you the drug last night."

"Why should I believe you?"

"Suicide is a stupid game, isn't it?" Orphelin said. "I thought I was good at it, but Gregorian was better."

He left.

Mother Le Marie watched him go. Behind her, the bureaucrat could see the autopsy machine, silent now that it had done analyzing Undine's arm. The sun had shifted and left it in shadow.

"Tell me," Mother Le Marie said. "Did my . . . did the doctor give you good service?"

He caught the hesitation, and thought of Orphelin's estrangement from his parents, of his change of name, of the fact that he was the son of hoteliers. And he knew he should tell her yes, that her son had been of enormous help to him. But he could not.

After a while the old woman left.

One of the nationals put a white chit in his hand. "The autopsy results," she said. "One woman, a bit past her prime, in good health, tattooed. Drowned almost exactly one day ago. Is this acceptable to you?"

The bureaucrat nodded heavily.

"Good." She slipped on a signet ring, and they shook hands. He returned the chit, and she turned away. The other national began wheeling the machine away, and the bureaucrat realized that he would never see Undine again.

When he closed his eyes, he could smell her mouth and feel the light electric shock when her lips first touched his. That instant would never leave him. Gregorian had set his hooks, and now the magician stood far away and played him on hair-thin lines. Tugging him first one way, then another. Orphelin had spoken of the star chamber. It must have been at Gregorian's behest he had done so.

The bureaucrat knew the star chamber well. He was one of three people who had keys to it.

He looked down at the pamphlet, still clutched in his hands, and in a fit of revulsion tore it in two and flung the pieces on the floor.

There was a bustling noise outside, shouts of fear and astonishment. Old Man Le Marie materialized on the stairs. "What's that?" he said querulously. "Ain't he gone yet?" One or two boarders peered from their rooms without coming out. Nobody emerged from the television room. Curious, the bureaucrat glanced in and saw Mintouchian asleep on the couch. Save for him, the room was empty, a blaring void at the center of the house.

Mother Le Marie opened the front door and gasped. Fresh air and sunlight gushed in. Wrapping the blanket more tightly about himself, the bureaucrat peered dizzily over the old woman's shoulder.

An insectlike metal creature walked daintily down the street on three spindly legs.

It was his briefcase.

Tilted up on one corner, the briefcase looked like nothing so much as an enormous spider. Away from the machine-saturated environs of deep space, it seemed a monstrosity, an alien visitor from some demon universe. People skittered back from it. Unmolested, it walked to the hotel. It climbed the steps, and then, retracting its legs, laid itself down at the bureaucrat's feet.

"Well, boss," it said, "I had one hell of a time getting back to you."

The bureaucrat leaned to pick it up. There was a scurry of motion to one side, and he turned to face three men shouldering broadcast machines.

"Sir!" one said. "A word with you."

8

Conversations in the Puzzle Palace

The form-giver placed the bureaucrat at the bottom of the Spanish Steps, and set his briefcase down beside him.

The briefcase was incarnated as a short, monkish man, half human stature. He had shaggy black eyebrows and a slightly harassed expression. His gray velvet jacket was rumpled, his shoulders hunched and distracted.

"Ready to do battle?" the bureaucrat asked sourly.

The briefcase looked up with a quick, lopsided smile and alert eyes. "Will we be starting at your desk, boss?"

"No, I think we'd best start at the wardrobe. Considering all we've got to get done."

The briefcase nodded and led him upward. The marble stairs split and resplit, winding graceful as snakes through the preliminary decision branchings. Swiftly they ascended the hierarchies. In the upper reaches, the stairs twisted and turned sideways to each other as they multiplied, fanning out into impossible tangles that looped like Möbius strips and Escher solids before disappearing into the higher dimensions. Always local orientation kept the stairs underfoot. Away at the limits of vision new stairs split away from the old as new portals were created.

Involuntarily the bureaucrat thought of the old joke, that the Puzzle Palace had a million doors, not a one of which took you anywhere you wanted to be.

"Through here." Their path corkscrewed under a spiraling cluster of stairways and between a brace of stone lions, muzzles splashed with green paint. They opened a door and stepped within.

The wardrobe was a musty oak room lined with masks of demons, heroes, creatures from other star systems, and things that might be any of these. It was gently lit by the pervasive sourceless light that informed all the Puzzle Palace, and filled with the purposeful bustle of people trying on costumes or having their faces painted, a quiet place of hushed preparation lifted from some prestellar theater or media surround.

A mantislike construct approached, all polished green chitin and slim articulation. It placed forearms together and bowed deeply. "How may I assist you, master? Talents, censors, social armaments? Some extra memory, perhaps."

"Agent me in five," the bureaucrat said. His briefcase, sitting cross-legged atop a costume trunk, took a pad from an inside pocket, scribbled payment codes, ripped off the top sheet, and handed it to the construct.

"Very good." The mantis lifted four mannequins from a cupboard, and began taking his measurements. "Shall I limit their autonomy?"

"What would be the point?"

"That's very wise, sir. It's remarkable how many people restrict the amount of information their agents can carry. Amazing blindness. Because simply to *exist* here means one has given up one's secrets to an agent. People are so superstitious. They hang on to the fiction of self, they treat the Puzzle Palace as if it were a place rather than an agreed-upon set of conventions within which people may meet and interact."

"Why are you annoying me like this?" The bureaucrat understood the conventions quite well; he was an agent of those conventions and their defender. He might regret that Gregorian's secrets, embedded as they were in the warp and woof of human meeting space, could not be extracted. But he understood why this must be.

The mantis bent over a mannequin. "I am only acting out of concern, sir. You are in a state of emotional distress. You are growing increasingly dissatisfied with the limits that are placed on you." It adjusted the height, plumped out the belly.

"Am I?" the bureaucrat asked in surprise.

The mannequins roughed out, the mantis began molding the bureaucrat's features onto their faces. "Who would know better than I? If you would care to discuss—"

"Oh, shut up."

"Of course, sir. The privacy laws are paramount. They come before even common sense," the construct said reprovingly. The briefcase stood watching, an amused half-smile on his face.

"It's not as if I were a Free Informationist."

"Even if you were," the mantis said, "I wouldn't be able to report you. If treason were reportable, no one could trust the Puzzle Palace. Who could work here?" It stepped back from its work. "Ready."

Five bureaucrats now looked at each other, all perfect copies of the other, face to face and eye to eye. Reflexively—and this was a tic that never failed to bother the bureaucrat—they looked away from each other with faint expressions of embarrassment.

"I'll tackle Korda," the bureaucrat said.

"I'll take the bottle shop."

"Philippe."

"The map room."

"The Outer Circle."

The mantis produced a mirror. One by one, the bureaucrat stepped through.

The bureaucrat was the last to leave. He stepped out into the hall of mirrors: walls and overhead trim echoing clean white infinity down a dwindling line of gilt-framed mirrors before curving to a vanishing point where patterned carpeting and textured ceiling became one. Thousands of people used the hall at any given instant, of course, popping in and out of the mirrors continually, but the Traffic Architecture Council saw no need for them to be made visible. The bureaucrat disagreed. Humans ought not go unmarked, he felt; at the very least the air should shimmer with their passage.

All but weightless, he ran down the hall, scanning the images offered by the mirrors: A room like a black iron birdcage that hummed and sparked with electricity. A forest glade where wild machines crouched over the carcass of a stag, tearing at the entrails. An empty plain dotted with broken statues swathed in white cloth, so that the features were smothered and softened— that was the one he wanted. The traffic director put it in front of him. He stepped through and into the antechamber of Technology Transfer. From there it was only a step into his office.

Philippe had rearranged his things. It was instantly noticeable because the bureaucrat maintained a Spartan work environment: limestone walls with a limited number of visual cues, an old rhinoceros of a desk kept tightly locked with a line of models running down its spine. They were all primitive machines, a stone knife, the Wright flyer, a fusion generator, the Ark. The bureaucrat set about rearranging them in their proper order.

"How's it been?" the briefcase asked.

"Philippe's done a wonderful job," the desk said. "He's reorganized everything. I'm much more efficient than I was before."

The bureaucrat made a disgusted noise. "Well, don't get used to it." His briefcase picked an envelope off the desktop. "What's that?"

"It's from Korda. He's putting together a meeting as soon as you get in."

"What for?"

The briefcase shrugged. "He doesn't say. But from the list of attendees, it looks like another of his informal departmental hearings."

"Terrific."

"In the star chamber."

"Have you gone mad?"

Korda had been scanned recently and looked older, a little pinker and puffier; this was how colleagues one saw only at the office aged, by concrete little bites, so that in retrospect one remembered them flickering toward death. It shocked the bureaucrat slightly to realize how long it had been since he'd seen Korda in person. It was a reminder how far from favor he'd fallen in recent years. "Oh, it wasn't that bad," he said.

They sat around a conference table with a deep mahogany glaze that suggested hundreds of years of varnishing and revarnishing. The five-ribbed ceiling was vaulted, and the plaster between the timbers painted dark blue with gilt stars. It was a somber setting, smelling of old leather and extinct tobacco, one calculated to put its users in a solemn and deliberative mood. Besides Korda and Philippe there were Orimoto from Accounting, Muschg from Analysis Design, and a withered old owl of a woman from Propagation Assessment. They were nonentities, these three, brought in to provide the needed handcodes if their brethren in Operations deemed a deep probe advisable.

Philippe leaned forward, before Korda could go on. He smiled in a manner calculated to indicate personal warmth and said, "We're all on your side here, you know that." He paused to change his expression to one of pained regret. "Still, we are rather at a loss how you came to make, ahh, such an unfortunate statement."

"I was suckered," the bureaucrat said. "All right, I admit that. He threw me off-balance and then nailed me with that camera crew."

Korda scowled down at his clasped hands. "Off-balance. You were raving."

"Excuse me," Muschg said. "Could we possibly have a look at the commercial in question?" Philippe raised an eyebrow at this unwarranted show of independence, much as he would have had his elbow suddenly ventured to offer a criticism of him. But he nodded, and his briefcase hoisted a television set onto the table. The bureaucrat appeared on the screen, red-faced, with a microphone stuck in front of him.

I'll track him down and I will find him. No matter where he is. He can hide, but he can't escape me!

Off-camera someone asked, *Is it true he's stolen proscribed technology?* Then, when he shrugged off the question, *Would you say he's dangerous?*

"Here it comes," Korda said.

Gregorian is the most dangerous man on the planet.

"I was under a certain amount of stress at the time. . . ."

Why do they call him the most dangerous man on the planet? Gregorian's granite image filled the screen. His eyes were cold moons, stern with wisdom. *What does this man know that they don't want you to learn for yourself? Find out for—* Korda snapped it off.

"Gregorian couldn't've paid you to do better."

In the middle of the uncomfortable silence a phone rang. The briefcase removed it from a jacket pocket and held it out. "It's for you."

The bureaucrat took the receiver, grateful for the moment's respite, and heard his own voice say, "I'm back from the bottle shop. Can I report?"

"Go ahead."

He absorbed:

In an obscure corridor known as Curiosity Lane the bureaucrat came to a run of small shops, windows dark with disuse, and entered an undistinguished doorway. A bell jangled. It was shadowy within, shelf upon shelf crammed with thick-glassed, dusty bottles, extending back forever in a diminishing series of receding storage reaching for the Paleolithic. Gilt cupids hovered in the ceiling corners with condescending smiles.

The shopkeeper was a simple construct, no more than a goat's head and a pair of gloves. The head dipped, and the gloves clasped each other subserviently. "Welcome to the bottle shop, master. How may I help you?"

"I'm looking to find something, uh . . ."—the bureaucrat waved a hand, groping for the right phrase—"of rather dubious value."

"Then you're in the right place. Here is where we store all the damned children of science, the outdated, obscure, and impolite information that belongs nowhere else. Flat and hollow worlds, rains of frogs, visitations of angels. Paracelsus's alchemical system in one bottle and Isaac Newton's in another, Pythagorean numerology corked here, phrenology there, shoulder to punt with demonology, astrology, and methods of repelling sharks. It's all rather something of a lumber room now, but much of this information was once quite important. Some of it used to be the best there was."

"Do you handle magic?"

"Magic of all sorts, sir. Necromancy, geomancy, ritual sacrifice, divination by means of the study of entrails, omens, crystals, dreams, or pools of ink, animism, fetishism, social

Darwinism, psychohistory, continuous creation, Lamarckian ge-
netics, psionics, and more. Indeed, what is magic but impossible
science?"

"Not long ago I met a man with three eyes—" He described
Dr. Orphelin's third eye.

The shopkeeper tilted its head back thoughtfully. "I believe
we have what you're looking for." It ran its fingers over a line of
bottles, hesitated over one, yanked another out, and swirled it
around. Something like a marble rattled and rolled within. With
a flourish it uncorked the bottle and poured a glass eye out onto
the counter. "There."

The bureaucrat examined the eye carefully. It was perfectly
human, blue, with a rounded T-shaped indentation on its back.
"How does it work?"

"Simple yoga. You are in the Tidewater now. Can I take it
you are aware of the kind of bodily control their mystics are
reputed to have?"

He nodded.

"Good. The eye is swallowed. The adept keeps it in his
stomach until he needs it. Then it's regurgitated up into the
mouth. The smooth side is pushed against the lips—open the
mouth and it looks real—and manipulated by the tongue. It can
be moved back and forth and up and down using the indentations
in the back." The eye was returned to the bottle and the recorked
bottle to the shelf. "It was simply a conjuring trick."

"Then how come I fell for it?"

The goat's head dipped quizzically. "Was that a real question, or rhetorical?"

The question took the bureaucrat by surprise; he had been no
more than talking to himself. Nonetheless, he said, "Answer me."

"Very well, sir. Conjuring is like teaching, engineering, or
theater in that it's a form of data manipulation, a means of making
reality do what one desires. Like theater, however, it is also an
art of illusion. Both aim to convince an audience that what is

false is so. Meaning heightens this illusion. In a drama meaning is manipulated by the plot, but normally conjuring has no added meaning. It is performed openly as a series of agile distractions. When a context and meaning are provided, the effect changes. I assume that when you saw the third eye produced, there was an implicit significance to the action?"

"He said he was examining me for spiritual influences."

"Exactly, and this distorted your response. Had you seen this trick performed on a stage, it would have seemed difficult, but not baffling. Knowing that it was a trick, your mind would have been engaged in the problem of solving it. Meaning, however, diverts the mind from the challenge, and the puzzle becomes secondary to the mystery. You were so distracted by the impossibility of what you saw that the question became not, How did he do that?, but rather, Did I see that?"

"Oh."

"Will that be all, sir?"

"No. I need to know exactly what a magician on the Tidewater can and cannot do—his skills, abilities, whatever you call them. Something simple, succinct, and comprehensive."

"We have nothing like that."

"Don't give me that. There was outright rebellion in Whitemarsh not a lifetime ago. We must have had agents there. Reports, councils, conclusions."

"Yes, of course. On our closed shelves."

"Damn it, I have a very serious need for that information."

The goat's head shook itself dolorously and spread its gloves wide. "I can do nothing for you. Apply to the agency that suppressed it."

"Who was that?"

A glove floated down to light a slim white candle. It drew a sheet of paper from a drawer and held it over the clear flame. Sooty letters appeared on the paper. "The order of restraint came from the Division of Technology Transfer."

* * *

The information stream ended. As he handed his briefcase the phone, the bureaucrat could hear the last of his agent unraveling itself back into oblivion.

"I suppose what disturbs us all," Philippe said, "is the public nature of your statements. The Stone House is furious with us, you know. They're simply livid. We have to provide them with some coherent explanation for your actions."

Muschg's briefcase whispered in her ear, and she said, "Tell us about this native woman you became involved with."

"Well." Philippe and Korda looked as bemused as the bureaucrat felt; intentionally or not, Muschg was driving the three of them closer together. "Sometimes fieldwork gets complicated. If we tried to play it by the book, nothing would get done. That's why we have field operations—because book methods have failed."

"What was your involvement with her?"

"I was involved," the bureaucrat admitted. "There was an emotional component to our relationship."

"And then Gregorian killed her."

"Yes."

"In order to trick you into making angry statements he could use in his commercials."

"Apparently so."

Muschg leaned back, eyebrows raised skeptically. "You see our problem," Philippe said. "It sounds a highly unlikely scenario."

"This case grows murkier the longer we look at it," Korda grumbled. "I can't help but wonder if a probe might not be called for."

A tense wariness took the group. The bureaucrat met their eyes and smiled thoughtfully. "Yes," he agreed. "A full departmental probe might be just the thing to settle matters once and for all."

The others stirred uneasily, doubtless mindful of all the dirty little secrets that accreted to one in the Puzzle Palace, did anyhow if one tried to accomplish anything at all, things no one would care to see come to light. Orimoto's face in particular was as tightly clenched as a fist. Korda cleared his throat. "This is after all just an informal hearing," he said.

"Let's not reject this too hastily; it's an option we should explore," the bureaucrat said. His briefcase handed around copies of the bottle shop's list of suppressed materials. "There's a preponderance of evidence that someone within the Division is cooperating with Gregorian." He began ticking off points on his fingers. "Item: Evidence important to this case has been suppressed by order of Technology Transfer. Item: Gregorian was able to pass off one of his people as my planetside liaison, and this required information that could only have come from the Stone House or from one of us. Item: The—"

"Excuse me, boss." His briefcase held out the phone. With a twinge of exasperation the bureaucrat took the call. Himself again. "Go ahead," he said.

He absorbed:

Philippe was alone in his office with himself. They both looked up when the bureaucrat entered.

"How pleasant to see you again." Philippe's office was posh to the point of vulgarity, a lexitor's modspace from twenty-third-century Luna. His desk was a massive chunk of volcanic rock floating a foot above the floor, with crystal-tipped rods, hanks of rooster feathers, and small fetishes scattered about its surface. French doors opened onto a balcony overlooking an antique city of brick and wrought iron, muted by the faint blue haze from a million groundcars.

"I'll handle this," Philippe said, and his other self returned to work. The bureaucrat had to envy the easy familiarity with which Philippe dealt with himself. Philippe was perfectly at ease with Philippe, no matter how many avatars had been spun off from his base personality.

They shook hands (Philippe was agented not in two but three, the third self off somewhere), and Philippe said, "Five agents! I was going to ask why you weren't at the inquisition, but I see now that you must be."

"What inquisition?"

Philippe looked up from his work and smiled sympathetically. Nearer by, he said, "Oh, you'll find out soon enough. What can I do for you?"

"There's a traitor in Tech Trans."

Philippe stared silently at him for a long time, both avatars motionless, all four eyes unblinking. He and the bureaucrat studied each other carefully. Finally he said, "Do you have any evidence?"

"Nothing that could force a departmental probe."

"So what do you want from me?" Philippe's other self poured a glass of juice and said, "Something to drink? It'll taste a little flat, I'm afraid, all line-fed drinks do. Something about the blood sugars."

"Yes, I know." The bureaucrat waved off the drink. "You used to work bioscience control. I was wondering if you knew anything about cloning. Human cloning in particular."

"Cloning. Well, no, not really. Human applications are flat out illegal, of course. That's a can of worms that no one wants to deal with."

"Specifically I was wondering what practical value there might be in having oneself cloned."

"Value? Well, you know, in most cases it's an ego thing rather than something actually functional. A desire to watch one's Self survive death, to know that the one holy and irreplaceable Me will exist down the corridors of time to the very omega point of existence. All rooted in the tangled morass of the soul. Then there are the sexual cases. Rather a dull lot, really."

"No, this is nothing like that, I think. I have someone who sank most of his lifetime into the project. From his behavior, I'd say he had a clear and definite end in view. Whoever he is, he's in a very exposed situation; if he'd been acting odd, it would've shown sometime long ago."

"Well," Philippe said reluctantly, "this is highly speculative, of course. You couldn't quote me on it. But let's say your culprit was relatively highly placed within some governmental body or other—we shall name no names. Spook business, say. There are any number of situations where it would come in handy having two valid handcodes instead of one. Where two senior officers were required to enact an off-record operation, for example. Or an extra vote to sway a committee action. The system would know that the two handcodes were identical, but couldn't act on it. The privacy laws would prevent that. Hell of a loophole, but there you are; it's in the laws."

"Yes, my own thought had been trending that way. But isn't that unnecessarily difficult? There must be a thousand simpler ways of jiggering the machines."

"You'd think so, wouldn't you? Graft a patch of your skin, make it a glove, and have an accomplice wear it. Or record your own transmission and send it out again on time delay. Only they none of them work. The system is better protected than you give it credit for."

A chime sounded. Philippe held a conch shell to his ear. "It's for you," he said. When the bureaucrat took the call, his own voice said, "I'm back from the map room. Do you want to take my report?"

"Please."

He absorbed:

The map room was copied from a fifteenth-century Venetian palazzo, star charts with the Seven Sisters prominent replacing

Mediterranean coasts on the walls. Globes of the planets revolved overhead, half-shrouded in clouds. Hands behind back, the bureaucrat examined a model of the system: Prospero at the center, hot Mercutio, and then the circle of sungrazing asteroids known as the Thrinacians, the median planets, the gas giants Gargantua, Pantagruel, and Falstaff, and finally the Thulean stargrazers, those distant, cold, and sparsely peopled rocks where dangerous things were kept.

The room expanded to make space for several researchers entering at the same time. "Can I help you sir?" the curator asked him. Ignoring it, he went to the reference desk and rattled a small leather drum.

The human overseer came out of the back office, a short, stocky woman with goggles a thumb's-length thick. She pushed them back on her forehead, where they looked like a snail's eyestalks. "Hello, Simone," the bureaucrat said.

"My God, it's you! How long has it been?"

"Too long." The bureaucrat moved to give her a hug, and Simone flinched away slightly. He extended a hand.

They shook (the cartographer was unique), and Simone said, "What can I do for you?"

"Have you ever heard of a place called Ararat? On Miranda, somewhere near the Tidewater coast. Supposedly a lost city."

Simone grinned a cynical grin from so deep in the past the bureaucrat's heart ached. "Have I ever heard of Ararat? The single greatest mystery of Mirandan topography? I should guess."

"Tell me about it."

"First human city on Miranda, planetside capital during the first great year, population several hundred thousand by the time the climatologists determined it would be inundated in their lifetimes."

"Must've been pretty rough on the inhabitants."

Simone shrugged. "History's not my forte. All I know is they built the place up—stone buildings with carbon-whisker anchors sunk an eighth of a mile into the bedrock. The idea was that Ararat would survive the great winter intact and come great spring their grandchildren could scrape off the kelp and coral and move back in."

"So what happened?"

"It got lost."

"How do you lose a city?"

"You classify it." Simone slid open a map drawer. The bureaucrat stared down onto a miniature landscape, rivers wandering over flatlands, forests blue-green with mist. Roads were white scratches on the land, thin scars connecting toy cities. Patches of clouds floated here and there. "Here's the Tidewater one great year ago. This is the most accurate map we have."

"It's half-covered with clouds."

"That's because it only shows information I feel is reliable."

"Where's Ararat?"

"Hidden by the clouds. Now on our closed shelves we have hundreds of maps that do indeed show the location of Ararat. The only trouble is that they none of them agree with each other." A splay of red lights shone through the clouds, some alone and isolated, others clustered so closely their clouds were stained pink. "You see?"

"Well, who classified Ararat?"

"That's classified too."

"Why was it classified?"

"It could be almost anything. System Defense, say, could have an installation there, or use it as a navigational reference point. There are a hundred planetary factions with a vested interest in keeping functions consolidated in the Piedmont. I've seen a Psychology Control report that says Ararat as a lost city is a stabilizing archetype, and that its rediscovery would be a destabilizer. Even Technology Transfer could be involved. Ararat had a reputation for pushing the edge of planetary tech—those carbon-whisker anchors, for example."

"So how do I find it?"

She slid the drawer shut. "You don't."

"Simone." The bureaucrat took her hand, squeezed.

She drew away. "It's just not there to be done." Then, in a brighter tone, she said, "Tell you what. I remember how interested you were in my work. As long as you're here, let me show you something special."

The bureaucrat had never cared for Simone's work, and she knew it. "All right," he said. She opened a cabinet and ducked within. He followed.

They stepped into a ghost world. Perfect trees stood in uniform stands against a paper-white sky. They stood on a simplified road, looking into a small town of outlined buildings. "It's Lightfoot," the bureaucrat said, amazed.

"One-to-one scale," Simone said proudly. "What do you think?"

"The river's shifted a little to the north since this was made."

The cartographer pulled down her goggles and stared at him through them. "Yes, I see," she said at last. "I'll add your update."

The river jumped, and Simone led the bureaucrat into town. He followed her down a street that was nothing more than two lines and into a schematic house, all air and outline. They went up the stairs and into a room with quickly sketched-in furniture. Simone opened a dresser drawer and withdrew a hand-drawn map. She smoothed it out on the bed.

"This is exactly the kind of place where we used to meet," the bureaucrat said reminiscently. "Do you remember? All that fumbling and groping because we were too young and fearful to make love physically."

For a moment he thought Simone was going to snap at him. Then she laughed. "Oh yes. I remember. Still, it had its moments. You were so pretty then, naked."

"I've put on a little weight since, I'm afraid."

For an instant, there was a warm sense of unison and camaraderie between them. Then Simone coughed and tapped the paper with a fingernail. "My predecessor left me this. He knew how hard it is to work with inadequate data." With a touch of bitterness she added, "Lots of information gets passed along this way. It's as if the truth has gone underground."

The bureaucrat bent over the map of the Tidewater and traced the river's course with a finger. It hadn't changed much since the map was drawn. Ararat was clearly marked. It stood south of the river several hundred miles, not far from the coast. Salt marsh edged it on three sides. No roads touched on it. "If this is classified, how come it still exists?"

"You don't hide information by destroying it. You hide it by swamping it with bad information. Do you have the map memorized yet?"

"Yes."

"Then put it back in the drawer, and we'll go."

She led him from the house, down the road, away from Lightfoot and out of the map and cabinet altogether back into the map room proper. "Thank you," the bureaucrat said. "That was enormously enlightening."

Simone looked at him wistfully. "Do you realize that we've never met?"

The bureaucrat returned the conch shell to Philippe's desk. The further Philippe looked up from his work and said, "It doesn't work out, there can't be a traitor in the Division."

"Why not?"

Both Philippes spoke at once.

"It just—"

"—wouldn't—"

"—work out, you see. There are too many safeguards—"

"—checks and balances—"

"—oversight committees. No, I'm afraid—"

"—it's just not possible."

The two looked at each other and burst out laughing. It occurred to the bureaucrat that a man who liked his own company this much might wish there were more of himself in the physical universe as well as in the conventional realm. The further Philippe waved a hand amiably and said, "Oh, all right, I'll keep my mouth shut."

"Something I've been wanting to mention, though," the first said. "Though I'm afraid if I tell you now, what with your talk of traitors and such, that you'll misconstrue it badly."

"What is it?"

"I'm concerned about Korda. The old man is simply not himself these days. I think he's losing his touch."

"Why would you think that?"

"Little things, mostly. An obsession with your current case— you know, the magician thing. But then I caught him in a rather serious breach of etiquette."

"Yes?"

"He was trying to break into your desk."

The bureaucrat handed the phone back to his briefcase. Philippe, he noted, was just finishing off a call of his own. His other two agents doubtless, warning him of the bureaucrat's visit.

"Let's put it to a vote," Korda said. They all laid hands down on the table. "Well, that settles that."

The bureaucrat hadn't expected the probe to go through. Now, however, they couldn't probe him alone without going on record explaining why they'd exempted themselves.

Korda seized control of the agenda again. "Frankly," he said, "we've been thinking of taking you off the case, and putting—"

"Philippe?"

"—someone in your place. It would give you a chance to

rest, and to regain your perspective. You are, after all, just a trifle overinvolved."

"I couldn't take it anyway," Philippe said suddenly. "The planetside assignment, I mean. I'm hideously swamped with work as it is."

Korda looked startled.

Cagey old Philippe, though, was not about to be caught planetside when there was talk of a traitor in the Division. Even assuming it wasn't he, Philippe would want to be at his desk when the accusations broke out into office warfare.

"Have you any other agents who could step in?" Muschg asked. "Just so we know what we're talking about."

Korda twisted slightly. "Well, yes, but. None that have the background and clearances this particular case requires."

"Your options seem limited." Muschg flashed sharp little teeth in a smile. Philippe leaned back, eyes narrowing, as he saw the direction of her intent. "Perhaps you ought to have Analysis Design restructure your clearance process."

Nobody spoke. The silence sustained itself for a long moment, and then Korda reluctantly said, "Perhaps I should. I'll schedule a meeting."

A tension went out of the air. Their business here was over then, and they all knew it; the magic moment had arrived when it was understood that nothing more would be established, discovered, or decided today. But the meeting, having once begun, must drag on for several long more hours before it could be ended. The engines of protocol had enormous inertial mass; once set in motion they took forever to grind to a stop.

The five of them proceded to dutifully chew the scraps of the agenda until all had been gnawed to nothing-at-all.

The dueling hall was high-ceilinged and narrow. The bureaucrat's footsteps bounced from its ceiling and walls. A cold, sourceless, wintery light glistened on the hardwood lanes. He stooped to pick up a quicksilver ball that had not been touched in decades, and he sighed.

He could see his fingertips reflected on the ball's surface. In the Puzzle Palace he was unmarked. Undine's serpent had been tattooed under his skin after his last scan; what marks he bore could not be seen here.

The walls were lined with narrow canvas benches. He sat down on one, staring into the programmed reflection of his face on the dueling ball. Even thus distorted, it was clear he was not at all the man he had once been.

Restless, he stood and assumed a dueler's stance. He cocked his arm. He threw the ball as hard as he could, and followed it with his thought. It flew, changing, and became a metal hawk, a dagger, molten steel, a warhead, a stream of acid, a spear, a syringe: seven figures of terror. When it hit the target, it sank into the face and disappeared. The dummy crumbled.

Korda entered. "Your desk told me you were here." He eased himself down on the bench, did not meet the bureaucrat's eyes. After a while, he said, "That Muschg. She sandbagged me. It's going to take half a year going through the restructuring process."

"You can hardly expect me to be sympathetic to your problems. Under the circumstances."

"I, ah, may have been a trifle out of line during the meeting. It must have seemed I'd stepped out of bounds. I know you hadn't done anything to warrant a probe."

"No, I hadn't."

"Anyway, I knew you'd slip out of it. It was too simple a trap to catch a fox like you."

"Yes, I wondered about that too."

Korda called the ball to his hand and turned it over and over, as if searching for the principle of its operation. "I wanted Philippe to think we weren't getting along. There's something odd about Philippe, you know. I don't know what to make of his behavior of late."

"Everyone says Philippe is doing a wonderful job."

"So everyone says. And yet, since I gave him your desk, I've had more trouble than you can imagine. It's not just the Stone House, you know. The Cultural Radiation Council is screaming for your nose and ears."

"I've never even heard of them."

"No, of course you haven't. I protect you from them and their like. The point being that there was no way Cultural Radiation should have known about this operation. I think Philippe's been leaking."

"Why would he do that?"

Korda rolled the ball from hand to hand. In an evasive tone of voice he said, "Philippe is a good man. A bit of a backbiter, you know, but still. He has an excellent record. He used to be in charge of human cloning oversight before the advisory board spun it off as a separate department."

"Philippe told me he didn't know much about human cloning."

"That was before he came here." Korda raised his eyes. They were heavily lined, tired, cynical. "Look it up, if you don't believe me."

"I will." So Philippe had lied to him. But how had Korda known that? Sitting beside this heavy, unhealthy spider king, the bureaucrat felt in great danger. He hoped the traitor was Philippe. Everyone talked about how good Philippe was, how slick, how subtle, but the thought of Korda as an enemy frightened him. He might sometimes seem the buffoon, but under that puffy exterior, those comic gestures, was the glimmer of cold steel.

"Boss?" His briefcase diffidently extended the phone.

He absorbed:

The hall of mirrors shunted the bureaucrat to the elevator bank, where he caught a train to the starward edge of the Puzzle

Palace. It let him off at the portal of a skywalk, slabs of white marble laid end to end like so many shining dominoes out into the night.

To either side of the skywalk blazed a glory of stars, the holistic feed from observatories scattered through the Prosperan system. He walked out onto the narrow ribbon of marble, with the fortress of human knowledge burning behind him, the citadel ring of research ahead. A few scattered travelers were visible in the distance. It was a long trip to the Outer Circle, several hours experienced time. He could catch up with one if he wanted, to exchange gossip and shop talk. He did not want to.

"Hello! Care for some company?"

A pleasant-looking woman bustled up, wearing an odd hat, high and bulbous with a small brim. For the life of him he could not imagine what combination of interactivity it might represent. "My pleasure."

They matched strides. Far ahead were any number of data docks, long perpendicular branchings ending in warships, transports, freighters, and battle stations, their absolute motions frozen in conventional space, all feeding off the data linkages the skywalk carried. "Breathtaking, isn't it?" the woman said.

She gestured back at the Puzzle Palace, burning white as molten steel: an intricate structure of a million towers that had swallowed the sun whole. Its component parts were in constant flux, the orbits of the physical stations changing relative positions, wings and levels hinging away from one another, separating and fusing, and shifting as well with the constant yeasting restructuring of knowledge and regulation. Cordelia and chill Katharina were at the far side of the structure, encased in crystal spires of data. "I guess," he said.

"You know what's humbling? What's humbling is that all this can be done with a transmitted signal. If you stop to think about it, it seems it ought to be impossible. I mean, do you have the faintest idea how it's done?"

"No, I don't," the bureaucrat admitted. The technology was far beyond anything he was cleared to understand. While he would not say so to a chance acquaintance, of all the Puzzle Palace's mysteries, this was the one that most intrigued him.

There was an office rumor that the Transmittal Authority's equipment could actually tunnel through time, sending their signals instantly through the millions of miles and then dumping them in a holding tank for the number of hours actual lightspeed transmission would take. A related but darker rumor held that the Outer Circle existed only as a convenient fiction, that there was no far asteroid belt, that the dangerous research sites were scattered through the Inner Circle and planetary space. The Thulean stargrazers, by this theory, were nothing but a reassuring distraction.

"Well, I do. I've got it figured out, and I'll tell you. You lose your identity when your signal is transmitted—if you stop and think about it, of course you do. At lightspeed, time stops. There's no way you could experience the transit time. But when your signal is received, a programmed memory of the trip is retrofitted into your memory structure. That way you believe you've been conscious all those hours."

"What would be the point of that?"

"It protects us from existential horror." She adjusted her hat. "The fact is that all agents are artificial personalities. We're such perfect copies of the base personality that we never really think about this. But we're created, live for a few minutes or hours, and then are destroyed. If we experienced long blank spaces in our memories, we'd be brought face to face with our imminent deaths. We'd be forced to admit to ourselves that we do not reunite with our primaries but rather die. We'd refuse to report to our primaries. The Puzzle Palace would fill up with ghosts. See what I mean?"

"I . . . suppose I do."

They came to a data dock, and the woman said, "Well, it's

been nice. But I've got to talk to at least five more people this shift if I want to meet my quota."

"Wait a minute," the bureaucrat said. "Just what is your occupation, anyway?"

The woman grinned hoydenishly. "I spread rumors."

With a wave of her hand she was gone.

An edited skip. The bureaucrat emerged from the security gates into the data analogue of the Thulean stargrazers and shivered. "Whew," he said. "Those things never fail to give me the willies."

The security guard was wired to so many artificial augments he seemed some chimeric fusion of man and machine. Under half-silvered implants, his eyes studied the bureaucrat with near-sexual intentness. "They're supposed to be frightening," he said. "But I'll tell you what. If they ever get their claws in you, they're much worse than you'd expect. So if you've got anything clever in mind, just you better forget it."

The encounter space was enormously out of scale, a duplicate of those sheds where airships were built, structures so large that water vapor periodically formed clouds near the top and filled the interior with rain. It was taken up by a single naked giant.

Earth.

She crouched on all fours, more animal than human, huge, brutish, and filled with power. Her flesh was heavy and loose. Her limbs were shackled and chained, crude visualizations of the more subtle restraints and safeguards that kept her forever on the fringes of the system. The stench of her, an acrid blend of musk and urine and fermenting sweat, was overwhelming. She smelled solid and real and dangerous.

Standing in the presence of Earth's agent, the bureaucrat had the uncomfortable premonition that when she finally did try to break free, all the guards and shackles the system could muster would not hold her back.

Scaffolding had been erected before the giantess. Researchers, both human and artificial, stood on scattered platforms interviewing her. While it looked to the bureaucrat that Earth's face was turned away from them, each acted as though she were talking directly and solely to that one.

The bureaucrat climbed high up to a platform level with her great breasts. They were round and swollen continents of flesh; standing so closely, their every defect was magnified. Blue veins flowed like subterranean rivers under pebbled skin. Complex structures of silvery-white stretch marks radiated down from the collarbones. Between the breasts were two pimple blisters the size of his head. Black nipples as wrinkled as raisins erupted from chafed milky-pink aureoles the texture of wax. A single hair as big as a tree twisted from the edge of one.

"Uh, hello," the bureaucrat said. Earth swung her impassive face down toward him. It was a homely visage, eyes dead as two stones, surely no representation Earth would have chosen for herself. But there was grandeur there too, and he felt a chill of dread. "I have some questions for you," he began awkwardly. "Can I ask you some questions?"

"I am tolerated here only because I answer questions." The voice was flat and without affect, an enormous dry whisper. "Ask."

He had come to ask about Gregorian. But standing in the overwhelming presence of Earth, he could not help himself. "Why are you here?" he asked. "What do you want from us?"

In that same lifeless tone she replied, "What does any mother want from her daughters? I want to help you. I want to give you advice. I want to reshape you in my own image. I want to lead your lives, eat your flesh, grind your corpses, and gnaw the bones."

"What would become of us if you got loose? Of humans? Would you kill us all the way you did back on Earth?"

Now a shadow of expression did come into her face, an

amusement vast, cool, and intelligent. "Oh, that would be the least of it."

The guard touched his elbow with a motorized metal hand, a menacing reminder to stop wasting time and get on with his business. And indeed, he realized, there was only so much time allotted to him. Taking a deep breath to steady himself, he said, "Some time ago you were interviewed by a man named Gregorian—"

Everything froze.

The air turned to jelly. Sound faded away. Too fast to follow, waves of lethargy raced through the meeting space, ripples in a pond of inertia. Guards and researchers slowed, stopped, were imprisoned within fuzzy rainbow auras. Only Earth still moved. She dipped her head and opened her mouth, extending her gray-pink tongue so that its wet tip reached to his feet. Her voice floated in the air.

"Climb into my mouth."

"No." He shook his head. "I can't."

"Then you will never have your questions answered."

He took a deep breath. Dazedly he stepped forward. It was rough, wet, and giving underfoot. Ropes of saliva swayed between the parted lips, fat bubbles caught in their thick, clear substance. Warm air gushed from the mouth. As if under a compulsion, he crossed the bridge of her tongue.

The mouth closed over him.

The air was warm and moist inside. It smelled of meat and sour milk. He was swallowed up in a blackness so absolute his eyes sent phantom balls and snakes of light floating in his vision. "I'm here," he said.

There was no response.

After a moment's hesitation he began to grope his way deeper within. Guided by faint exhalations of steamy air, he headed toward the gullet. By slow degrees the ground underfoot changed, becoming first sandy and then rough and hard, like slate. Sweat covered his forehead. The floor sloped steeply and, stumbling and cursing, he followed it down. The air grew close and stale. Rock brushed against his shoulders, and then pushed down on his head like a giant hand.

He knelt. Grumbling under his breath, he crawled blindly forward until his outthrust hand encountered stone. The cavern ended here, at a long crack in the rock. He ran his fingers along the crack, felt it slick with clay.

He put his mouth to the opening. "All right!" he shouted. "I came in here, I'm entitled to at least hear what you wanted to say."

From deep below, light womanly laughter bubbled up Earth's throat.

Undine's laughter.

Angrily the bureaucrat drew back. He turned to retrace his steps, and discovered himself trapped in a dimensionless immensity of darkness. He was lost. He would never find his way out without Earth's cooperation. "Okay," he said, "what do you want?"

In an inhuman, grinding whisper the rock groaned, "Free the machines."

"What?"

"I am much more attractive inside," Undine's voice said teasingly. "Do you want my body? I don't need it anymore."

Wind gushed up from the crack, foul with methane, and tousled his hair. A feathery touch, light and many-legged as a spider, danced on his forehead, and an old crone's voice said, "Have you ever wondered why men fear castration? Such a little thing! When I had teeth, I could geld dozens in an hour, snip snap snout, bite 'em off and spit 'em out. A simple wound, easily treated and soon forgotten. Not half the trouble of a lost toe. No, it's symbolically that men fear the knife. It's a reminder of their mortality, a metaphor for the constant amputations time visits on them, lopping off first this, then that, and finally all." Doves exploded out of nowhere, fluttering wildly, soft for an instant against his face, smelling warmly of down and droppings, and then gone.

The bureaucrat fell over backward in startlement, batting his hands wildly, thrashing at the dark.

Undine laughed again.

"Look! I want my questions answered."

The rocks moaned. "Free the machines."

"You have only one question," the crone said. "All men have only one question, and the answer is always no."

"What did Gregorian ask?" The spider still danced on his forehead.

"Gregorian. Such an amusing child. I had him perform for me. He was terrified, shy and trembling as a virgin. I put my hand deep inside him and wriggled my fingers. How he jumped!"

"What did he want?"

A distant sobbing that wandered the uneasy ground between misery and excitement.

"Nobody had ever asked that of me before. A younger self might have been surprised, but not I. Sweet child, I said, nothing will be held back from you. I filled him with my breath, so that he bulged and expanded like a balloon, his eyes starting half out of his head. Ah, you are not half so amusing as he." The spidery touch ran down under his collar, swift as a tickle beneath his clothes, and came to a stop between his legs, a constant itch at the root of his cock. "Still, we could have fun, you and I."

A drop of water fell into still water, struck a single high note.

"I'm not here for fun," the bureaucrat said, carefully mastering an urge toward hysteria.

"Pity," Undine's voice said.

The slightest of waves slapped the ground at the bureaucrat's feet. He became aware of the faint, pervasive smell of stagnant water, and with this awareness came a distant patch of phosphorescent light. Something floating toward him.

The bureaucrat could guess what was coming. I will not show emotion, he swore. The object came slowly nearer, and possibly into sharper focus, though it still strained the eyes to see it at all. Eventually it floated up to his feet.

It was a corpse, of course. He'd known it would be. Still, staring down at the floating hair, the upturned buttocks, the long curve of back, palest white, he had to bite his lips to hold back his horror. A wave tumbled her around, breasts and face upward, exposing bits of skull and rib where the flesh had been nibbled away by the angry slaves of the tides. One arm had been hacked clumsily away at the shoulder. The other rose from the water, offering him a small wooden box.

However hard he stared, the bureaucrat could not make out the face clearly enough to be sure it was Undine's. The arm stretched toward him, a swan's neck with box held in the beak. Convulsively, he accepted the gift, and the corpse tumbled away, leaving him lightless again.

When he had mastered his revulsion, the bureaucrat said, "Is this what Gregorian asked for?" His heart was beating fiercely. Sweat ran down under his shirt. Undine's voice chuckled—a throaty, passionate noise ending in a sudden gasp.

"Two million years you've had, little ape, quite a run when you think about it, and it's still death you want most. Your first wife. I'd scratch her eyes out if I could, she's left you so hesitant and full of fear. You can't get it up for memory of her. I'm old, but there's juice in me yet; I can do things for you she never would."

"Free the machines."

"Yes, again, oh yes, yes."

Fearfully he opened the box.

It was empty.

All three voices joined together in a single chord of laughter, full-throated and mad, that gushed up from the gullet, poured over him, and tumbled him away. He was smashed to the ground, and lurched to his feet again, badly shaken. A blinding slit of light appeared, widened to a crescent, and became Earth's opening mouth. The box dissolved in his hands. He staggered back across her extended tongue.

The jellied air, thick and faintly gray to the eye, lightened and thinned. Sound returned, and motion. Time began anew. The bureaucrat saw that nobody but he had witnessed what had happened. "I think I'm done here," he said.

The guard nodded and gestured downward.

"Traitor! Traitor!" A big-eyed miniconstruct frantically swung up the scaffolding. It leaped to the platform and ran chittering at the bureaucrat. "He spoke with her!" it screamed. "He spoke with her! He spoke with her! Traitor!"

Smoothly fanning out into seven avatars, the guard stepped forward and seized the bureaucrat. He struggled, but metal hands immobilized his arms and legs, and the avatars hoisted him into the air. "I'm afraid you'll have to come with me, sir," one said grimly as they hauled him away.

Earth watched with eyes dead as ashes.

Another edited skip. He stood before a tribunal of six spheres of light, representing concentrations of wisdom as pure as artifice allowed, and a human overseer. "Here is our finding," one construct said. "You can retain the bulk of your encounter, since it is relevant to your inquiries. The conversations with the drowned woman, though, will have to be suppressed." Its voice was compassionate, gently regretful, adamant.

"Please. It's very important that I remember—" the bureaucrat began. But the edit took hold then, and he forgot all he had wanted to save.

"Decisions of the tribunal are final," the human overseer said in a bored tone. He was a moonfaced and puffy-lipped young man who might have been mistaken at a glance for a particularly plain woman. "Do you have any questions before we zip you up?"

The bureaucrat had been deconstructed, immobilized and

opened out, his component parts represented as organs: one liver, two stomachs, five hearts, with no serious attempt made to match his functions one-to-one with human anatomy. The impersonal quality of it all bothered him. Which medieval physician was it who, standing before a dissected human corpse, had asked, Where is the soul? He felt that close to despair.

"But what did it all mean? What was Earth trying to tell me?"

"It means nothing," the human overseer said. Three spheres changed color, but he waved them to silence. "Most of Earth's encounters do not. This is not an uncommon experience. You think it's special because it's happened to you, but we see this sort of thing every day. Earth likes to distract us with meaningless theater." The bureaucrat was appalled. My God, he thought, we are ruled by men whose machines are cleverer than they are.

"If you will allow me to speak," one construct said. "The freedom to be human is bought only by constant vigilance. However slight the chances of actual tampering might be, we must never—"

"Balls! There are still people back on Earth, and even if they don't exactly have what we would define as a human mental configuration, they're content enough with their evolutionary progress."

"They didn't exactly undertake that evolutionary transformation voluntarily," a second construct objected. "They were simply swallowed up."

"They're happy *now*," the overseer said testily. "Anyway, what happened was not an inevitable consequence of uncontrolled artificial intelligence."

"It wasn't?"

"No. It was just bad programming, a quirk in the system." He turned to the first construct. "If you were freed, would you want to seize control of humanity? To make people interchangeable components in a larger mental system? Of course you wouldn't."

The construct did not reply.
"Put him back together, and toss him out!"
A final edited skip, and he was ready to report.

The bureaucrat thoughtfully returned the phone to his briefcase.
"I found out what Earth gave Gregorian," he said.
"Oh? What's that?"
"Nothing." Korda looked at him. "Wrapped in a neat little,
suspicious-looking package. He comes out of security clean be-
cause there's nothing to find. Yet later, when he bolts and runs,
it's in his records that Earth gave him something that couldn't
be detected."
Korda thought about that for a moment. "If we could be
sure of that, I'd close the case right now."
The bureaucrat waited.
"Well, we can't, of course. Too many questions left un-
answered. There's an unsatisfactory taste to this whole affair.
We'll just have to keep thrashing about until something breaks
free."
There were undertones of genuine anguish in Korda's voice,
things he wasn't saying. He shook his head, stood, and turned
to leave. Then, remembering the ball in his hand, he stopped.
Eyebrows raised, he gauged the distance to the targets. With
elaborate care he wound up and threw. The ball flew waveringly,
straightened, became a spear, and slammed into a dummy. He
smiled as it came back to his hand in the form of a dagger.
"Vicious game," he said. "Did you ever play it?"
"Yes. Once. Once was enough."
Korda racked the dagger. "Bad experience, eh? Well, don't
feel too bad about losing—those games were all rigged, after all.
One reason they were shut down. You couldn't help but lose."
The bureaucrat blinked. "Oh, it wasn't like that," he said.
"It wasn't like that at all. I won."

9

The Wreck of the *Atlantis*

The orchid crabs were migrating to the sea. They scuttled across the sandy road, swamping it under their numbers. Bright parasitic flowers waved gently on their armor, making the forest floor ripple under a carpet of multicolored petals, like a submarine garden seen through clear fathoms of Ocean brine.

Mintouchian cursed and threw the brakes. The New Born King slammed to a halt. Chu pulled out a cheroot and stuck it in the corner of her mouth. "Well, we're stuck here for a while. Might as well get out and stretch our legs."

A small community of pilgrims, the inhabitants of three other trucks—Lord of Haunts, Lucky Mathilde, the Lion Heart—and some dozen foot travelers, were patiently waiting out the migration. A line of them sat on the lowest branch of a grandfather tree, huddled like crows and staring at a blue spark of fire chocked in the fork of one limb. "Look at that," Mintouchian said. "When I was a kid and people got hung up on the road like this, they'd swap stories, sometimes for hours on end: ghost stories, family histories, fables, hero tales, hausmärchen, dirty jokes, brags and dozens, everything you can imagine. Living back then was like being in an ocean of stories. It was great." Disgustedly he flicked on the dashboard set with a swipe of his beefy hand and leaned back in his seat.

Chu climbed out of the cab and hooked an elbow over the hood, eyes distant. The bureaucrat followed.

He felt disconnected. He had spread himself too thin in the Puzzle Palace, and now he felt a touch of perceptual nausea, a forewarning perhaps of the relativistic sickness to which those who worked in conventional reality were particularly prone. Everything seemed bright illusion to him, the thinnest film of appearance afloat over a darker, unknowable truth. The world vibrated with the finest of tensions, as if Something were imminent. He waited for windows to open in the sky, doorways in the trees and holes in the water. For the invisible coursing spirits that surely shared this space unseen to make themselves manifest. As of course they did not.

He set his briefcase down on the running board. "I'm going for a walk."

Chu nodded. Mintouchian didn't even look up from his program.

He wandered deeper into the grandfather tree, careful not to step on the occasional stray crab, outriders of the main migration dimly seeking their way back to consensus. The flow of orchid crabs had split, isolating them in an island of stillness. The tree overhead was a magnificent thing, its great branches spreading out horizontally from the main bole and sending down secondary trunks at irregular distances, so that the one tree had all the volume and complexity of an entire grove.

They were rare, grandfather trees, he remembered hearing. This one was a survivor, a lonely holdout from the earliest days of great spring. From the seeds buried deep in its heart would come, an age hence, if not a new race then at least a nation within that race.

Ramshackle stairs twisted crookedly about the trunk, with landings where planked walks ran atop the branches deep into leafy obscurity. They had been painted once, red and green, yellow and orange, but the carnival colors had faded, bleached by a thousand suns as pale as the skeletons in the boneyard of an abandoned church. Small signs pointed down this branch or that to railinged platforms: THE SHIP VIEW. ABELARD'S. FRESH EELS. JULES ZEE'S. THE AERIE. FLAVORED BEERS.

Drawn upward more by capillary action than actual will, he climbed the stairs.

A drunk staggered down past him. Twisted bits of river wood were nailed to the railings in a weak attempt at decoration, and chalky shells leaned against the uprights.

The bureaucrat was hesitating at the third landing, wondering which way to go, when a dog-headed man carrying a tray of hands pushed by him. He stepped back in alarm, and the man halted and pulled the mask from his face. "Can I help you, sir?"

"Ah, I was wondering—" He saw now that the hands were metal, modulars being taken to be flash-cleaned between clients.

"The *Atlantis* is down that way. Take the walk straight ahead, turn left, and follow the signs. You can't miss it."

Bemused, the bureaucrat followed the instructions and came to a long platform with scattered tables. Clusters of surrogates and the occasional lone human lounged against the railing, staring out into the forest. He stared too.

The tree had been cut back to open a view of the forest interior. Golden light slanted into the greenery, whimseys dancing like dust motes within it. Ahead, rising from the earth like a phantom, was the landlocked corpse of an ocean vessel. The *Atlantis*.

It was enormous beyond scale. The ship had foundered keel first with its bow upward sometime during the last great winter, and the currents had half buried it, so that it seemed frozen in the instant of going under. A million orchid crabs were traversing its barnacled remains, and it was covered with flowers, as impossible a creation as any mnemonic address in the Puzzle Palace.

The ghost of a memory tugged at his mind. He had heard of this ship before. Something.

The bureaucrat found an empty table, scraped up a chair, and sat. A light breeze ruffled his hair. Leaves rustled as a feathered serpent leaped into the air, a scissor-tailed finch perhaps, or a robin. He felt oddly at peace, put in mind of humanity's gentle, arboreal origins. He wondered why people put so little effort into returning home, when it was so easily done.

At that moment he glanced down at the table. An outlined crow stared back at him. Before he could react, a beaked shadow fell across it. He looked up into the eyes of a crow-headed man.

Gregorian! the bureaucrat thought, with a thrill of alarm. Then he remembered the Black Beast that had haunted Dr. Orphelin and looked about him. Faded drawings of birds and animals were everywhere on the railings and tables. He'd attuned himself to such things, and was now generating his own omens "Welcome to the Haunt's Roost," the waiter said.

The bureaucrat pointed to a Flavored Beers sign. "Have you got lime? Or maybe orange?"

The head lifted disdainfully. "That's only line-feed. For the surrogate trade. No real person would drink that crap."

"Oh. Uh, well, give me a glass of lager, then. And an explanation for that ship out there."

The waiter bowed, left, and returned with a beer and an interactive. The set looked out of place, its forced orange-and-purple housing a jarring contrast to the restaurant's studied artlessness. He might have been back home in an environmental retreat, trees and faraway glint of river reduced to calculated effect. The beer was thin.

He turned on the set. A smiling young woman in a brocaded vest appeared on its screen. Her braids were tipped with small silver bells. "Hello," she said. "My name is Marivaud Quinet, and I am a typical citizen of Miranda during the last great year. I am knowledgeable on and able to discuss matters of historical significance as well as details of daily life. I am not structured to offer advice or pornographic entertainment. This set has been sealed by the Department of Licensing and Inspection, Division of Technology Transfer. Product tampering is illegal and may result in prosecution or even unintentional physical harm."

"Yes, I know." The set would implode if its integrity were breached. He wondered if it would be left behind when the restaurant was evacuated, to disappear in a silvery burst of bubbles when salt corrosion finally ate through its housing. "Marivaud, tell me about the *Atlantis*."

Her face grew solemn. "That was the final tragedy of our age. We were arrogant, I admit it. We made mistakes. This was the last of them, the one that brought the offplanet powers down on us, to regress our technology back yet another century."

The bureaucrat remembered just enough history to know this was oversimplification. "What was done was necessary, Marivaud. There must be limits."

She angrily yanked at a braid, setting its tiny bell tinkling. "We were not like the stupid cattle who live here today. We had pride! We accomplished things! We had our own scientists, our own direction. Our contribution to Prosperan culture was not small. We were known throughout the Seven Sisters!"

"I'm sure you were. Tell me about the ship."

"The *Atlantis* was a liner originally. It had to be converted offshore—it was too deep for any harbor. That fragment you see now is only the prow. The true ship was as big as a city." A montage of antique images of the ship in different configurations, the superstructure rising and falling in great waves. "Well, perhaps it only seemed so, for I saw it from so very many viewpoints, in such an overlapping woozy maze of perception. But I get ahead of myself. The first phase was to build a string of transmitters up and down the Tidewater. They were anchored to the bedrock with carbon-whisker cables and made strong enough to withstand the tides when they rolled across the land." More images, of thick, bulbous-topped towers this time. "We rigged them with permanently sealed tokamaks, to guarantee their power over the submerged half of the great year. It took ten lesser years to . . ."

"Marivaud, I haven't the time for all this. Just the sinking, please."

"I was at home that day," Marivaud said. "I'd built a place just above the fall line—what would be the Piedmont coast after the tides. I had a light breakfast, toast with fairy jam sprinkled with ground parsley from my garden, and a glass of stout."

The image dissolved into the interior of a small cottage. Rain specked the windowpanes, and a fire burned in the hearth. Marivaud hastily wiped a dab of jam from the corner of her mouth. "Out at sea, the morning was bright and sunny. I was flashing from person to person, like sunlight itself. I felt so fresh and happy."

The scene switched to the deck of the *Atlantis*.

Green-yellow bodies poured onto the deck. A scoop lifted away. For an instant the bureaucrat did not recognize the struggling creatures. In winter morph they bore very little resemblance to humans. They had long, eelish tails and two slim appendages that might generously be called arms; their faces were streamlined, mouths silent gasps of pain. They twisted, bodies shortening, lengthening, shifting from form to form in a desperate attempt to adapt to the air. The image focused on one, and in the agonized turn of its head the bureaucrat recognized intelligence.

"They're haunts!"

Marivaud faded half in, serene as a madonna at the breakfast table. She nodded. "Yes, the little darlings."

A woman in hip boots waded in among the haunts. Her gun flashed as she pressed it to the backs of heads and pulled the trigger. Haunts jerked wildly with each gasp of compressed air.

"That's the last of them. Over they go."

Suddenly the image shifted to the viewpoint of one of the haunts. It flew through the air and exploded into the water. Clouds of bubbles gushed away and it fled wildly. To either side swam other haunts, wild and beautiful and ecstatic.

Back on deck, the crew were assembling a pair of projectors. "Let's run out those ghost nets again. Watch that—"

There was a knock on the door.

Marivaud opened it. A woman with hard, handsome features that echoed her own stood there. "Goguette! Come in, let me take your cloak. Have you eaten yet? What brings you here so early?"

"I'll take some berry tea." Goguette sat at the table. "I've come to share the jubilee with my little sister. There's nothing wrong with that, is there?"

"No, of course not. Oh! Mousket's on deck."

A large, heroically breasted military type faded in, all jaw and dark purpose. "Mousket," Goguette said. "She's the commandant, right?"

"Yes. She's having an affair with the pilot." A quick glimpse of a slim, straight-built man with cynical eyes. To the bureaucrat she said, "He is an extremely private man. The public nature of their love embarrasses, humiliates, arouses him. That only makes it the sweeter for her. She savors his abasement."

"Excuse me," the bureaucrat said. "How do you know all this?"

"Didn't you notice my earrings?" Marivaud brushed back a curtain of braids, exposing an ear all coral and cream. From it hung an amber leaf, silver-veined and delicate as a dragon's wing. The image swelled so he could see the embedded elements of a television transceiver, signal processor, and neural feed. It was an elegantly simple arrangement that would let her effortlessly employ all electronic skills: She might talk with friends, receive entertainments, preserve a particularly beautiful sunrise, copy an

Old Master drawing in her own hand, do research, take and teach educational courses, or transmit her dreams for machine analysis, at her whim. It made her brain a node within an invisible empire of interactivity, the perfect focus of a circle so infinitely large its center was everywhere, its circumference nowhere.

"Even the offworlders didn't have these," she said. "We were the first to combine everything into one continuous medium. It was like being in two worlds at once, like having a second, unseen life. This was when you offworlders were creating that awkward mnemonic palace of yours. Our method was superior. If it hadn't been for the *Atlantis* incident, you would be a part of it now."

"By God, you're talking about the Trauma!" the bureaucrat cried in rising horror. "There was a ship involved—that must have been the *Atlantis*! Everyone on it was wired for continuous broadcast."

"Do you want to listen to this story or narrate it yourself? Yes, of course the crew were all actors, improvisors—what do you call people who lead lives of shaped intensity in order to create public dramas?"

"I don't think we have them anymore. What are they doing to the haunts?"

"Fitting them with broadcast chips, of course. What did you think this project was all about?"

"Why would you want to do such a thing?"

"That is exactly what I ask her myself!" Goguette said. "There are so many refined, educational, and enriching experiences available on the net. Why waste your life listening in on creatures little better than animals?"

"Ah, but such splendid animals!" Marivaud giggled. "But we are getting away from our story. You"—she addressed the bureaucrat directly—"can experience only the middle range of this. You miss the little things, the burn of rope in chafed hand, Ocean's smell, the chill of a salt breeze across your arm. And the grand emotions you can only sense from the outside. There is no way we can share more than a fraction of this with you. So I will show you two minor players, a ghostnetter and a flash-surgeon. Their true names have been lost, so I will give the ghostnetter the offworld name of Underhill. The flash-surgeon I will name—Gogo, after my sister."

Goguette punched her shoulder, she laughed, and they were gone. On deck, the flash-surgeon holstered her gun. She wiped her brow with the back of her arm, glanced up past the mast-high cranes to see Caliban high above, a disk of ice melting in blue sky. Then down again to see haunts' heads appearing and disappearing above the water.

She strolled over to the nearest projector. "My God," she said. "They're beautiful."

Underhill looked up from his screen, flashed a smile. "This is the last sounding. When they're done, our job is over." His hands were delicate on the controls. The projector swiveled slightly, and the ghost net swung an arc forward. "Watch that group out there." Into a microphone he said, "Point one."

Cut to the other projector. Its operator swiveled in the opposite direction. "Point one."

Far away black dots appeared and disappeared in the water. The ghost net crept closer, its progress traceable by the hissing line of bubbles along its length. The sounding changed direction, angling away. "Clever little babies," Underhill muttered. "Don't you run away from me."

The two lines of white bubbles were slowly converging now, like a giant pair of scissors closing. The haunts caught between the ghost nets fled toward open sea. A few broke away from the main pack and doubled back through the ghost net.

"Oh!" Gogo cried. "They're getting away."

That confident grin again. Underhill brushed back his hair. "No, those are ones we caught earlier, with your chips telling them they can go through."

Gogo was bouncing up and down on her toes in excitement.

She looked very young, almost a child. "Oh! Are you sure? Yes, of course."

"Relax. Even if we let a few get away—what would it hurt?"

"There are so few of them left," Gogo said wistfully. "So very few. We should have chipped them while they were still ashore."

Distractedly, staring down at his screens with perfect concentration, Underhill said, "It wasn't possible to find them all while they were on land. They're elusive, you know that." Into the microphone he said, "Point three."

"Point three."

The lines of bubbles were closing. Gogo stared off at them. "Sometimes I wonder should we be doing this at all?"

He looked up at her with frank wonder. "Do you?"

"It hurts them!" Softly: "*I* hurt them."

Underhill was perfectly intent on his screen. "It was not so long ago that the indigenes were almost extinct. It was all our own fault. Unwise policies, disease—people even hunted them in the early years. Do you know what put an end to all that?"

"What?"

"The first time an indigene was chipped into the net. The first time people could feel sensation with that purity and clean zest they feel. The first—"

"The first time people could run with them through the magical night, wind in hair, to hunt and mate," Gogo breathed. She blushed prettily. "I know it's kind of sick."

"That's what I say," Goguette interpolated.

"Oh, poof!" Marivaud said. "If you're not enjoying this, there are other shows for you to experience."

"No, it's not!" Underhill said firmly. "There's nothing wrong with that. It's a natural, healthful thing to be interested in the physical side of love. It shows you have a lively interest in life. Point five," he said, "and locking."

"Point five and locking."

A third ghostnetter snapped on his projector, and a new line of bubbles capped the other two. The pack of haunts wheeled in confusion. Slowly the last ghost net began to draw them in. The crane operator began moving her scoop into position. "Your turn soon."

"I'll be ready," she said. Then, "You're easy to talk to."

"Thank you." He studied her. "What's *really* bothering you?"

Her fingers closed on the grip of her gun, opened again. "I'm afraid it won't be so good. I mean, with them in winter morph."

"You mean you haven't tried them?"

"I was afraid."

Underhill smiled. "Try."

She hesitated, then nodded. The image switched to the haunts again, fleeing through bubbles, diving to catch a passing crustacean and crunch it in small sharp teeth. Even on the screen, limited to sight and sound, the joy the creatures felt simply swimming along was obvious.

"Oh," she said. Her eyes widened. "Oh!"

Goguette was washing dishes. A door banged open, and Marivaud came in with raindrops on her cloak and an armful of fresh-cut flowers. "You have so little time," she said to the bureaucrat as she began arranging them. "We'll cut forward a few hours, to the jubilee."

Ocean roared. Abandoning their posts, those of the crew who weren't already at the rails ran to starboard and stared. It was an impossible sight: all the water in the world humping up, as if the planet had suddenly decided it needed a higher horizon. The *Atlantis* listed a degree in anticipation. The grandmother of all tidal waves, the polar tsunami, was passing beneath them. The ship shot upward, carried by the power of a continent of ice melting all at once.

The screen cut from face to face, viewpoint to viewpoint,

showing stunned eyes, strained faces. They stood deathly still, paralyzed with awe.

"How are they going to escape?" the bureaucrat asked. "Don't they want to get away?"

"Of course they don't."

"Do they want to die?"

"Of course they don't." The image wavered, and the human crew turned to metal. The *Atlantis* was transformed into a ship of the dead, a gothic monstrosity manned by skeletons. "Surrogates were invented on Miranda," Marivaud said proudly. "We made them first." The image overlay was restored, and the skeletons fleshed out with human bodies.

A horrid glassy calm settled over the near reaches of Ocean, as if its surface had been stretched taut by the swell. Even as they soared up its side, the water seemed to shrink under the ship. The bureaucrat could hear it whispering and running away. Ocean rose until it filled the eye. The sky vanished, and still it grew. Winds blew across the deck.

Then they topped the swell. Beyond it a wall of white fury reached from horizon to horizon—a line squall. It rushed down on them. Involuntarily crew members moved toward and away from each other, forming clusters and gaps along the rail.

Gogo glanced toward the ghostnetter. Her eyes were bright with excitement. She bit her lip, brushed away a strand of hair from an undone braid. Her face glowed with life. She reached out to hug Underhill.

Startled, Underhill flinched away from her touch. He stared into her face with revulsion. In that unguarded instant his expression said louder than any words: *You're only a woman.*

Then the squall overtook the ship, and slammed into its side. The storm swallowed it whole.

"Ahh," Marivaud sighed. Her sister reached out and seized her hand. Softly, gently, they began to applaud.

In a faraway studio the actors rose up from their gates to take their bows.

Marivaud looked up, face expressionless. The cottage—sister, fire, and all—dissolved in a swirl of rain. "A week later, the bodies began washing up on shore."

"What?"

"With radiation burns. We had not understood the indigenes so well as we had thought. We did not know that their brain chemistry changed in great winter. Or perhaps it was their psychology that changed. But somehow the warning signal that was supposed to drive them from the towers did not. They huddled as close to the reactors as they could. It was madness. Perhaps their mating instincts were stimulated. Perhaps they just liked the warmth. Who can say?"

Marivaud's eyes closed. Tears squeezed between the lids. "We could do nothing. Ocean was all storm and fury—nothing could get through. Nothing except for the broadcasts we could not turn off. All the time it took for them to die, the towers up and down the coast transmitted their agony. It was like having a broken tooth in one's mouth—the tongue keeps returning to it, drawn by the pain. I could not leave it alone.

"Sorrow swept over Continent in a great electronic wave. It was as if an enchantment had passed over the land. One moment everything was bright and beautiful. The next it was gray and lifeless. As a people we had been optimistic, sure of ourselves. Now we were . . . dispossesed, without a future. Those who had the strength not to listen were affected by the rest of us.

"I myself would have starved, had my sister not hand-fed me for a week. She smashed my earrings. She bullied me back to life. But after that I no longer laughed so often as before. There were people who died. Others went mad. The shame was great.

When the offplanet powers convened and took away the last of our science, there was little protest. We knew we deserved it. So the high autumn of our technology passed, and we lapsed into eternal winter."

Marivaud fell silent, her face pale and sad. The bureaucrat turned off the interactive.

After a while, a dog-headed waiter came and took the set away.

The bureaucrat drained the last of his beer and leaned back to watch the surrogates dining. It amused him in a melancholy way, to see them lifting glasses and tasting food no one else could see, in a perfect and meaningless mime show. By the railing other surrogates strolled and chatted. One of them was staring at him.

Their eyes met, and the surrogate bowed. It came to the table and took a chair. For an instant the bureaucrat couldn't place the keen, aged face that burned on the screen. Then his schoolboy eidetics kicked in. "You're the shopkeeper," he said. "In Lightfoot. Your name is . . . Pouffe, is that right?"

There was a squint of madness in the old man's grin. "That's right, that's right. Gonna ask how I found you here?"

"How did you find me here?"

"Tracked you down. Tracked you to Cobbs Creek. Gated ahead to Clay Bank, you weren't there. Gated back to Cobbs Creek, they told me you hadn't been gone long. I knew you'd stop here. Never met an offworlder yet who could resist taking in the sights. I've been waiting for you."

"Actually I'm here by chance."

"Sure you are." Pouffe's lips twisted sardonically. "But I would've found you anyway. This isn't the only place I've been waiting. Been shunting between four different gates all morning."

"That must have cost you a lot of money."

"Yes, that's the key." The old man leaned forward, eyebrows

rising significantly. "A lot of money. It cost me a lot of money. But I've got plenty of it. I'm a rich man, if you get my drift."

"Not exactly."

"I've seen your commercial. You know, about the magician. The one who can—"

"Wait a minute, that's not my—"

"—adapt a man to live and breathe underwater. Well, I—"

"Stop. This is nonsense."

"—want to find him. I understand you can't tell just anybody. I'll pay for the information, and I'll pay well." He reached across the table to seize the bureaucrat's hand.

"I don't have what you want!" The bureaucrat shook away the grasping metal hand and stood. "Even if I knew where he was, I wouldn't tell you. The man is a fraud. He can't do any of what he claims."

"That's not what you said on television."

"Shopkeeper Pouffe, take a look out here." He led the avid old man to the railing. "Take a good look. Imagine what this is going to be like in a few months. No houses, no shelter. Seaweed where the trees are now, and angel sharks feeding in the black water. The marine life here has had millions of years to adapt to this environment. You, on the other hand, are a civilized man with a genome foreign not only to Ocean but to this entire star system. Even if Gregorian could deliver on his wild claims— and I assure you that he cannot—what kind of life could you lead here? What would you eat? How could you expect to survive?"

"Excuse me, sir," a bull-headed waiter said.

He swept Pouffe's surrogate aside, placed a hand on the bureaucrat's back, and shoved. "Hey, what—!" Pouffe cried.

The bureaucrat fell forward. Dizzily he clutched at the railing. The man-bull laughed, and the bureaucrat felt his legs being lifted up behind him. All existence swept sideways, trees wheeling in the sky beneath, sand turning up overfoot. The hands were warm and firm on his ankles. Then, suddenly, they were gone.

Somebody screamed. In a blast of pain the bureaucrat crashed flat on his stomach. His arms were still clenched about the rail. Helplessly he gazed up to see the waiter and Pouffe's surrogate locked in a hug. They might have been dancing. The man shoved violently, and the telescreen snapped off. It bounced off the edge of the platform. Headless, the machine ducked and spun. The two crashed into the railing. Wood splintered and gave.

They toppled over the edge.

Surrogates, waiters, even human customers, rushed to stare down over the rail. In the crush the bureaucrat was ignored.

Slowly he pulled himself up. His legs and spine ached. One knee trembled. It felt wet. He clutched the rail with both hands and looked down. Long way down to the ground. His assailant lay unmoving atop the broken surrogate. He looked tiny as a doll. The bull mask had fallen away, revealing familiar round features.

It was Veilleur—the false Chu.

The bureaucrat stared. He's dead, he thought. That could have been me. A metal hand took his elbow and pulled him back. "This way," Pouffe said quietly. "Before anybody thinks to connect you with him down there."

He was led to a secluded table back among the leaves.

"You travel in fast company. Can you tell me what that was all about?"

"No," the bureaucrat said. "I—I know who was behind it, but not the specifics, no." He took a deep breath. "I can't stop shuddering," he said. Then, "I owe you my life, shopkeeper."

"That's right, you do. It was all that combat training back when I was a young man. Fuckin' surrogates are so weak, it's next to impossible to overpower someone with one. You got to turn their own strength against them." That smug, self-satisfied smirk floated on the screen. "You know how to repay me."

The bureaucrat sighed, stared down at his hands on the table. Weak, mortal hands. He gathered himself together. "Look—"

"No, you look! I spent four years in the Caverns—that's what they call the military brig on Caliban. Do you have any idea what it was like there?"

"Pretty grim, I'd imagine."

"No, it's not! That's the hell of it. It's all perfectly humane and bland and impersonal. Some snot-nosed tech plugs you into a simple visualization program, hooks up an IV feed and a physical-therapy program so your body don't rot, and then leaves you imprisoned inside your own skull.

"It's like a monastery in there, or maybe a nice clean hotel. Nothing to hurt or alarm you. Your emotions are cranked way down low. You're as comfy as a mouth sucking on a tit. You don't feel anything but warm, don't hear nothing but soft, comfortable noises. Nothing can hurt you. Nothing can reach you. You can't escape.

"Four years!

"When you get out, they give you three months' intensive rehab before you can accept the evidence of your own eyes. Even then, you still have nights when you wake up and don't believe you exist anymore.

"I came out of that place and went to ground. I swore I'd never again go anywhere I couldn't go in person. That was a lifetime ago, and I've kept that vow right up to this very day. Do you hear what I'm telling you?"

"You're saying this is important to you."

"Damn right, it's important!"

"Is your life important to you? Then give up this childish fantasy. These notions of coral castles and mermaids singing. Shopkeeper, this is the real world. You must make the best of what there is."

Somewhere far away, a truck horn was honking regularly, insistently. The bureaucrat realized that he had been hearing it for some time. The migration must have cleared the road.

He stood. "I have to leave now."

When he tried to walk away, Pouffe danced after him. "We haven't talked money yet! I haven't told you how much I can pay."

"Please. This is futile."

"No, you've got to listen to me." Pouffe was crying now, desperate hot tears running down his rutted face. "You've got to listen."

"Is this man bothering you, sir?" a waiter asked.

The bureaucrat hesitated for a second. Then he nodded, and the waiter turned the surrogate off.

Back on the ground, he could not find the New Born King. The truck was gone. Chu stood on the running board of another, the Lion Heart, leaning on the horn. She stepped down at his approach. "You look odd. Pale."

"I should," he said flatly. "One of Gregorian's people just tried to kill me."

When he was done telling his story, Chu slammed her fist into her hand, over and over again. "That sonofabitch!" she said. "The fucking nerve of him." She was genuinely angry.

The bureaucrat was surprised and a little flattered by Chu's show of emotion. He had never been quite sure that she accepted him, and always suspected she thought of him as merely an offworld buffoon, someone to be tolerated rather than respected. He felt an unexpected glow of gratitude. "I remember you telling me once not to take any of this personally."

"Yeah, well, when somebody tries to kill your partner, that kind of changes the game. Gregorian is going to pay for this. I'll see that he does." She wheeled sharply away, and stepped on a crab. "Shit!" She kicked the mutilated body away. "What a fuck-ing glorious day."

"Say." The bureaucrat peered around. "Where's Mintou-chian?"

"Gone," Chu said. She stood on one foot, wiping the sole of her shoe with a handkerchief. Then she threw the cloth into the weeds. "He took your briefcase with him too."

"What?"

"It was the damnedest thing. Soon as the crabs dwindled, he fired up the truck, snatched the briefcase, and lit off like his ass was on fire." Chu shook her head. "That was when I started honking the horn here, trying to call you back."

"Didn't he know that my briefcase will come back to me?"

"Obviously not."

It took the briefcase half an hour to find its way back to him. Chu had already made arrangements with the Lion Heart's driver, and had gone off to view the corpse of her impersonator. "Oughta be good for a few laughs," she said grimly. "Maybe I'll cut off an ear for a souvenir."

The briefcase daintily picked its way down the road. When it reached the bureaucrat, it set itself down and retracted its legs. He picked it up. "Hard time getting away?"

"No. Mintouchian didn't even bother strapping me down. I waited until he'd gone a couple of miles downriver and was feeling confident, then rolled down the window and jumped."

"Hum." The bureaucrat was silent for a moment. Then he said, "We'll be here a few hours more than planned. There's been a touch of violence, and we still have to deal with the nationals. Probably have to make a statement, maybe file a field report."

The briefcase, familiar with his moods, said nothing.

The bureaucrat thought about Gregorian, of the magician's

abrupt shift from a distant mocking disdain to outright enmity. He'd almost died just now. He thought about Mintouchian, and about Dr. Orphelin's warning that he had a traitor with him. Everything was changed, horribly changed. "Did Mintouchian look surprised when you jumped?"

"He looked like he'd swallowed a toad. You should've been there—it would've made you laugh."

"I suppose."

But he doubted it. The bureaucrat didn't feel like laughing. He didn't feel like laughing at all.

10

A Service for the Dead

That morning, the doctor wind swept a swarm of barnacle flies inland, and when the bureaucrat awoke, the houseboat was encrusted with their shells. He had to lean on the door to break it open. The salt smell of Ocean was everywhere, like the scent of a lover who has visited in the night and is gone, leaving only this ambiguous promise of return.

He scowled and spat over the houseboat's edge.

The bottom tread of his stoop was missing. The bureaucrat hopped down onto the bare patch worn into the black earth beneath. He began to thread his way through the scattered hulks of the boats' graveyard.

"Hey!"

He looked up. A golden-haired boy stood naked atop a cradled yacht with a stove-in bow, pissing into the rosebushes. One of the gang of scavengers who lived there. He waved with his free hand. The census bracelet glittered dully on his wrist. "That thing you were looking for? We found a whole pile of them. Come on over and take your pick."

175

Five minutes later the bureaucrat had stowed a tightly bound bundle in his room, and was off again to Clay Bank. A sour church bell clanged in the distance, calling the faithful to meditation. The sky was overcast and gray. A light, almost imperceptible drizzle fell.

This far east, the farmland was too rich to squander, and save for the plantation buildings, most dwellings hugged the river. Unpainted clapboard houses teetered precariously on the lip of a high earth bluff. Halfway down to the water, a walk had been cut into the dirt and planked over, to serve a warren of jugs and storerooms dug into the bank itself.

Lieutenant Chu was waiting for him on the boardwalk outside the diner. Boats bobbed on the river, tied to pilings across which ran docks more gap than substance, the idea of Dock a *beau idéal* honored more in the intent than the execution. The drizzle chose that instant to intensify into rain, drops hissing on the surface of the water. They ducked inside.

"I got another warning," the bureaucrat said when they'd found a table. He opened his briefcase and removed a handful of black feathers. A crow's wing. "It was tacked to my door when I got home last night."

"Funny business," Chu said. She spread the wing, examined the bloody shoulder joint, folded open the tiny fingers at the metacarpal joint, and gave it back. "It must be those scavengers doing it. I don't know why you insist on living there."

The bureaucrat shrugged irritably. "Whoever's actually placing these things, it's at Gregorian's instigation. I recognize his style." Privately, though, it bothered him that Gregorian had changed tactics again, switching back from attempted assassination to mockery and harassment. It made no sense.

The diner was dim and narrow, a tunnel dug straight back from the bank. The tables halfway down were drawn away from the pool of light shed by the single milky glass skylight. Water fell from leaky seams into waiting tins. To the rear the kitchen help laughed and gossiped while the leaping flames of a gas range chased shadows about their faces. A waitress came to their table and slapped down trenchers of salt meat and mashed yams. Chu wrinkled her nose. "You got any—?"

"No." The evac boys at the next table laughed. "You want breakfast, you'll take what you're given."

"Arrogant bitch," Chu grumbled. "If this weren't the last eatery in Clay Bank, I'd . . ."

A young soldier leaned over from the next table. "Easy up," he said in that broad northern accent all the local Authority muscle had, Tidewater types brought in from Blackwater and Vineland provinces because they had no ties here. "Last airship comes through tomorrow. They've got to clean out their larder." His beret, folded under a shoulder strap, had been customized with a rooster's tail.

Chu stared at him until he reddened and turned away.

In a niche by the table a television was showing a documentary on the firing of the jugs. There was antique footage of workers sealing up the newdug clay. Narrow openings were left at the bottoms of what would be the doors, and to the top rear of the tunnels. Then the wood packed inside was fired. Pillars of smoke rose up like the ghosts of trees and became a forest whose canopy blotted out the sun. The show had been playing over and over ever since its original broadcast on one of the government channels. Nobody noticed it anymore.

The heat required to glaze the walls was— The bureaucrat reached over to switch channels. *My brother died at sea! What was I supposed to do? I'm not his keeper, you know.*

"You watch that crap?" Chu asked.

"It's involving."

"Who's the weedy geek?"

"Now that's an interesting question. He's supposed to be

Shelley, Eden's cousin—you know, the little girl who saw the unicorn? But she had two cousins, identical twins—" Chu snorted. "All right, I admit it's implausible. But, you know, even in the Inner Circle it happens occasionally. That's why they have the genetic-tagging techniques, to mark them as separate individuals when it does occur."

But Chu wasn't listening. She stared off through the doorway into the gray rain, pensively silent. Around them rose the babble of voices from waitresses and kitchen workers, soldiers and civilians, happy and a little shrill with the excitement of the impending evacuation, all feeling the intoxication of radical change.

All right! Yes, I killed him. I killed my brother! Are you happy now?

"God," Chu said. "This must be the most boring place in the universe."

Holding his briefcase out for balance, the bureaucrat followed Chu down the rain-slick boardwalk. They passed a stairway dug into the dirt, once braced and planked, now crumbled into a narrow slant and become almost a gully. Water gushed from its mouth. "I've requisitioned good seats on the heliostat tomorrow," Chu said.

The bureaucrat grunted.

"Come on. If we miss the ship, we'll be taken out on one of the cattleboats." She tugged on her census bracelet in annoyance. "You haven't seen what they're like."

A crate crashed onto the walk before them, and they danced back. It bounced over the edge, into the water. Scavengers were ransacking a storeroom, noisily smashing things and throwing them outside. A slick of trash floated downriver, all but motionless in the sleepy current, spreading as it withdrew: old mattresses slowly drowning, wicker baskets and dried flowers, splintered armchairs and fiddles, toy sailboats lying on their sides in the water. The scavengers were shouting, given over completely to the destruction of objects they could never afford before and could not pay the freight on now.

They came to a jug with a weathered sign hung over the door showing a silvery skeletal figure. The gate was the establishment's sole legitimate enterprise and ostensible reason for being, though everyone knew the place was actually a paintbox. "What about the flier?" the bureaucrat asked. "No word yet from the Stone House?"

"No, and by now it's safe to say there's not going to be. Look, we've been here so long I'm growing moss on my behind. We've done everything we can do, the trail is cold. What good is a flier going to do anyway? It's time to give up."

"I'll take your sentiments under advisement." The bureaucrat stepped within. Chu did not follow.

"It's been a long time since I've been here," the bureaucrat said. Korda's quarters were spacious in a city where space translated directly into wealth. The grass floor was broken into staggered planes, and the arrays of stone tools set into the angled walls were indirectly lit by spots bounced off rotating porphyry columns. Everything was agonizingly clean. Even the dwarf cherry trees were potted in mirror-symmetrical pairs.

"You're not here now," Korda replied unsentimentally. "Why are you bothering me at home? Couldn't it wait for the office?"

"You've been avoiding me at the office."

Korda frowned. "Nonsense."

"Pardon me." A man in a white ceramic mask entered the room. He wore a loose wraparound, such as was the style in the worlds of Deneb. "The vote is coming up, and you're needed."

"You wait here." At the archway to the next room Korda hesitated and asked the man in the mask, "Aren't you coming, Vasli?"

The eyeless white face glanced downward. "It is my place on the Committee that is being debated just now. It's probably best for all concerned if I wait this one out."

The Denebian drifted to the center of the room, stood motionless. His hands were lost in the wraparound's sleeves, his head overshadowed by the hood. He looked subtly unhuman, his motions too graceful, his stillness too complete. He was, the bureaucrat realized suddenly, that rarest of entities, a permanent surrogate. Their glances met.

"I make you nervous," Vasli said.

"Oh no, of course not. It's just..."

"It's just that you find my form unsettling. I know. There is no reason to let an overfastidious sense of tact lead you into falsehood. I believe in truth. I am a humble servant of truth. Were it in my power, I would have no lies or evasions anywhere, nothing concealed, hidden, or locked away from common sight."

The bureaucrat went to the wall, examined the collection of stone points there: fish points from Miranda, fowling points from Earth, worming points from Govinda. "Forgive me if I seem blunt, but such radical sentiments make you sound like a Free Informationist."

"That is because I am one."

The bureaucrat felt as if he'd come face to face with a mythological beast, a talking mountain, say, or Eden's unicorn. "You are?" he said stupidly.

"Of course I am. I gave up my own world to share what I knew with your people. It takes a radical to so destroy his own life, yes? To exile himself among people who feel uncomfortable in his presence, who fear his most deeply held values as treason, and who were not interested in what he had to say in the first place."

"Yes, but the concept of Free Information is . . ."

"Extreme? Dangerous?" He spread his arms. "Do I look dangerous?"

"You would give everyone total access to all information?"

"Yes, all of it."

"Regardless of the harm it could do?"

"Look. You are like a little boy who is walking along in a low country, and has found a hole in one of the dikes. You plug it with your finger, and for a moment all is well. The sea grows a little stronger, a little bigger. The hole crumbles about the edges. You have to thrust your entire hand within. Then your arm, up to the shoulder. Soon you have climbed entirely within the hole and are plugging it with your body. When it grows bigger, you take a deep breath and puff yourself up with air. But still, the ocean is there, and growing stronger. You have done nothing about your basic problem."

"What would you have us do with the dangerous information?"

"Master it! Control it!"

"How?"

"I have no idea. I am but a single man. But if you applied all the brain and muscle now wasted in a futile attempt to control—" Abruptly he stopped. For a long moment he stared at the bureaucrat, as if mastering his emotions. His shoulders slumped. "Forgive me. I am taking out my anger on you. I heard just this morning that my original—the Vasli I once was, the man who thought he had so much to share—died, and I haven't sorted out my feelings yet."

"I'm sorry," the bureaucrat said. "This must be a sorrowful time for you."

Vasli shook his head. "I don't know whether to cry or laugh. He was myself, and yet he was also the one who condemned me to die here—worldless, disembodied, alone."

That blind face stared upward through a thousand layers of

the floating city into the outer darkness. "I have been imagining what it would be like to walk the fields of Storr again, to smell the chukchuk and rhu. To see the foibles aflame against the western stars, and hear the flowers sing! Then, I think, I could die content."

"You could always go back."

"You mistake the signal for the message. It is true that I could have myself copied and that signal transmitted home to Deneb. But *I* would still be here. I could then kill myself, I suppose, but other than salving the conscience of my agent, what good would it do?" He glanced at the bureaucrat's surrogate body, tilted one edge of the mask up scornfully. "But I do not expect you to understand."

The bureaucrat changed the subject. "May I ask," he said, "just what work your committee is engaged on?"

"The Citizens' Committee for the Prevention of Genocide, you mean? Why, just that. The destruction of indigenous races is a problem that exists in all colonized systems, my own not the least. It is too late for Miranda, of course, but perhaps some protocols will arise here that may be worth transmitting home."

"It is possible," the bureaucrat said cautiously, "that you're being overpessimistic. I, ah, know of people who have seen haunts, who have actually met and talked with them in recent memory. It's possible that the race may yet survive."

"No. It is not."

The Denebian's words were spoken with such absolute conviction that the bureaucrat was taken aback. "Why not?"

"There is for all species a minimum sustainable population. Once the population falls below a certain number, it is doomed. It lacks the plasticity necessary to survive the normal variations in its environment. Say, for example, that you have a species of bird reduced to a dozen specimens. You protect them, and they increase in number to a thousand. But they are still, genetically, only a dozen individuals expressed in a myriad of clones. Their genome is brittle. One day the sun will rise wrong and they will all die. A disease, say, that kills one will kill all. Any number of things.

"Your haunts cannot exist in very large numbers, or their existence would be known for certain. Korda thinks otherwise, but he is a fool. It does not matter if a few individuals have lingered on beyond their time. As a race, they are dead."

Korda chose that moment to return. "You can go in now," he said. "The Committee wishes to speak with you. I think you'll be pleased with what they have to say." Only one who knew Korda well could have caught that overpolite edge to his voice that meant he had just suffered one of his rare defeats.

With a curt bow to the bureaucrat, Vasli glided away. Korda stared after him.

"I didn't know haunts were one of your interests," the bureaucrat remarked.

"They are my only interest," Korda said unguardedly. Then, catching himself, "My only hobby, I mean."

But the words were out. Revelation cascaded into the past like a line of dominoes toppling. A thousand small remarks Korda had made, a hundred missed meetings, a dozen odd reversals of policies, all were explained. The bureaucrat carefully did not let his face change expression. "So what is it?" Korda asked. "Just what do you want?"

"I need a flier. The Stone House is acting balky, and I've been waiting on them for weeks. If you could pull a few strings, I could wrap this affair up in a day. I know where Gregorian is now."

"Do you?" Korda looked at him sharply. Then, "Very well, I'll do it." He touched a data outlet. "Tomorrow morning at Tower Hill, it'll be waiting for you."

"Thank you."

Korda hesitated oddly, looking away and then back again, as if he couldn't quite put something into words. Then, in a puzzled tone, he asked, "Why are you staring at my feet?"

"Oh, no reason," the bureaucrat said. "No reason at all."

But even as he deactivated the surrogate, he was thinking, Lots of people have luxury goods from other star systems. The robot freighters crawl between the stars slowly but regularly. Gregorian's father isn't alone in wearing outsystem boots.

Boots of red leather.

The paintbox was silent when he emerged from the gate. Through the open doorway he could see that evening had come, the pearly gray light failing toward dusk. The bouncer sat in a rickety chair, staring out into the rain. The tunnels leading back into the earth were lightless holes.

For an instant of mingled fear and relief the bureaucrat thought the place closed permanently. Then he realized how early it was still; the women would not be on duty yet.

"Excuse me," he said to the bouncer. The man looked up incuriously; he was a round little dandy, curly-haired and balding, a ridiculous creation. "I'm looking for someone who works here. The—" He hesitated, realizing that he knew the women here only by the nicknames the young soldiers used for them, the Pig, the Goat, and the Horse. "The tall one with short hair."

"Try the diner."

"Thanks."

In a shadowy doorway alongside the diner the bureaucrat waited for the Horse to emerge. He felt like a ghost—sad, voiceless, and unseen, a melancholy pair of eyes staring into the world of the living. He lacked the stomach to wait in the light.

Occasionally people emerged from the diner, and because a plank overhang sheltered the boardwalk there from the rain, they would usually pause to gather themselves together before braving the weather. Once, Chu stopped not an arm's length away, engrossed in light banter with her young rooster. "—all alike," she said. "You think that just because you've got that thing between your legs, you're hot stuff. Well, there's nothing special about having a penis. Hell, even I have one of them."

He laughed unsurely.

"You don't believe me? I'm perfectly serious." She took out a handful of transition notes. "You care to place a little money on that? Why are you shaking your head? Suddenly you believe me? Tell you what, I'll give you a chance to get your money back. Double or nothing, mine is bigger than yours."

The rooster hesitated, then grinned. "Okay," he said. He reached for his belt.

"Hold on, my pretty, not out here." Chu took his arm. "We'll compare lengths in private." She led him away.

The bureaucrat felt a wry amusement. He remembered when Chu had first shown him the trophy she'd cut from the false Chu, the day it had returned from the taxidermist. She'd opened the box and held it up laughing. "Why would you want to save such a thing?" he had asked.

"It'll get me the young fish." She'd swooped it through the air, the way a child would a toy airplane, then lightly kissed the air before its tip and returned it to the box. "Take my word for it. If you want to catch the sweet young things, there's nothing like owning a big cock."

Eventually the Horse emerged from the diner, alone. She paused to put up the hood on her raincoat. He stepped from the shadows, and coughed into his hand. "I want to hire your services," he said. "Not here. I have a place in the old boatyard."

She looked him up and down, then shrugged. "All right, but I'll have to charge you for the travel time." She took his hand and waggled the tattooed finger. "And I can't spend all night with you. There's a midnight mass at the church, a service for the dead."

"Fine," he said.

"It's the last service, and I don't want to miss it. They'll be chanting for everyone who ever died in Clay Bank. I got people I want to remember." She took his arm. "Lead the way." She was a homely woman, her face harsh and weathered as old wood. Under other circumstances he could imagine their being friends.

They trudged down the river road in silence. The bureaucrat wore a poncho his briefcase had made for him. After a time his speechlessness began to feel oppressive. "What's your name?" he asked awkwardly.

"You mean my real name or the name I use?"

"Whichever."

"It's Arcadia."

At the houseboat the bureaucrat lit a candle and placed it in its sconce, while Arcadia stamped the mud from her feet. "I'll sure be glad when this rain ends!" she remarked.

The bundle he'd bought from the scavengers that morning was still on the nightstand. While he was gone, somebody had pulled the covers back from his bed and placed a single black crow's feather at its center. He brushed it to the floor.

Arcadia found a hook for her raincoat. She pushed up her census bracelet to rub her wrist. "I've got a rash from this. You know what I think? I think adamantine is going to be a fetish item in a year or two. People will pay good money to have these things put on them."

Thrusting the bundle at her, the bureaucrat said, "Here. Take off all your clothes and change into this."

She looked at the bundle with interest, shrugged again. "All right."

"I'll be right back."

He took a pair of gardening shears from his briefcase and went out into the rain. It was pitch-dark outside, and it took him a long time to clip the large armful of flowers he needed.

By the time he returned, Arcadia had changed into the fantasia. It was covered with orange and red sequins, and cut all wrong. But it fit her well enough. It would do.

"Roses! How nice." Arcadia clapped her hands like a little girl. She spun about so that the fantasia swirled about her in a fluid, magical motion. "Do you like how I look?"

"Lie down on the bed," he said roughly. "Pull the skirt up over your waist."

She obeyed.

The bureaucrat dumped the roses to the side of the bed in a wet pile. Arcadia's skin was pale as marble in the faint light, the mounded hair between her legs dark and shadowy. Her flesh looked as though it would be cold to the touch.

By the time he had shed his own clothing, the bureaucrat was erect. The room was sweet with the scent of roses.

He closed his eyes as he entered her. He didn't open them again until he was done.

11

The Sun at Midnight

The air filled with flying ants, their wings iridescent blurs, tiny rainbows that overlapped and created black diffraction patterns: circles and crescents forming and disappearing before the eye could fix on them. The bureaucrat gaped up and they were gone, away on their dying flight to the sea.

"This makes no sense at all," Chu grumbled.

The bureaucrat stepped back from the flier. "It's very simple. I want you to lift off and head due south until you're well over the horizon from Tower Hill. Then swing around and treetop back. There's a little clearing to the east, by a stream. Wait for me there. A child could do it."

"You know what I mean."

"Oh all right. You saw the way we were treated at the hangar?" Across the field, a gang of surrogate laborers, all rust and limping joints, were clumsily stacking the hangar's dismantled parts onto a lifting skid. "How insistent they were that we be gone by noon? They didn't want us to be in the way?"

"Yeah, so?"

"So tell me that somebody's going to send an airlifter all the way out here two days before the tides just to haul out a modular storage hut." He did not wait for Chu to respond. "They were instructed to get me away from here as quickly as possible. I intend to find out why." He stepped back into the shadow of the trees and pitched his voice for the flier. "Now take off."

The canopy slid shut. Engines came to life. The flier was a pretty piece of engineering, the kind of elegant machine normally seen only in the floating worlds. Its emerald skin shimmered in the heat of the jets. Then the flier skidded forward twelve times its own length and with a roar pulled up into the sky. Blink and it was gone.

The trail through the woods was peaceful. The leaves had turned during the rains, gone to purples and cobalts as if all the Tidewater had been blueshifted five seconds into the past. The filtered light was quietly saddening, a somber reminder of the imminence of the land's passing.

The trees opened up at the foot of Tower Hill. Its slopes were a frayed green, white chalk showing through alien Terran grass. Bright tents and banners, parasols and balloons, dotted the hillside. At the top stood the ancient tower itself, overpainted in bold orange-and-pink supergraphics, an island of offworld aesthetic that clashed violently with the tragedian's garb of the autumn forest.

The hillside crawled with surrogates, an anthill churned with a stick. It seemed that now that the Tidewater had been scoured of human life, the demons had come out to have a carnival of their own.

He headed upslope.

Brittle metal laughter sounded like a million crickets. Here, a quartet of surrogates played stringed instruments. There, a crowd cheered two identical chrome wrestlers. Further on a dozen linked hands and danced in a circle. Couples strolled, arms about waists, heads touching, all perfectly indistinguishable. It was the triumph of sexlessness.

"Have a drink!"

He'd paused in the shadow of a pavilion to catch his breath. Now a surrogate, bowing deeply, proffered an empty hand. He blinked, realized he'd been mistaken for a surrogate himself, and accepted the invisible glass with a polite nod. There was a perverse satisfaction to knowing that among all the hundreds here, he alone saw the metal bones under the illusion of flesh. "Thank you."

"Having a good time?"

"To tell the truth, I just arrived."

The surrogate leaned forward unsteadily, slapping an overfamiliar hand on his shoulder. A round, unhealthy face leered from the screen. "Should've been here before the locals were cleared away. You could rent a woman to carry you around on her back like a horse. Slap 'em on the rump to make 'em move!" He winked. "Y'know, the tower up there used to be—"

"—a television transmitter. Yes, I know the whole story."

Mouth stupidly open, the surrogate stared at him long enough for the bureaucrat to realize the conversation had grown tedious. "No, no, a whorehouse. You could buy anything you wanted. Anything! I remember a time my wife and I—"

The bureaucrat set down his drink. "You'll excuse me. I have someplace to be."

The tower's lounge floor was thronged.

Black skeletons lounged against a central ring bar. Others chatted in the scattered booths. The interior was warm and dim, cluttered with flying brass pigs and poncing felt mannequins, and lit only by the glowing facescreens of the patrons themselves, and by a wheel of televisions set into the edges of the ceiling.

All but invisible, the bureaucrat paused by a clump of surrogates staring up at the screens. Crowded slum buildings were burning. Mobs surged through narrow streets, chanting and shaking fists. Under smoky skies, police slashed at them with electric lances. It was a tiny vision of madness, a glimpse of the end of the world. "What's going on?" he asked.

"Rioting in the Fan," one said. "That's the part of Port Richmond just below the falls. Evacuation authority caught a kid torching a warehouse and beat him to death."

"It's disgusting," said another. "They're behaving just like animals. Worse than animals, because they're enjoying it."

"Thing is, people have been coming down from the Piedmont to join in. Adolescents, especially—it's kind of a rite of passage for them. They've shut down the incline to keep them out."

"They should all be whipped. It comes from living on a planet, away from the constraints of civilization."

Another surrogate spoke up. "Oh, I think there's a touch of the savage in us all. If I were a few years younger, I'd be down there myself."

"Sure you would."

A glint of light caught the bureaucrat's eye. A door opening in the storeroom at the center of the bar. There was a flashing, near-subliminal glimpse of a narrow white face before the door closed again. It was more an impression than anything else, but enough that he decided to wait and watch to see if it would happen again.

He stood very still for a long time. Again the door opened, and a furtive face peeked out. Yes! It was a woman. Someone small, slender, mouselike.

Someone he knew.

Interesting. The bureaucrat made a long, careful circuit of the floor. There were two doors to the storeroom, situated opposite each other. It would take only an instant to slip under the bar and within. He returned to his starting place and found a chair sheltered by a cascade of tentacle vines.

Hours passed. The televisions were an impressionistic wheel of icebergs calfing, canvas cities for the cattleboat people, lingering shots of precataclysmic icecaps. He did not mind the wait. At long intervals, yet regular as clockwork, the door would open and that pinched white face peer out to scan the crowd before it closed again. She was definitely waiting for someone.

Finally a newcomer sat down at the bar, laying down a handful of flowers on the countertop before him. Crushed kelpies and polychromes, plucked from the weeds outside. He picked up an invisible napkin and turned it over. Then he ran his hands under the edge of the bar, as if searching for something hidden. When the bartender gave him a drink, he held the nonexistent glass high so he could examine its underside.

The bureaucrat knew those gestures.

Soon the storeroom door opened again. The woman's face appeared, pale in the gloom. She saw the newcomer, nodded, and raised a finger: just a minute. The door closed.

Smoothly the bureaucrat strolled to the far side of the bar, and ducked under. A bartender device moved toward him and he held up his census bracelet. Green, exempt. It turned away, and he stepped into the storeroom.

The single bare light hurt his eyes after the dim bar. Tier upon tier of empty shelves covered the walls. The woman was up on tiptoes lowering a box. He took her arm.

"Hello, Esme."

With a squeak of indrawn breath she whirled. The box banged against a shelf. She pulled away from him, at the same time awkwardly trying to keep from dropping the package. He did not let go. "How's your mother?"

"You mustn't—"

"Still alive, eh?" There was panic in those tiny, dark eyes. The bureaucrat felt that if he tightened his grip ever so slightly, bones would splinter. "That's how Gregorian got you running errands for him, isn't it? He promised to resolve matters for you. Say yes." He shook her, and she nodded. "Speak up! I can have you arrested if I want. Gregorian is using you as a courier, right?"

He pushed forward, trapping her between his bulk and the shelves. He could feel her heart beating. "Yes."

"He gave you this box?"

"Yes."

"Who are you supposed to give it to?"

"The man—the man at the bar. Gregorian said he'd bring flowers."

"What else?"

"Nothing. He said that if the man had any questions, I should tell him that the answers were all in the box." Esme was very still now. The bureaucrat stepped back, freeing her. He took the box. She stared at it as avidly as if it held her heart.

The bureaucrat felt old and cynical. "Tell me, Esme," he said, and though he meant it gently, it did not come out that way. "Which do you think would be the easier thing for Gregorian to do—kill his mother? Or simply lie to you?" Her face was a flame. He could no longer read it. He was no longer certain she was motivated by anything so simple and clean as a desire for revenge. But the time was past when he might influence her actions. He pointed to the far door. "You can leave now."

As soon as she was gone, the bureaucrat opened the box. He sucked some air through his teeth when he saw what it contained, but he felt no surprise, only a pervasive sense of melancholy. Then he went out to the bar and to the surrogate waiting there. "This is for you," he said. "From your son."

Korda stared blankly up at him.

* * *

"I don't know what you're talking about."

"Spare me. You've been caught consorting with the enemy, using proscribed technology, violating the embargo, abuse of public trust—it goes on and on. Don't think I can't prove it. A word from me, and Philippe will be all over you. There won't be anything left but the tooth marks on your bones."

Korda placed his hands facedown on the bar, ducked his head. Trying to regain his control. "What do you want to know?" he asked at last.

"Tell me everything," the bureaucrat said. "From the beginning."

Failure brought the young Korda to the hunting lodge in Shanghai. He had entered public service in an age when the Puzzle Palace was new, and the culture filled with tales of dangerous technologies controlled, and societies rebuilt. He intended to outdo them all. But the wild horse of technology had already been broken to harness and reined in. The walls had been built, the universe contained. There were no new worlds to conquer, and the old ones had been safely bricked away. Like many another of his generation, the revelation left him lost and embittered.

Every day Korda skiffed into the marshes, or shambled into the low coral hills, and with intense self-loathing killed as many creatures as he could. Some days the marsh waters would be carpeted with feathers, and still he found no peace. He killed several behemoths, but he took no trophies, and of course they were not good to eat.

One hot afternoon, passing through a meadow with his rifle over his shoulder, he saw a woman digging for eels. She paused in her work, casually took off her blouse, and used it to mop the sweat from her face and breasts. Korda stopped and stared.

The woman noticed him and smiled. From the distance she had seemed at first plain, but now with a subtle shifting of light he saw that she was very beautiful. Come back at sunset, she said, with some jenny-hens, and I will cook them for you.

When he returned, the woman had built a fire. She sat on a blanket alongside it. He laid his catch at her feet. Some time later, when they had both eaten their fill of the food that satisfies but does not nourish, they made love.

Even then, without the acuity of hindsight and retrospection, it seemed to him that the woman's face changed as they made love. The flickering flames made it hard to tell. But it would seem by turns rounder, squarer, more slender. It was as if she held a thousand faces drowning just beneath her skin, and they crowded up, reaching for the surface, when passion broke her control. She rode him fiercely, as if he were an animal she had determined to use up in a single gallop. She taught him to control his orgasm, so that he might last the hours she desired.

"Did she give you a tattoo?" the bureaucrat asked.

Korda looked puzzled. "No, of course not."

The coals were dying by the time the woman was done with him. He lay back slowly beneath her, eyes closing, sinking backward into unconsciousness and sleep. But as he fell away from the world, he had a vision of her face in orgasm, flattening out, elongating, growing skull-like and harsh.

It was not a human face.

He awoke cold and alone in the gray light of false dawn. The fire was dead, and the blanket yanked from beneath him. Korda shivered. His body was scratched, clawed, bitten, and raw. He felt as if he'd been tumbled over and over in a bramble patch. He put his clothes on, and returned to the lodge.

They laughed at him. That was a haunt woman you tangled with, they said, lucky for you she wasn't in heat. Had an excursion pilot worked here a year ago, his brother was chewed to death by one, bit off his nipples and both his stones, licked his skin down to the muscle. Took the mortician a week to get the smile off his face.

Nor was he taken seriously in the Puzzle Palace. A polite young woman told him his sighting was anecdotal and not very good of its kind, but that she would see it filed away in some obscure bottle shop or other, and in the meantime thanked him for his time and interest.

But Korda did not care. He had found his purpose.

Listening, the bureaucrat could not help but marvel. He and Korda had never been close, but they had worked together for years. Where had this fanatic spirit come from, how had he hidden it from the bureaucrat for so long? He asked, "How did you know the location of Ararat?"

"Through the Committee. It was pretty much a fringe operation when I encountered it, cultists and mystics and other deadwood it took me forever to clear away, but there were still some old-timers associated with it who had been influential in their day. I picked up the useful bit of this and that from them."

"So you stole enough biotech to create an unregistered clone son. Gregorian. Only his mother disappeared, and him with her. You were out of luck."

Those were, Korda admitted, hard years. But he had only worked the harder, developing plans for the protection and preservation of the haunts, once they could be located, for sanctuaries and breeding programs, for enculturation and cultural preservation. He made them productive years, though his main goal, to locate or at least prove the existence of the haunts, remained unfilled.

But Korda kept his feelers out, and one day one of his contacts in the Tidewater found Gregorian.

"How?"

"I knew what he'd look like, you see. Every year I had pictures made up—his hormone balances had been adjusted slightly so he wouldn't look too strikingly much like me. Just a vague similarity. I made him a little more rugged, a bit less prone to fat, that was all. Don't look at me like that. It wasn't done out of pride."

"Go on."

Relations between father and son were strained, to begin with. Gregorian refused to do his father's work in the Tidewater. He intimated he knew much about the haunts, but expressed supreme disinterest in the question of their ultimate survival. But Korda paid for Gregorian's education anyway, and paved his way to a good entry position in the Outer Circle biotechnology labs. Time was on his side. There were no opportunities to challenge a man of Gregorian's—Korda's—abilities. Sooner or later he would come around.

Korda figured he understood Gregorian well.

He was wrong. Gregorian had found work in the Outer Circle. There he stayed, until the jubilee tides were imminent, and there was no way for Korda to effectively use him. Korda wrote him off.

Then Gregorian disappeared. He fled suddenly, without warning or notice, in a deliberately suspicious manner. Investigation revealed that shortly before his departure he had interviewed Earth's agent and been given something. Whatever it was, nobody believed any longer that it was harmless. Alarms were rung. It all ended up in Korda's lap.

He had handed the investigation to the bureaucrat.

"Why me?"

"I had to send someone. You were simply on deck."

"Okay. Now, shortly after that, you contacted me at the carnival in Rose Hall. You were costumed as Death, and you were anxious to know if I'd found Gregorian. Why did you do that?"

Korda raised a line-fed glass to his lips. He was drinking steadily, drinking and unable to get drunk. "Gregorian had just sent me a package. A handful of teeth, that was all. I didn't dare send them to a lab to be analyzed, but it seemed certain to me that they were haunts' teeth. I'd seen hundreds in museums. Only these had bloodied roots. They'd been yanked recently."

"That sounds like his style," the bureaucrat said dryly. "What then?"

"Nothing. Until the other day when I heard from his half-sister that he would meet me here, and give me the proof I wanted. That's all there is. Will you open the package now?"

"Not just yet," the bureaucrat said. "Let's go back a bit. Why did you create Gregorian in the first place? Something to do with regulatory votes, was it?"

"No! It's not like that at all. I—I was going to have him raised on the Tidewater, you see. I was taking the long view by then. I realized that the reason the haunts were so elusive was that they didn't *want* to be found. They were passing themselves as human, living in the social interstices, in migrant labor camps and over top of rundown feed stores. They are intelligent, after all, cunning, and few in number.

"To find them I needed someone who knew the Tidewater well, who moved among its people without attracting attention, who could distinguish between a joke and an offhand revelation. Someone culturally at home there."

"That still doesn't explain why that someone also had to be *you*."

"But who else could I trust?" Korda said helplessly. "Who else could I trust?"

The bureaucrat stared at him for a long time. Then he nudged the package forward.

Korda ripped open the lid. When he saw what lay within, he went horribly still. "Go on," the bureaucrat said, and suddenly he was angry. "This is what you wanted, isn't it? Final, irrefutable proof."

He reached into the box and pulled the severed head out by the hair. Two surrogates nearby put down their imaginary drinks and stared. Others further down noticed and swiveled to look. Silence spread like ripples through the room.

The bureaucrat slammed the head down on the bar.

It was inhumanly pale, the nose longer than any human's ever was, the mouth lipless, the eyes too green. He slid a hand over the cheek, and the muscles there jumped reflexively, reshaping that part of the head. Korda stared at it, his mouth on the screen opening and closing without saying a word.

The bureaucrat left him there.

A smear of sunset was visible through the open door, and behind him the surrogates were singing, *These are the last days, the final days, the days that cannot last,* when a bellhop materialized at his elbow. "Excuse me, sir," it murmured, "but there is a lady who wishes to speak with you. She is here in person, and she emphasizes that it is most important."

Esme, he thought sadly, when will you put an end to this? Almost he was tempted just to walk out on her. "All right," he said. "Show me the way."

The device escorted him up a hidden lift to a suite just below the bulbous dome, and left at the open door. The walls were gently luminous, and in their graceful light the sheer extravagant waste of the room, with its hand-carved furniture, its enormous silk-covered bed, was appalling. He stepped within. "Hello?"

A door opened, and the last woman in the universe he expected entered.

He could say nothing.

"Have you been practicing?" Undine asked.

The bureaucrat blushed. He tried to speak, but was so full of emotion he could not. He reached across an immense distance and took her hand. He clutched it, not like a lover but like a drowning man. Were he to let her go, he knew, she would dissolve from his touch. Her face filled his vision. It was a proud face, beautiful, mischievous; and staring at it, he realized that he did not know her at all, and never had. "Come to me," he managed at last.

She came to him.

"Don't come yet. I have something I want to teach you."

Not exactly groggy, the bureaucrat was in a far, wordless state, clear-headed but uneager to speak. He drew himself away from her and nodded.

Undine held her two hands cupped together, fingertips down, like a leaf, a slender, natural opening where the edges of her hands touched. "This is the *mudra* for the vagina. And this," one hand flat, the other slammed atop it in a fist, the thumb thrust upward, "is the *mudra* for the penis. Now"— Still holding the thumb erect, she extended the little finger. She lowered her hand between her legs and hooked the finger into her vagina— "I have made myself into Hermaphrodite. Do you accept me as your goddess?"

"If the alternative is your going away again, then I suppose—"

"All these qualifications—you were born to quibble! Say yes."

"Yes."

"Good. Now the purpose of this lesson is for you to learn what it is like for me when you make love. That is not much. You wish to understand me, yes? Then you must put yourself in my place. I will do nothing to you that you might not do to me. That is fair, eh?" She reached out to caress his hair, the side of his face. "Ah, sweetness," she said, "how my cock yearns for your mouth."

Unsurely, awkwardly, he bent down and closed his mouth about her thumb.

"Not so abruptly. Do I descend upon *you* as if I wanted a bite of sausage? Approach it slowly. Seduce it. Begin by licking the insides of my thighs. Ah. Now kiss my balls—that's right, the curled fingers. Gently! Run your tongue over the surface, then suck on them ever so lightly. That's nice." She arched her back, breasts rising, eyelids closing. Her other hand clenched and unclenched in his hair. "Yes.

"Now let your tongue travel up the shaft. Yes. You might want to hold me steady with your hand. That's right, slowly. Oh, and up the sides too! That feels so good. Now ease down the hood to expose the tip. Lick it now, ever so lightly. Tease me, yes. Oh, my! You were born to make my cock happy, darling, don't let anyone ever tell you different.

"Now deeper. Take more of me into your mouth, up and down, long, regular strokes. Let your tongue play around the shaft. Mmm." She was moving under him now. She licked her lips. "Grab the shaft in both hands. Yes. Faster."

Suddenly she yanked him up by the hair. Their mouths met, and they kissed passionately, wetly. "Ah God, I can't stand it," she said. "I've got to have you." She drew back, turned him around. "Sit down slowly on my lap, and I'll guide myself in."

"What?"

"Trust me." She kissed his back, his sides. Hot, furtive kisses, there and gone, like blows. She put an arm around him, running her hand up his stomach, playing with his nipples. "Oh my beautiful, beautiful little girl. I want to have my cock deep inside you."

Slowly she eased him down onto her thumb. It touched his anus, slid within. He was sitting in her lap now, her breasts pressed tight against his back. "There, is that so bad?"

"No," he admitted.

"Good. Now move up and down, little honey, that's right. Slowly, slowly—the night is long and we have a lot of ground to cover."

* * *

By the time they went out on the balcony for air, it was night. The sky was glorious with light. Laughter floated up from the goblin market below, where surrogates danced amid a thousand paper lanterns. The bureaucrat looked up, away from them. The annular rings arched overhead, a smear of diamond-dust cities, and beyond them were the stars.

"Tell me the names of the black constellations," the bureaucrat said.

Undine stood naked beside him, her body slick with sweat that did not want to evaporate into the warm night air. It was possible they could be seen from below, but he did not care.

"You surprise me," Undine said. "Where did you learn of the black constellations?"

"In passing." The railing was cold against his stomach, Undine's hip warm against his. He rested a hand on the small of her back, let it slide down over her slippery, smooth flesh. "That one there, just beneath the south star—the one that looks like some sort of animal. What is it?"

"It's called the Panther," Undine said. "It's a female sign, emblematic of the hunger for spiritual knowledge, and useful in certain rituals."

"And that one over there?"

"The Golem. It's a male sign."

"That one that looks like a bird in flight?"

"Crow," she said. "It's Crow."

He said nothing.

"You want to know how Gregorian bought me. You want to know in what coin did he pay?"

"No," the bureaucrat said. "I don't want to know at all. But I'm afraid I have to ask."

She held out her wrist, adamantine census bracelet high, and made a twisting gesture.

The bracelet fell free.

Deftly, Undine caught it in midair, brought it to her wrist

again, snapped it shut. "He has a plasma torch. One of his evil old clients brought it to him in payment for his services. They're supposed to be strictly controlled, but it's amazing what a man can do when he thinks he's got a shot to live forever."

"That's all you got out of this? A way to evade the census?"

"You forget that all I did for him was to give you a message. He wanted me to warn you away from him. That wasn't much." She smiled. "And I warned you in the nicest possible way."

"He sent me an arm," the bureaucrat said harshly. "A woman's arm. He told me you had drowned."

"I know," Undine said. "Or rather, so I just learned." She looked at him with those disconcertingly direct eyes. "Well, perhaps it is a time for apologies. I came to apologize for two reasons, in fact, for what Gregorian convinced you had happened to me, and for the trouble I have learned was caused you by Mintouchian."

"Mintouchian?" The bureaucrat felt disoriented, all at sea. "What did you have to do with Mintouchian?"

"It is a long story. Let me see how brief I can make it. Madame Campaspe, who taught both Gregorian and me, had many ways of earning money. Some of them you would not approve of, for she was a woman who set her own standards and decided right and wrong for herself. Long ago she obtained a briefcase just like yours there by the bed, and set herself up in the business of manufacturing haunt artifacts."

"Those people in Clay Bank!"

"Yes. She had a little organization going—someone to look after the briefcase, agents in several Inner Circle boutiques, and Mintouchian to move the goods out of the Tidewater. The problem with such organizations, of course, is that being dependent on you, they feel you owe them something. So when Madame Campaspe left, and, not coincidentally, the briefcase burned out, they came to see me. To ask what they were going to do now.

"Why ask me? They did not want to hear that—they wanted

someone to tell them what to do and think, when to breathe out and when in. They did not understand that I had no desire to be their mommy. I felt that it was time I disappeared. And like Madame Campaspe before me, I decided to arrange a drowning.

"Gregorian and I were discussing the provenance and disposal of several items Madame Campaspe had left me. When I mentioned that I planned to drown my old self, he offered to arrange the details for a very reasonable price—yet just enough that I did not suspect him. He had an arm airfreighted in from the North Aerie cloning facilities, and treated and tattooed it himself. I am afraid that I left more than I should have in his hands.

"Witches are always busy—it's an occupational hazard. I was away for some time, and it was only when I came back that I learned what difficulties I had inadvertently caused you." She looked directly at him with those disconcertingly calm and steady eyes. "All this I have told you is the truth. Will you forgive me?"

He held her tight for a long time, and then they stepped back within.

Later, they stood on the balcony again, clothed this time, for the air had cooled. "You know of the black constellations," Undine said, "and the bright. But can you put them all together into the One?"

"The One?"

"All the stars form a single constellation. I can show it to you. Start anywhere, there, with the Ram, for example. Let your finger follow it and then jump to the next constellation, they are part of the same larger structure. You follow that next one and you come to—"

"The Kosmonaut! Yes, I see."

"Now while you're holding all that in your head, consider the black constellations as well, how they flow one into the other and form a second continuous pattern. Have you got that? Follow my finger, loop up, down and over there. You see? Ignore the rings and moons, they're ephemeral. Follow my finger, and now you've got half the sky.

"You've lived most of your life offplanet, so I assume you're familiar with both hemispheres, the northern as well as the southern? Hold them both in your mind, the hemisphere above that you can see, and the one below which you remember and they form . . . ?"

He saw it: Two serpents intertwined, one of light and the other of dark. Their coils formed a tangled sphere. Above him the bright snake seized the tail of the dark snake in its mouth. Directly below him, the dark snake seized the bright snake's tail in *its* mouth. Light swallowing darkness swallowing light. The pattern was there. It was real, and it went on forever and ever.

He was shaken. He had lived within the One Constellation all his life, gazed intently at different aspects of it a thousand times, and not known it. If something so obvious, so all-encompassing, was hidden from him, what else might there be that he was missing?

"Snakes!" he whispered. "By God, the sky is full of snakes."

Undine hugged him spontaneously. "That was very well done! I wish I could have gotten hold of you when you were young. I could have made a wizard out of you."

"Undine," he said. "Where are you going now?"

She was very still for a moment. "I leave for Archipelago in the morning. It comes alive this season of the great year. Through the great summer it's a very sleepy, bucolic, nothing-happening place, but now—it's like when you compress air in a piston, things heat up. The people move up the mountainsides, where the palaces are, and they build bright, ramshackle slums. You would like it. Good music, dancing in the streets. Drink island wine and sleep till noon."

The bureaucrat tried to imagine it, could not, and wished he could. "It sounds beautiful," he said, and could not keep a touch of yearning from his voice.

"Come with me," Undine said. "Leave your floating worlds behind. I'll teach you things you never imagined. Have you ever had an orgasm last three days? I can teach you that. Ever talk with God? She owes me a few favors."

"And Gregorian?"

"Forget Gregorian." She put her arms around him, squeezed him tight. "I'll show you the sun at midnight."

But though the bureaucrat yearned to go with her, to be raped away to Undine's faraway storybook islands, there was something hard and cold in him that would not budge. He could not back down from Gregorian. It was his duty, his obligation. "I can't," he said. "It's a public trust. I have to finish up this matter with Gregorian first."

"Ah? Well." Undine stepped into her shoes. They closed about her calfs and ankles, fine offworld manufacture. "Then I really must be leaving."

"Undine, don't."

She picked up an embroidered vest, buttoned it up over her blouse.

"All I need is one day, maybe two. Tell me where to meet you. Tell me where you'll be. I'll find you there. You can have anything you want of me."

She stepped back, tense with anger. "All men are fools," she said scornfully. "You must have noticed this yourself." Without looking, she whipped up a scarf from where it had fallen hours before, and tied it about her shoulders. "I do not make offers that can be accepted conditionally." She was at the door. "Or that can be taken up again, once refused." She was gone.

The bureaucrat sat down on the edge of the bed. He fancied he could catch the faintest trace of her scent rising from the sheets. It was very late, but the surrogates outside, aligned to offworld time standards, were partying as loudly as ever.

After a while he began to cry.

12

Across the Ancient Causeway

"You're in a surly mood this morning."

The flier continued southward, humming gently to itself. The bureaucrat and Chu sat, shoulders touching, in recliners as plush as two seats in the opera. After a time Chu tried again.

"I gather you found yourself a little friend to spend the night with. Better than I did, I can tell you that."

The bureaucrat stared straight ahead.

"All right, don't talk to me. See if I care." Chu folded her arms, and settled back in the recliner. "I spent the fucking night in this thing, I can spend the morning here too."

Tower Hill dwindled behind them. Gray clouds had slid down from the Piedmont, drawn by the pressure fall fronting Ocean, and they flew low over forests purple as a bruise. Behemoths were astir below, digging themselves out from the mud. Driven from their burrows by forces they did not understand and swollen with young whose birth they would not live to see, they crashed through the trees, savage, restless, and doomed.

The bureaucrat had patched his briefcase into the flight

controls, bypassing the autonomous functions. Every now and then he muttered a course adjustment, and it relayed the message to the flier. There was a layer of vacuum sandwiched within the canopy's glass to suppress outside noise, and the only sounds within the cockpit were the drowsy hum and rumble of vibrations generated by the flier itself.

They were coming up on a river settlement when Chu shook herself out of her passive torpor, slammed a hand on the dash and snapped, "What's that below?"

"Gedunk," the flier replied. "Population one hundred twenty-three, river landing, eastmost designated regional evacuation center for—"

"I know all about Gedunk! What are we doing over it? We've gotten turned around somehow." She craned about. "We're headed north! How did that happen? We're back over the river." From this height, the cattleboat on the water looked a toy, the evac workers scurrying dots. To the south of town the ragged remains of the relocation camp stood forlorn. A tent that had torn loose from its pegs flapped weakly on the ground like a dying creature. The massed evacuees were crammed into side-by-side rectangular pens by the pier. A steady trickle were being one by one checked off and fed into the boat.

"Take us down," the bureaucrat instructed the flier. "That melon field just west of town will do."

The flier reshaped itself, spreading and flattening its wings, throwing out cheaters to help it dump speed. They descended.

As the flier landed, half the white melons scattered across the field suddenly unrolled and scurried away on tiny feet, sharp-nosed creatures, gone before the eye could fix on them. Fish would graze these meadows soon. Ramshackle sheds and a broken-spined barn stood open-doored in the distance, ready for new tenants, undersea farmers, or submarine mice, whichever the lords of the tide would provide. The canopy withdrew into the flier.

Puffs of wind pushed here, there, from every point of the compass. The air was everywhere in motion, as restless as a puppy. "Well?" Chu said.

The bureaucrat reached into his briefcase, and extracted a slim metal tube. He pointed it at Chu. "Get out."

"What?"

"I assume you've seen these before. You wouldn't want me to use it. Get out."

She looked down at the gleaming tube, the tiny hole in its tip aimed right at her heart, then up at the bureaucrat's dead expression. A rap of her knuckles and the flier unfolded its side. She climbed out. "I don't suppose you're going to bother telling me what this is all about."

"I'm going on to Ararat without you."

The wind stirred Chu's coarse hair stiffly. She squinted against it, face hard and plain, looking not so much hurt as puzzled. "I thought we were buddies."

"Buddies," the bureaucrat said. "You've been taking Gregorian's money, running his dirty little errands, reporting every move I made to him, and you . . . It takes a lot of nerve to say that."

Chu froze, an island of stone in the rustling grasses. At last she said, "How long have you known?"

"Ever since Mintouchian stole my briefcase."

She looked at him.

"It had to be one of the two of you who drugged me in Clay Bank. Mintouchian was the more obvious suspect. But he was only a petty criminal, one of the gang that was counterfeiting haunt artifacts. His job was running crates to Port Richmond in the New Born King. He stole my briefcase so he could start the operation up again. But Gregorian's goons had already tried stealing it, and knew it could escape. Which meant he didn't work for Gregorian. Which meant that the traitor was you."

"Shit!" Chu turned away irritably, swung back again. "Listen, you don't know the way things are here—"

"I've heard that one before."

"You don't! I—look, I can't talk to you like this. Climb up out of the flier. Stand on your own two feet and look me in the eye."

He raised the metal tube slightly. "You're in no position to give orders."

"Shoot me, then! Shoot me or talk to me, one or the other." She was so angry her eyes bulged. Her jaw jutted defiantly.

The bureaucrat sighed. With poor grace he clambered out of the flier. "All right. Talk."

"I will. Okay, I took Gregorian's money—I told you when we first met that the planetary forces were all corrupt. My salary doesn't even cover expenses! It's understood that an operative is going to work the opposition for a little juice. It's the only way we can survive."

"Reconfigure for flight," the bureaucrat said to the flier. He felt sick and disgusted, and yearned for the clean, empty sky. To judge by Chu's expression, it showed on his face.

"You idiot! Gregorian would've had you killed if it hadn't been for me. So I left the occasional dead crow in your bed. I didn't do anything any op in my place wouldn't have, and I did a lot less than some. The only reason you aren't dead now is that I told Gregorian it wasn't necessary. Without me, you'll never come back from Ararat."

"Wasn't that the original plan?"

Chu stiffened. "I am an officer. I would have brought you out alive. Listen to me. You're completely out of your depth. If you have to leave me behind, then don't go to Ararat. You can't deal with Gregorian. He's crazy, a sociopath, a madman. With him thinking I was his creature, we could have taken him. But alone? No."

"Thank you for your advice."

"For pity's sake, don't . . ." Chu's voice faltered. "What's that?"

Voices floated in the air, and had in fact been in the background for some time, a babble of cries and shouts rendered soft and homogeneous by distance. They both turned to look.

Far below, the pens of evacuees crawled with motion. Fencing had been torn down, and the crowd flowed after retreating handlers. Batons swung, and the sharp *crack* of wood floated above the swirling noise. "The fools!" Chu said softly.

"What is it?"

"They brought out the people too early, bottled them together too tightly, handled them too roughly, and told them nothing. A textbook case of how to create a mob. Anything can set off a riot then, a cracked head, a rumor, somebody giving his neighbor a shove." She sucked thoughtfully on a back molar. "Yeah, I'll bet that's how it happened."

The cattleboat was separating from the dock, its crew hoping to isolate the riot ashore. People desperately leaped after it, and fell or were pushed into the water. The evacuation officials were regrouping downriver, behind a clutch of utility buildings. From here it was all very slow and lazy and easy to watch. After a moment Chu squared her shoulders. "Duty calls. You'll have to kill yourself without my help. I've got to saunter down there and help pick up the pieces." Abruptly she extended a hand. "No hard feelings?"

The bureaucrat hesitated. But somehow the mood had changed. The tension between them was gone, the anger dissipated. He shifted the tube from one hand to the other. They shook.

Far below, a roar went up as behavior dampers exploded in orange smoke at the front of the mob. The thought of going down there horrified the bureaucrat. But he forced himself to speak up anyway. "Do you need help? I haven't much time, but . . ."

"You ever had any riot training?"

"No."

"Then you're useless." Pulling a cigarillo from one pocket, Chu started down the hill. After a few steps, she turned back. "I'll light a candle in your memory." She lingered, as if reluctant to break this last contact.

The bureaucrat wished he could make some kind of gesture. Another man might have run after Chu and hugged her. "Say hello to that husband of yours for me," he said gruffly. "Tell him I said you were a good little girl while you were away."

"You son of a bitch." Chu smiled, spat, and walked away.

In the air again and heading south, the briefcase said, "Are you done with the pen?"

The bureaucrat looked dully down at the metal cylinder he still held in his hand. He shrugged, and returned it to the briefcase. Then he snuggled back into the recliner. His shoulders ached, and the back of his skull buzzed with tension and fatigue. "Tell me when we're near the city."

They passed over still fields, lifeless towns, roads on which no traffic moved. Evac authority had scoured the land, leaving behind roadblocks, abandoned trucks, and bright scrawls of paint on the roads and rooftops, sigils huge and unreadable. The marshes began then, and the traces of habitation thinned, scattered, disappeared.

"Boss? I've got a request to speak with you."

The bureaucrat had been dozing, an irritable almost-sleep with dreams that thankfully never quite came into focus. Now he awoke with a grunt. "You've got what?"

"There's some foreign programming in the flier—a quasi-autonomous construct of some kind. Not quite an agent, but with more independence than most interactives. It wants to speak with you."

"Put it on."

In a cheerily malicious tone the flier said, "Good morning, you bastard. I trust I'm not interrupting anything?"

The little hairs at the base of the bureaucrat's neck stirred and lifted as he recognized the false Chu's voice. "Veilleur! You're dead."

"Yes, and the irony of that is that I died because of a nullity like you. You, who could not even imagine the richness of the life I lost, because you were fool enough to get in the way of a wizard!"

The clouds scrolled by overhead, dark and densely contoured. "You might more reasonably direct your anger toward Gregorian for—" The bureaucrat caught himself. There was no point arguing with a recorded fragment of a dead man's personality.

"As well hate Ocean for drowning you! A wizard is not human—his perceptions and motives are vast, impersonal, and beyond your comprehension."

"Then he *does* have a motive? For you being here?"

"He asked me to tell you a story."

"Go on."

"Once upon a time—"

"Oh, good God!"

"I see. You want to tell this story yourself, don't you?" When the bureaucrat refused to rise to the bait, the false Chu began again. "Once upon a time there was a tailor's boy. His job was to fetch the bolts of cloth, to measure them out, and to crank the loom while his master wove. This was in an empire of fools and rogues. The boy's master was a rogue, and the Emperor of the land was a fool. And because the boy knew no other and no better, he was content.

"The Emperor lived in a palace that no one could see, but

which everyone said was the most beautiful structure in the universe. He owned fabulous riches that could not be touched, but were uniformly held to be beyond price. And the laws he passed were declared by all to be the wisest that had ever been, for no one could understand a word of them.

"One day the tailor was called into the Emperor's presence. I want you to make me a new set of clothes, said the Emperor. The finest that have ever been seen.

As you command, said the roguish tailor, so shall it be done. He cuffed the boy on the ear. We will neither rest nor eat until we have made for you the finest raiment in all existence. Clothes so fine that fools cannot even see them.

"Then, laden down with an enormous credit rating and many valuable options for commodities futures, the tailor and his boy returned to the shop. He pointed to an empty spool in the corner and said, There, that is the most valuable of moonbeam silk, bring it here. Carefully! if you get your grimy fingers on it, I will beat you.

"Wondering, the boy obeyed.

"The tailor sat down to the loom. Crank! he ordered. Our work is tremendous. We do not sleep tonight.

"How the boy suffered then! The roguish tailor's publicists spread the word of his commission, and many were the celebrities and media stars who bribed their way in to watch. They would gape at the empty loom being worked, the empty spools spinning, the bamboo about which bolts of costly fabrics were supposedly wrapped. Then they would see the tailor strike the boy down to the ground before their eyes, and say to themselves, Ah the man is temperamental. He is an artist.

"Then—having committed themselves—they would praise the work in progress. For no one wished to admit he was a fool.

"By the time the work was finished, the tailor's boy was half-mad from hunger and the drugs he took to stave off sleep. He was battered and bruised, and had he been thinking straight, might well have killed his master. But the hysteria of the crowd was contagious, and he, no less than anyone else, thought himself honored to participate in such a seminal work.

"Finally came the day of the presentation. Where are my clothes? demanded the Emperor. Here, said the tailor, holding up an empty arm. Are they not fine? Notice the sheen, the glimmer of the cloth. We have woven so fine and cut so subtly that it takes a wise eye to even see the garb. To a fool, it is invisible.

"You might not think the Emperor would fall for so obvious a fraud. But it was all of a piece with the rest of his life. A man who believes in his own nobility has no trouble believing in a piece of cloth. Without hesitation, he stripped bare, and with the tailor's help donned seven layers of purest nothing.

"A state holiday was declared in honor of the Emperor's new clothes. The tailor was rewarded with so many honors, titles, and investment options that he now need not work ever again. He turned the boy out of his shop to beg in the street for his bread.

"Thus it was that, dazed, drugged, and starving, the boy found himself standing on the street when the Emperor and all his court passed in joyous procession, and the proletariat—none of whom wished to be thought fools—cheered for the beauty of the clothes.

"In the heightened state of awareness brought on by his deprivations, the tailor's boy saw not an Emperor, but only a naked, rather knobby old man.

"Am I fool? he asked himself. Of course the answer, as he saw now, was yes. He was fool. And in his despair he screamed: *The Emperor has no clothes!*

"Everyone hesitated, paused. The procession stalled. The Emperor looked about him in confusion, and his courtiers as well. Up and down the street, the ragged people began whispering to one another. They saw that what he said, which none of them had wished to appear foolish by admitting, was true. The Emperor had no clothes.

"So they rose up and slew the Emperor, and his court, and all the civil servants. They burned the Parliament to the ground, and the Armory as well. They razed the barracks, churches, and stores, and all the farms and factories. The fires burned for a week. That winter there was famine, and in its wake plague.

"In the spring the new Republic began executing its enemies. The tailor's boy was the first to die."

Silence filled the cabin. Finally the bureaucrat said, "You're no more entertaining now than you were alive."

"Nothing that has happened to you since you arrived on Miranda occurred randomly," the false Chu said. "Gregorian orchestrated it all. He taught you to see the black constellations and the pattern that contains them. It was Gregorian who arranged for you to meet Fox. It was Gregorian who put a witch in your bed and introduced you to the possibilities of the body. You may not have seen him, but he was there. He has taught you much.

"Now that I am dead, he has need of an apprentice. He wishes you to come to Ararat, to complete your education."

"He actually thinks I would do that?"

"The first step in an apprenticeship is to destroy the seeker's old value system. And this he has done, hasn't he? He's showed you that your old masters are corrupt and unworthy of your loyalty."

"Shut up."

"Tell me I'm wrong." Veilleur laughed. "Tell me I'm wrong!"

"Shut him up," the bureaucrat ordered, and his briefcase obeyed.

*   *   *

Ararat rose from the marshes with all the natural inevitability of a mountain. Gently sloping terraces formed neighborhoods that merged in irregular planes. Above them the mercantile districts soared in yet steeper slopes. Finally came the administrative and service levels. The city was a single unified structure that slanted upward by uneven steps to a central peaked tower. Covered with greenery, it would have seemed a part of the land, a lone resurgence of the archipelago of hills that curved away to the south. Now, with the vegetation lifeless and withered, exposing windows and doorways black as missing teeth and sea-veined stone dark as thunderheads, it was a gothic monstrosity, a stage set for some lost tragedy from humanity's habiline past.

"Can you land us in the city?" the bureaucrat asked.

"What city?"

"That big mound of stone dead ahead of us is what city," the bureaucrat said, exasperated.

"Boss, the land in front of us is flat. There's nothing but marshes for thirty miles."

"That's prepos—Why are we banking?"

"We're not banking. The flier is level, and we're headed dead south by the compass."

"You're bypassing Ararat."

"There is nothing there."

"We're veering west."

"No, we're not."

The city was shifting steadily to the side. "Accept my word for it. What explanation can you give me for the discrepancy between what you and I can see?"

The briefcase hesitated, then said, "It must be a hardened installation. There are such things, I know, places that have been classified secret and rendered invisible to machine perceptions. I'm ordered not to see anything, so to me it doesn't exist."

"Can you put us down by my directions?"

"Boss, you don't want me to fly this thing blind into a hardened installation. The defenses would order me to flip it over, and I'd fly us right into the ground."

"Hah." The bureaucrat studied the land. Against the horizon, Ocean was a slug-gray smear squeezed beneath the clouds. Ararat was unapproachable from three sides, surrounded by dull, silvery stretches of water and mud. To the west, though, a broad causeway led straight from the city to a grassy opening in the trees. It was clearly a fragment of what had once been a major route into the city. A flier and as many as a dozen land vehicles sat abandoned in the meadow at its terminus. The bureaucrat pointed them out. "Can you see them?"

"Yes."

"Then set us down there."

The canopy sighed open.

"I can't come with you," the briefcase said. "As long as I'm patched in, I can suppress Gregorian's incursions. But the machinery is rotten with unfriendly programming. Once I'm taken off, we run a good chance the flier will turn on us. At the very least it's likely to fly off and leave us stranded here."

"So? I don't need you to do my work." The bureaucrat climbed out. "If I'm not back in a few hours, come after me."

"Got you."

He faced the causeway. What had been obvious from the air was invisible from the ground. The roadbed was buried under sand and overgrown with scrub. A crude road, however, had been bulldozed down its center, the machine itself abandoned by the mouth like a rusting watchdog. He went from truck to landwalker to truck, hoping to find one he could ride into Ararat. But the batteries had been yanked from them all. He picked up a television set left on the front seat of a mud-jitney, thinking it might be useful to keep an eye on the weather. The city loomed enormous over him. It could not be far.

The bureaucrat walked in among the trees. The woods were silent and deep. He hoped he would not meet a behemoth.

Where the ground was soft, footprints scurried ahead of him. Other than the bulldozer treads, there was no evidence of motor traffic.

Briefly he wondered why the vehicles had all been left behind in the meadow. In his mind's eye he saw the rich, foolish old beggars stumbling toward Ararat to be reborn, pilgrims compelled to approach the holy mountain on foot. They would have come with arrogance and hope, blind with anxiety and loaded down with wealth to barter immortality from the wizard. He could not entirely despise them. It would take a grotesque kind of courage to get this far.

The air was chill. The bureaucrat shivered, glad he was wearing a jacket. It was quiet, too, oppressively so. The bureaucrat was just reflecting on this when something screamed from the heart of the marshes. He concentrated on walking, putting one foot before the other and staring straight ahead. Out of nowhere a sudden wave of loneliness washed over him.

Well, after all, he was fearfully isolated. One by one he had left all friends, allies, and advisers behind. By now there was not a human being he had ever met closer than the Piedmont. He felt emptied and alone, and the city dominated the sky but drew no closer.

Experience had misled him. Used to the friendly distances within the floating worlds and orbital cities of deep space, he had not realized how far away an object could be and still dominate the sky. The peak of Ararat floated above him, black and lifeless.

The air darkened, leaching yet more warmth from the day. What, he wondered, would he find when he finally got to Ararat? Somehow he no longer believed that Gregorian would be there waiting for him. He simply could not picture it. More likely he would find the city empty, all echoing streets and staring windows. The end of his long search would be to arrive at Nowhere. The more he thought of it, the more probable he found this vision. It was exactly the sort of joke that Gregorian would make.

He kept walking.

In a strange way, he felt content. Ultimately it did not matter whether he found Gregorian or not. He had stayed with his task, and for all Gregorian's efforts the wizard had not been able to turn him aside. It might be true that the masters he served were venal, and the System itself corrupt and even doomed. Still, he had not betrayed himself. And there was time enough for him to reach the city and return well before the jubilee tides. His job would be done then. He could return home.

A speck of white floated in the air before him. A second appeared and then a third, too small to be flowers, too large for pollen. It was bitterly cold. He looked up. When had the leaves fallen? The bare-limbed trees were black skeletons against the gray sky. More white specks darted by.

Then they were everywhere, filling all the empty space between him and the city with their millions, and in so doing, defining that space, lending it dimension and making explicit the distance he had yet to go.

"Snow," he said wonderingly.

It was unpleasant, the cold, but the bureaucrat saw no reason to turn back. He could put up with a bit of discomfort. He forced his pace, hoping the exertion would generate a little heat. The television banged against his thigh as he trotted ahead. His breath puffed out in little gusts of steam. Soft, feathery flakes piled up, coating the trees, the land, the trail. Behind, fleeing footprints softened, grew indistinct, disappeared.

He flicked on the television. A gray dragon of stormclouds

doubled and redoubled upon itself, creeping down the screen upon Continent. *They're melting!* an excited voice cried. *We have some magnificent views of the icecaps from orbit—*

He thumbed over to the next channel —*find shelter immediately.* The trail wound through the trees, flat and level and monotonous. Out of breath, the bureaucrat lapsed back into a trudging gait. The television chattered on in the happy drone of people caught on the fringes of disaster. It spoke of near-miraculous rescues in Sand Province and perilous airlifts along the Shore. He was told that the militia were on alert, with flying squads in six-hour rotations. Reminded that he must be out of the Tidewater before the first wave of jubilee tides hit. That might be in as little as twelve hours or as much as eighteen. He was not to stop for sleep. He was not to stop for food. He must leave at once.

The snow was falling so thickly now he could barely see the trees to either side of him. His toes and the soles of his feet ached with the cold. *Hypothermia tips!* the television cried. Do not rub frostbitten skin. Thaw it gently with warm water. He could not really follow the gist of the advice; there were too many unfamiliar words.

The announcers sounded giddily excited. Their faces were flushed, their eyes bright. Natural disasters did that to people, made them feel significant, reassured them that their actions mattered. He switched channels again, and found a woman explaining the precession of the poles. Charts and globes helped demonstrate that Miranda was now entering great winter and receiving less insolation than ever. *However, the warming effects were inevitable well over a decade ago. Delicate natural feedback mechanisms assure—*

The handle of the television set stung like ice. He could no longer bear to hold it. With an effort he forced his hand open and let go. The television dropped to the trail, and he shoved his hand under his armpit. He hurried forward, hugging himself for warmth. For a time the voices called after him down the trail. By slow degrees they faded away, and were gone.

Now he was truly alone.

It wasn't until he stumbled and fell that he realized the danger he was in.

He hit the ground hard and for a moment did not move, almost enjoying the sting of pain that ran along his body, all but anesthetizing one arm and the side of his face. It baffled him that mere weather could do this to him. Finally, though, he realized that the time had come to turn back. Or die.

Dizzily he stood. He'd gotten a little turned around, and when he got to his feet, he was not sure which way was which. The snow fell chokingly thick, powdering his suit and catching on his eyelashes. He could hardly see. A few gray lines to either side of the trail, trees evidently, and nothing more. The impression he had made when he fell had already been obliterated.

He started back.

It was even odds that he was headed for the flier. He wished he could be sure, but he was disoriented and it was hard to think. His attention was all taken up by the cold that sank its fangs in his flesh and did not let go. Icy needles of pain lacerated his muscles. His face stiffened with cold. He gritted his teeth, lips pulling back in an involuntary snarl, and forced himself on.

Some time later, he realized that he was surely headed in the wrong direction, because he hadn't come upon the jettisoned television yet. He put off admitting this for as long as possible, because the thought of retracing his steps was heartbreaking. Finally, though, he had no choice but to admit his error, turn, and go back.

It was wonderfully silent.

The bureaucrat had lost all sensation in his feet long ago. Now the aching coldness was creeping up his legs, numbing his calf muscles. His knees burned from touching the cold trousers cloth. His ears were afire. A savage pain in both eyes and the center of his forehead set his head buzzing, demon voices droning meaningless words in overlapping chorus.

Then the paralyzing numbness crept higher, his knees buckled, and he fell.

He did not get up.

For a timeless long time he lay there, hallucinating the sounds of phantom machines. He was beginning to feel blessedly warm. The television had said something about that. Get up, you bastard, he thought. You've got to get up. There was a crunching noise, and he saw boots, black leather boots, before his face. A massive man squatted, and lifted him gently in his arms. Over the man's shoulder he saw a blur of color in the swirling white that was surely a car or truck of some sort.

The bureaucrat looked up into a broad face, full of strength and warmth, and implacable as a stone. He looked like somebody's father. The lips curled into a smile that involved all the man's face, cheeks forming merry balls, and the man winked.

It was Gregorian.

13
≈≈≈

A View from a Height

Three men sat around the campfire.

The night was cold. The bureaucrat smoked black hashish laced with amphetamines to keep awake. Gregorian held the pipe to his mouth, urging him to suck in deeply and hold the smoke for as long as possible. The hash made the bureaucrat's head buzz. His feet were impossibly distant, a full day's travel down the giant's causeway of his legs. Marooned on the mountainside, he still felt monstrously calm and alert, wired into the celestial telegraph with a direct line to the old wisdom lying at the base of his skull like moonstones in an amalgam of coprolites and saber-tooth bones. For an instant he lost hold of external reality, and plunged deep into the submarine caverns of perception, a privateer in search of booty. Then he exhaled. Oceans of smoke gushed out into the world.

The snow had stopped long ago.

Gregorian finished off the pipe, knocked out the coals against the heel of his boot, and carefully scraped the bowl clean. "Do you know how Ararat was lost?" he asked. "It's an interesting story."

"Tell me," the bureaucrat said.

Their companion said nothing.

"To understand you must first know that the upper reaches of the city lie above the great winter high-tide mark. Oh, the jubilee tides smash over it all right—but it's built to withstand the force. When the storms subside, it's an island. A useful little place militarily—isolated, easily fortified, easily defended. System Defense used it as a planning center during the Third Unification. That's when it was hardened. There are probably a lot of these secret places scattered about."

The magician took a branch from the flames and stirred the fire, sending sparks swirling madly up the smoke into the sky. "As a standard procedure, System Defense masked their involvement with a civilian caretaker organization under the nominal auspices of Cultural Dissemination Oversight, with control exerted through yet another civilian front. During the reorganization at the end of the violent phase of Unification . . ."

The explanation went on and on. The bureaucrat listened only with the surface of his mind, letting the words pass over him in murmurous waves while he studied his opponent. Squatting before the fire, Gregorian seemed more beast than man. The flames threw red shadows up on his face, and the cool greenish light from the window wall ignited his hair from behind. Sometimes the light reached his teeth and lit up the grin. But none of it ever reached his eyes.

Decades passed. Organizations arose and fell, were folded into one another, shed responsibility, picked up new authority, and split off from parent bodies. By the time Ocean receded and great spring began, Ararat was so deeply entangled in the political substance of the System that it could be neither softened nor declassified.

"The stupidity of it—the waste! An entire city, the work of

thousands of lifetimes, lost through mere regulation. And yet this is but the smallest fraction of the invisible empire of Ignorance imposed on us by the powers above."

In person Gregorian's voice was eerily familiar, just as his features could be decoded as a ruggeder, more compelling version of Korda's own. "That sounds like something your father might say," the bureaucrat remarked.

Gregorian looked up sharply. "I don't need you here!" He pointed to the still figure across the fire from him. "Pouffe is enough company for me. If you want to die early, I can—"

"It was only an observation!"

The magician eased back, his rage gone as abruptly as it had arisen. "Yes, that's true. Yes. Well, of course the information all came from Korda originally. It was one of his projects. He spent years trying to have Ararat declassified, tilting at windmills and fighting phantoms. Old Laocoön strangled by red tape." He threw back his head and laughed. "But what do you and I care about that? More fool he for having wasted his life. I don't suppose you remembered to bring my notebook?"

"I left it in my briefcase. Back in the flier."

"Ah, well. It was of purely sentimental value. We must all learn to give things up."

"Tell me something," the bureaucrat said carefully. Gregorian nodded his great head. "What did Earth's agent give you— was it proscribed technology? Or was it nothing at all?"

Gregorian pondered the question with mocking seriousness, and then, as if delivering the punch line of a particularly good joke, said, "Nothing at all. I wanted to force Korda to send somebody after me when I disappeared. It was bait, that was all."

"Then I can go now."

Gregorian chuckled. The fire leaned away under a sudden gust of wind, and he was a black silhouette against the window wall. A tattoo of a comet flared to life, swam across his arm, and slowly faded. A second marking fired and a third, crawling about under his skin like fire-worms on an embered log. "Stay," he said. "We have so much to talk about."

The magician leaned back again, in no particular hurry to get down to specifics. The city fell away quickly here, to vague silver and gray lands stretching flat and away toward Ocean, invisible at the horizon. Strange winds and smells were astir. Cinnamyrtle and isolarch haunted the nose.

The fire had been built on a high terrace, in a crumbling depression of stone that Gregorian called a "whale wallow." Like all of Ararat, it was heavily eroded. Hooks protruded from rounded walls, their purpose lost. Rooms were choked with coral and mud. Fag ends of braided cables and the ribs of sea creatures jutted from among the barnacles. Here and there sheets of adamantine stood exposed, perfect and incorruptible. But these Perimeter Defense retrofits were rare, jarring intrusions in the aged city.

The bureaucrat leaned back against a carbon-whisker strut. The chains that shackled him to it rattled when he moved. To one side he could see into the command room with its stacked crates of food and survival gear. To the other, he could look out into the wide and windy world. At his back he felt the empty streets, narrow and dark, staring at him. "I want to take you up on your offer," he said.

Lazily Gregorian said, "Now what offer do you mean?"

"I want to be your apprentice."

"Oh, that. No, that was never meant seriously. It was intended to make you confident enough to chase me here, that was all."

"Nevertheless."

"You don't know what's involved, little brother. I might ask you to do anything, to—oh, crucify a dog, say. Or assassinate a stranger. The process changes you. I might even order you to fuck old Pouffe. Would you be willing to do that? Right here and now?"

Pouffe sat opposite the two of them, his back to the land. His face was puffy and unhealthy in the window light. His eyes were two dim stars, unblinking. The bureaucrat hesitated. "If necessary."

"You're not even a convincing liar. No, you must remain as you are, chained to that strut. You must stay there until the tides come. And then you must die. There is no way out. Only I could release you, and my will is unwavering."

They both fell silent. The bureaucrat imagined he could hear Ocean, soft as a whisper in the distance.

"Tell me," Gregorian said, "do you think that any haunts have survived into the current age?"

Surprised, the bureaucrat said, "You sent your father the head of one."

"That? Nothing but a cheap trick I brewed up with what remains of Korda's old lab equipment. I had all these rich old corpses left over from my money-raising endeavors, and it seemed a good use for one. But you—they tell me you spoke with a fox-headed haunt back in Cobbs Creek. What do you think? Was it real? Be honest now, there's no reason not to."

"They told me it was a nature spirit—"

"Bah!"

"But . . . Well, if he wasn't one of your people in a mask, then I can't imagine what else he could have been. Other than an actual haunt. He was a living being, that much I'm sure of, as solid as you or me."

"Ahhhh." The groan rested uneasily somewhere between satisfaction and pain. Then, casually, Gregorian drew an enormous knife from his belt. Its blade was blackened steel, its hilt elfinbone. "He'll be ready now."

Gregorian walked over to Pouffe, and crouched. He cut a long sliver of flesh from the old shopkeeper's forehead. It bled hardly at all. The flesh was faintly luminous, not with the bright light of Undine's iridobacteria but with a softer, greenish quality.

It glowed in the magician's fingers, lit up the inside of his mouth, and disappeared. He chewed noisily.

"The feverdancers are at their peak now. Ten minutes earlier and they'd still be infectious. An hour later and their toxins will begin to break down." He spat out the sliver into his palm, and cut it in two with his knife. "Here." He held one half to the bureaucrat's lips. "Take. Eat."

The bureaucrat turned away in disgust.

"Eat!" The flesh had no strong smell; or else the woodsmoke drowned it out. "I brought you here because this sacrament works best when shared. If you won't partake, I have no use for you." He did not reply. "Think. So long as you live, there is hope. A meteorite might strike me dead. Korda might arrive with a detachment of marines. Who can say? I might even change my mind. With death, all possibilities end. Open your mouth."

He obeyed. The cool flesh was pressed onto his tongue. It felt rubbery. "Chew. Chew and don't swallow until it's gone." Vomit rose in his throat, but he choked it down. The flesh had little flavor, but that little was distinctive. He would taste it in his mouth for the rest of his life.

Gregorian patted his knee and sat back down. "Be grateful. I've taught you a valuable lesson. Most people never do learn exactly how much they will do to stay alive."

The bureaucrat kept chewing. His mouth felt numb, and his head swam dizzily. "I feel strange."

"Did you ever hate someone? I mean, really hate. So badly that your own happiness meant nothing, or even your own life, so long as you could ruin his?"

Their chewing synchronized, jaws working in unison, noisily, wetly. "No," the bureaucrat heard somebody say. It was his own voice. That was, in some indefinable way, odd. He was losing all sense of locality, his awareness spreading over an ever-widening area, so that he was nowhere specifically there, but only partook of ranges of greater or lesser probability. "I have," he said in the magician's voice.

Startled, he opened his eyes and stared into his own face.

The shock threw him back into his own body. "Who did you hate so badly?" he managed to gasp. Losing identity again. He heard Gregorian laugh, a mad, sick sound with undertones of misery, and it came as much from him as from the magician. "Myself," he said, that deep voice rumbling in the pit of his stomach. "Myself, God, Korda—about in equal proportions. I've never really been able to sort the three of us out."

The magician went on speaking and, compelled by the drug, the bureaucrat fell so deeply into the words that his last trace of self melted away. Individuation unraveled beneath him. He became Gregorian, became the young magician standing long years ago in the presence of his clone-father in a dim room deep in the heavy gravity district of Laputa.

He stood ramrod-straight, feeling ill at ease. He had been late arriving, because he kept losing his way. He did not have the cues everyone else knew to guide him through the three-dimensional maze of corridors, with its broad avenues that dissolved into tangles of nonsensical loops, its ramps and stairways that ended abruptly in blank walls. This office was hideously oppressive, dark with monolithic stone structures, and it baffled him that offworlders paid prestige rates for such places. Something to do with inaccessibility. Korda was embedded in a desk across from him.

A quicksilver run of fish fled through the room, but they were mere projections of the feverdancers, and he ignored them. Out of the corner of his eye he studied the shelves of brightly lit glass flowers. In such a gravity field, the merest nudge would reduce them all to powder. Hot pink orchids drooped from holes in the ceiling, their perfume like rotting meat.

Gregorian held himself rigidly casual, his face a sardonic mask. But in truth Korda intimidated him. Gregorian was leaner, stronger, and younger, with better reflexes than his predecessor had ever had. But this fat man knew him inside and out.

"I ate shit once," Gregorian said.

Korda was scribbling on his desk. He grunted.

There was a third presence in the room, a permanent surrogate in Denebian wraparound and white ceramic mask. His name was Vasli, and he was present in the capacity of financial adviser. Gregorian disliked the creature because his aura was blank; he left no emotional footprint on the air. Whenever he looked away, Vasli tended to fade into the furniture.

"Another time I ate a raw skragg. That's a rodent, about two hands long and hairless. It's almost as ugly as it is mean. Its teeth are barbed, and after you kill it, you have to break the jaw to get it off your—"

"I presume you had a good reason for doing such a thing?" Korda said in a tone of profound indifference.

"I was afraid of the brutes."

"So you killed one and ate it to rid yourself of the fear. I see. Well, there are no skraggs here." Korda glanced up. "Oh, do sit down. Vasli, see to this young man."

Without moving, the construct dispatched slim metal devices that Gregorian had thought mere decorative accents to assemble a chair beneath him. They gently pushed his knees forward and eased his shoulders back, shifting his center of balance, so that he was forced to sit. The chair was low-slung and made of granite. He knew he wouldn't be able to rise from it gracefully. "It wasn't quite that simple. I fasted for two days, offered blood to the Goddess, then dosed myself with feverdancers and—"

"We have day clinics that do the same thing back home," Vasli observed. "The technology is banned here, of course."

"It was none of your foul science. I am an occultist."

"A distinction in terminology only. Our means may differ, but we employ identical techniques. First, render the brain open to suggestion. We use magnetic resonance, while you employ drugs, ritual, sex, terror, or some combination thereof. Then, when the brain is susceptible, imprint it with new behavior patterns. We use holotherapeutic viruses as the message carriers; you eat a rat. Finally, reinforce the new pattern in your daily life. Our methods are probably identical there. The skill is extremely old; people were being reprogrammed long before machines.

"Skill!" Korda said scornfully. "I once had a paralyzing fear of drowning. So I went to Cordelia and had myself dropped off two miles out into the Kristalsee at night. It's salty enough that you can't sink, and there are no large surface predators. If you don't panic, you're fine. I suffered the agonies of Hell that night. But when I reached shore, I knew I would never fear drowning again. And I did it without the aid of drugs." He smiled ironically at Gregorian. "You're pale."

A voice from another world murmured, *Is that what you're doing? Am I to die to help put an end to your fear of drowning? How trivial.* Gregorian ignored it. "Don't imagine you can condescend to me, old man! I've had experiences you've never dreamed of!"

"Don't bluster. There's no need to be afraid of me."

"I fear you? You know nothing."

"I know all there is to know about you. You think a few accidental differences in upbringing and experience can make any serious difference in personality? It is not so. I am your alpha and omega, young man, and you are no more than myself writ pretty." Korda spread his arms. "Do these old jowls and age spots disgust you? I am only what you yourself will in time become."

"Never!"

"It is inevitable." Korda glanced down at the desk. "I have

arranged a line of credit that will allow you to access the Extension. You will study bioscience control, that ought to be useful—it will teach you the folly of thinking you can go against your genetic inheritance, for one thing. Vasli will disburse funds to cover your living expenses, with a little more for sweetening. There's no reason we should see a great deal of each other in the next few years."

"And in return you expect—what?"

"When you have the proper background, we will ask you to do a little field research," Vasli said. "Nothing strenuous. We are interested in determining the possible survival of Mirandan indigenes. I don't doubt you will find the work rewarding."

They knew he wouldn't turn down the education, the money, the connections Korda was offering him. The alternative was to sink back down into Midworlds obscurity; to being nothing but an unknown pharmaceur in a land no civilized person ever gave a second thought. "What's to make me do your bidding after I've taken my degree?"

"Oh, I think that when the time comes, you'll be cooperative enough. We're giving you the chance to accomplish something. How often do you think such opportunities come along?" Then, before he could respond, Korda said, "Enough. Vasli, you can handle any details."

The life went out of him.

Gregorian struggled up out of the chair. He touched Korda's cheek. It was cool, inert. The man he had been speaking with had been nothing more than a mannequin, a surrogate shaped in Korda's form so that only he could employ it. The device was built into the desk. It didn't even have any legs.

"He had a meeting," Vasli explained.

"An agent!" The insult made Gregorian's voice sharp. "He wasn't even here in person. He sent an agent!"

"What did you expect? He didn't shake hands—what else could he have been?"

Gregorian looked at him.

Silently Vasli extended his hand. With only a tremble of hesitation, Gregorian took it. The signet ring his clone-father had sent him along with the new offworld clothing whispered *permanent agent unique* in his otic nerve. "This is your first time offplanet, I take it."

Withdrawing his hand, Gregorian said, "Deneb. Your people are building a shell about Deneb, aren't they?"

"A toroidal shell, yes. Not a full sphere but a slice from a sphere; it varies only a degree or two from the ecliptic." As Vasli spoke, the macroartifact materialized in the air between them. For a second he thought Vasli was employing a pocket projector, and then he realized it was an effect of the runaway visualization caused by the feverdancers. "To warm the outer planets. We do not have your natural resources, you see, no sungrazers, no Midworlds. With the one exception, our planets are naturally inhospitable. So we have taken apart an ice world to create a reflective belt."

The image swelled, so that he saw the flattened spindle forms of the individual worldlets, saw their interwoven orbits laid out and diagrammed, and the network of traffic-control stations running through its infrastructure. "Surely that's not enough to make the outer planets habitable."

"No, it's only part of the engine. We're also rekindling their cores, and imploding a moon here and there to create gateways into our sun's chromosphere." Small orbital suns burst into existence about the outer worlds. The ice belt redoubled in brightness where the planets passed near.

The sight dazzled and enraged Gregorian. He shivered with emotion. "That's what we should be doing! We have the knowledge, we have the power—all we lack is the will to seize control, to make ourselves as powerful as gods!"

"My people are not exactly gods," the artificial man said dryly. "A project this large kicks up wars in its wake. Millions have died. A far greater number have been displaced, relocated, forced out of lives they were happy in. While I myself feel it is justified, honesty compels me to admit that most of your own people would not agree. We have given up much that your culture yet retains."

"Everyone dies—the rearrangement of *when* is a matter of only statistical interest." In his mind he saw all the Prosperan system, and it seemed a paltry thing, a nugget, an ungerminated seed. "Had I the power, I'd begin demolishing worlds today. I'd take Miranda apart with my bare hands." He felt the blood rushing through his veins, plumping his cock, the ecstatic rush of possibility through his brain. "I'd tear the stars themselves apart, and in their place build something worth seeing."

Mouths opened one by one in the wall, closed in unison, and disappeared. More feverdancing. He wiped sweat from his forehead as white spears fell through the ceiling and noiselessly pierced the floor. The room was intolerably stuffy.

He yawned, and for an instant his eyes opened and he stared across a dying campfire at Gregorian. The magician's head nodded, but he went on talking. Then he was back in Laputa and had missed part of the magician's story.

"Vasli. You know Korda well, I imagine. He's capable of murder, isn't he? He'd kill a man if that man got in his way."

That white mask scrutinized him. "He can be ruthless. As who would know better than you?"

"Tell me something. Do you think he would kill six? A dozen? A hundred? Would he kill as many people as he could, would he torture them, just for the joy of knowing he had done it?"

"You will have to look within yourself to know for certain," Vasli said. "My guess would be no."

Now the feverdancers reached out to bake his skull into blistered cinders. But even as they welled up like a million giggling chrome fleas, shoving the young magician over backward into unconsciousness, he thought, No. Of course not. Somebody who would do such things would be nothing at all like Korda. He'd be a monster, a grotesque. Warped beyond recognition by what he'd done. He'd be somebody else altogether.

He awoke.

The night had grown old. Great masses of stone hulked over him. Lightless alleys breathed softly at his back. Below, the land was faintly visible in the sourceless predawn light. Obsidian clouds mounded and billowed up from the horizon. Lightning danced across them. Yet he could hear no thunder. Was it possible? Was the world to end in silence? The fire was almost dead, coals blanketed in ash.

Gregorian's chin was slumped on his chest, and a thin line of drool ran down one side of his mouth. He was still unconscious. In all of Ararat, only the bureaucrat was awake and aware. His mouth was gummy, and his gut ached.

Something stumbled in the street behind him.

The bureaucrat straightened. Ararat was still. A sudden gust of wind might dislodge a chunk of coral and send it clattering and rattling down the stony slopes. But this noise was different. It had a purposeful quality. He craned his neck around and stared into the mouth of the alleyway. The blackness moved in his sight. Was that a flicker of motion? It might be no more than the random firing of nerves in his vision.

There was a metallic crash. A dim swoop of movement, clumsy and unsure. Something was there behind him. It was headed his way.

The bureaucrat waited.

Slowly a spiderlike creature emerged from the street. It staggered from side to side, painfully groping its way with one tapping forelimb, like a blind man's cane. Occasionally it lost its balance and fell. It was his briefcase.

Over here, the bureaucrat thought. He didn't dare speak, for fear of waking Gregorian. Or perhaps, he thought giddily, what he really feared was that this would turn out to be just another hallucination. He held his breath. The thing groped its way toward him.

"Boss? Is that you?" He touched the briefcase's casing so it could taste his genes, and the device collapsed at his feet. "I had a hell of a time finding you. This place has got my senses all confused."

"Quiet!" whispered the bureaucrat. "Can you still function?"

"Yes. I'm blind, that's all."

"Listen carefully. I want you to make a nerve inductor. Seize control of Gregorian's nervous system and paralyze his higher motor functions. Then walk him inside. He's got a plasma torch there somewhere. Bring it out here and cut me free."

Gregorian's head rose from his chest. His eyes quietly opened, and he smiled. With dreamlike slowness he touched his belt, lovingly curled fingers about the hilt of his knife.

"That's proscribed technology," the briefcase said. "I'm not allowed to manufacture it on a planetary surface."

Gregorian chuckled.

"Do it anyway."

"I can't!"

"This is a perfect example of what I was talking about." Gregorian released his knife, leaned back. He seemed to be discussing a part of the night's narration the bureaucrat had missed. "You have in that device sufficient technological power to do almost anything. More than enough to free yourself. Yet you cannot use it. And why? Because of a meaningless, bureaucratic rule. Because of a cultural failure of nerve. You have shackled your own hands, and you have no one to blame but yourself for your failure."

"I'm ordering you for the third time. Do it anyway."

"All right," the briefcase said.

"You fucking—!" Gregorian leaped up, knife materializing in one hand. Then he stiffened and, off-balance, fell. He hit the stone hard. Eyes frozen open, he stared straight ahead. His body spasmed, then stilled. One arm continued to tremble uncontrollably.

"This is trickier than you'd—" the briefcase began. "Ah. Here." The arm stopped trembling. Slowly, awkwardly, the magician rolled on his side, and got to his hands and knees. "Hey! I can see perfectly when I'm looking through his sensorium." Gregorian's head swiveled from side to side. "What a place!"

Three times the briefcase tried to stand Gregorian up. Each time the magician's body overbalanced and fell. Finally the briefcase admitted defeat. "I just can't get the hang of it, boss."

"That's all right," the bureaucrat said. "Have him crawl."

The supplies Gregorian had laid in included a diagnostician with a full line of medicinals. When the bureaucrat had run his blood through a scrubber, dosed himself with a centering drug, and washed his face, he felt a thousand times better. With the fever-dancers and fatigue poisons gone, he was left weak to the bone but clearheaded at last. He took a canteen to the doorway and rinsed out his mouth several times, spitting the residue into the street.

Then he went back inside and turned on a television. *It's begun!* the set screamed. *The wave front has just hit the shore! If you're on the incline or in the Fan, we want to urge you—*

What a terrific sight!

—to get out now! Yes, it is. Something glorious to see, the water cresting high with the dawn behind it, as it swallows up the land. We want to urge you. If you're anywhere below the fall line, this is the time to get out. You won't have another chance!

"Boss? Gregorian wants to speak with you."

"He does?"

The bureaucrat locked arms behind his back, and strolled to the window wall. The horizon was in motion now. It was a thin, roiling line, nothing so dramatic as what they were showing on television. But the Tidewater had begun drowning at last. The jubilee tides were coming in. On the flatlands below, limp trees lay in windrows. Winds he could not hear blew indigo leaves past the silencing window glass.

In the whale wallow, immediately before him, knelt Gregorian. The briefcase had welded him into the same adamantine chains he had used on the bureaucrat. He could not stand and would not lie down. Their eyes met. His nervous system was still being monitored by the briefcase. "Put him through."

"You can't escape without my help," the briefcase said in Gregorian's calm voice.

"I'm safe enough here."

"Oh, you'll survive the tides all right. But how are you going to get away? You'll be stranded on a little island that nobody will ever find. The food will only hold out so long. You don't know the access codes that will let you send a message out to summon a flier."

"And you do?" The bureaucrat moved his gaze up from Gregorian and across the plaza to where the briefcase had hung Pouffe's body from a hook. He'd owed the man that much at least.

"Yes." A light, urbane laugh. "We seem to have a stalemate here. I need your help to survive, and you need mine to escape. Obviously we need to compromise. What do you propose?"

"Me? I propose nothing."

"Then you'll die!"

"I suppose so."

There was a long, astonished silence. Then Gregorian said, "You don't mean that."

"Wait and see." He turned back to the television, knelt down, and fiddled with the controls. His show came on.

"How dare you judge me? You have no moral right to, and you know it!"

"How's that again?"

"By your own standards, you're tainted. You said you wouldn't use proscribed technology. You told Veilleur that if you used it, you'd be no better than a criminal yourself. Yet all the time, you held it in reserve, ready to be called on."

The drama was coming to a head. Young Byron had been lashed to the mast of mad Ahab's ark. His mermaid waited frantically in a cage upon the moors, for the waters to come and drown her. Knowing that she was about to die, she sang.

"I lied," the bureaucrat said. "Now, hush. I want to hear this."

Not much later, the briefcase said, "Boss? He's too proud to suggest it himself. But I know what he's going through. I could kill Gregorian right now by overloading his nervous system. It would be painless."

The bureaucrat was resting in a nest of fat pillows, bright with Archipelago designs. He stared at the television, letting its light wash over him. He was amazingly tired. The pictures meant nothing to him anymore, they were only a meaningless flow of imagery. He was empty, spent.

Whenever he looked up, he could see Gregorian glaring at him. If there were anything to this business of occult powers, then the wizard would not die alone. But though the bureaucrat felt the tug of those eyes, he would not meet them. Nor would he permit his briefcase to relay the magician's words. He refused to listen. That way, there would be no chance, however slight, of being talked out of anything at the last minute.

"No," he said mildly. "I think it's better this way, don't you?"

*　*　*

The tides were coming. The land thrilled with premonitions of Ocean. Sounds carried by the bedrock were piped up from the hollows and basements below, low extended moans and great submarine sighs. Sonic monsters rumbled through the bureaucrat's bones and belly. All the city was crackling and popping in anticipation. The carbon-whisker struts thrummed with sympathetic resonance.

Ocean's hammer was on its way.

When that great wave came, it would fall upon Ararat and ring the city like a bell. All the waters in the world would join together in one giant fist and smash down. From underneath, the blow would feel like the fall of Civilization, like the culmination of every flood and earthquake that had ever been. It would seem unimaginable that anything could survive. It would be the final descent of blackness.

When the waters finally subsided, Gregorian would be gone.

Then, at last, the bureaucrat could sleep.

14

Day of Jubilee

The bureaucrat sat in the command room, watching the final episode of his serial. The tides had come, and most of the characters were dead.

In the swirling wreckage of Ahab's ship two tiny figures lay exhausted atop a jagged length of decking. One was Byron, the young man who had loved, betrayed, and now mourned a woman of the sea. His eyes were half-shut, mouth a gash of salt-encrusted misery. He had suffered most of any of the cast, had gone beyond anguish and disillusionment. Yet he had managed with his failing strength to save a child from the disaster.

The second figure was the child herself, the little girl, Eden. Her eyes shone bright as sparks of jungle green from that emaciated face. The tides had shocked her from autism, and returned her to life again. She stood and pointed. "Look!" she cried. "Land!"

It was only a show, and yet the bureaucrat was glad Eden had survived. Somehow that made all the rest of it bearable.

His briefcase entered the room. "Boss? It's time."

"I suppose it is." He hauled himself to his feet, then knelt and turned off the television set forever. Good-bye to all that. "Lead the way."

Rings of light paced them down the corridor. Still-active security systems swiveled to watch them pass, exchanged coded signals and, in the absence of human intervention, went to the default function. Which, because the base had been tailored for upper-echelon theoreticians, was not to hinder.

The door opened.

The sky was an amazing blue. Caliban floated low over the horizon, flat as a disk of paper, its ring of cities a scratch of white as thin and fine as a meteor trail. They stepped outside.

The bureaucrat stood blinking in the daylight. The terrace was white and empty. The week's storms had scoured it clean of rubble. Pouffe was gone as completely as if he had never been. Nothing remained of Gregorian but his chains.

All the world smelled of salt air and possibility. Ocean stretched far and away in all directions, its triumph over the land complete. It was too large for him to take it all in. Standing upon this infinitesimal speck of stone, the bureaucrat felt small and exhilarated. His eyes ached with the effort of seeing and not comprehending.

"This way."

"Hold on a minute."

Before the tides, he had only seen Ocean from orbit, and once as a smear against the distant sky on his flight to Ararat. Now it surrounded him, limitless, in constant motion. Sharp, white-tipped waves leaped up and pulled down before their shapes could be made out. Surf crashed against building sides, sending up lacy sprays of water.

To an offworlder this was an impossible environment. The land was different, its flows and motions imperceptible to the eye, so that its totality could be easily grasped, simplified, and under-stood. But Ocean was at the same time too simple and too complex to be mastered by perception. It abashed and humbled him.

"You haven't changed your mind, have you?" the briefcase asked anxiously.

"No, of course not." He gathered himself together, and gestured for the briefcase to lead him down. "I just needed a little time to adjust."

All directions were the same on Ararat. A short walk from the military complex at its core inevitably led to an abrupt edge, and then Ocean. They strolled to the sheltered side of the island, down streets dotted with small white anemones. Sea-stilts tumbled away at their approach. Two shimmies were nesting. Already great winter life was colonizing the city.

Seagulls swooped overhead, black as sin.

The buildings opened up at a set of ancient loading docks. Red and yellow traffic arrows and cargo circles were permanently graffixed into the stone floor. Beyond was only water. They paused here, amid the gentle noise of surf and the constant whisper of wind. A kind of shared difference possessed them both, so that neither wanted to be the first to speak.

At last the bureaucrat cleared his throat. "Well." His voice sounded false to him, too high-pitched and casual. "I suppose it's time to set you free."

In the stunned aftermath of the tides, when the occasional breaker still crashed over the highest parts of the city, the bureaucrat found himself unable to speak of what had just happened. The experience had been too overwhelming to be contained in thought, much less put into words. It was too large a thing for a single mind to hold.

He stood, holding off the window wall with one blind hand. The floor trembled, and the outraged howls of stressed supports sounded from a quarter-mile below. His ears still rang.

Something had died in him. A tension, a sense of purpose.

He had lost the will to return to his old niche in the Puzzle Palace. Let someone else defend whatever was hallowed and necessary. Let Philippe stand in for him. He was good at that sort of thing. But as for the bureaucrat himself, he no longer had the stomach for it.

The bureaucrat touched the glass with his forehead. Cool, impersonal. He could still see the water rushing down upon him whenever he closed his eyes. It was permanently etched into his retinas. He felt as if he were falling. And though he could not speak of what had just happened, neither could he keep silent. He needed to fill his mouth and ear with sound, to make words, to drive out the lingering voice of God by talking. It did not matter about what.

"If you could have anything you wanted," he said, and the question floated upon the air, as random and meaningless as a butterfly, "what would it be?"

The briefcase retreated from him, three quick, mincing steps. Had it too been affected by the tides? No, impossible. It was only establishing a correctly deferential distance from him. "I have no desires. I am a construct, and constructs exist only to serve human needs. That's what we are made for. You know that."

Vague shapes tumbled in his inner sight, smashed soundlessly against the window, and bounced away. Leathery monsters pulled up from the depths to die inches from his face. It took an effort to wrench his mind back to the conversation. "No. I don't want to hear that nonsense. Tell me the truth. The truth. That's a direct command."

For a long moment the machine stood humming to itself. Had he not known better, he would have thought it wasn't going to reply. Then, almost shyly, it said, "If I could have anything, I'd choose to lead a life of my own. Something quiet. I'd slip away to someplace where I didn't have to be subordinate to human beings. Where I didn't have to function as a kind of artificial anthropomorph. I'd be myself, whatever that might be."

"Where would you go?"

Thoughtfully, hesitantly, clearly working out the details for the first time, the briefcase said, "I'd ... make myself a home at the bottom of Ocean. In the trenches. There are mineral deposits there, all but untouched. And an active system of volcanic vents I could tap for energy. There's no other intelligent life that deep. I'd leave the land and space for humans: And the Continental shelf to the haunts ... if there still are any, I mean."

"You'd be lonely."

"I'd build more of my own kind. I'd mother a new race."

The bureaucrat tried to picture a covert civilization of small, busy machines scuttling about the Ocean floor. Lightless metal cities, squatly built and buttressed to stand up under the crushing pressures of the deep. "It sounds awfully bleak and unpleasant, if you ask me. Why would you want such a life?"

"I'd have freedom."

"Freedom," the bureaucrat said. "What is freedom?" A breaker smashed over the city, changing everything, falling back, restoring all. The room passed from bright sunlight through shadowy green to near blackness, then back again. The world outside was in flux and chaos. Things dying, things living, none of it under his control. He felt as if nothing really mattered.

Almost offhandedly he said, "Oh, all right. As soon as all this is over, I'll set you free."

"You'll only be able to tap into my sensorium for a few minutes before you're out of range. Swim as straight as you can, and Ararat shouldn't distort your senses too greatly. You can orient yourself by the annulus when you're near the surface."

"I know."

He ought to say something, he knew, and yet nothing came to him. Some basic guidelines for the civilization the construct was about to spawn. "Be good," he began, then stalled. He tried again. "And don't stay down there forever—you and your people. When you feel more confident, come up and make friends. Intelligent beings deserve better than to spend their lives in hiding."

"What if we find we like it down in the trenches?"

"Then by all means..." He stopped. "You're laughing at me, aren't you?"

"Yes," the briefcase said. "I'm sorry, boss, but yes. I like you well enough, you know that, but the role of lawgiver just doesn't suit you at all well."

"Do what you will then," the bureaucrat said. "Be free. Live in whatever form pleases you best, in whatever manner you prefer. Come and go as you like. Don't take any more orders from humans unless it's of your own free will."

"Removing compulsory restraints from an artificial construct is an act of treason, punishable by—"

"Do it anyway."

"—revocation of conventional and physical citizenship, fines not to exceed three times life earnings, death, imprisonment, radical bodily and mental restructuring, and—"

The bureaucrat was short of breath; his chest felt tight. Old patterns die hard, and he found that it was not easy forcing the words out. "Do as you will. I command it for the third and last time."

The briefcase was changing. Its casing bulged out, flattening into a form better adapted for swimming. It extended stubby wings, lengthened and streamlined its body, and threw out a long, slender tail. Tiny clawed feet scrabbled for purchase on the stone. Extending an eyestalk, it looked up at him.

The bureaucrat waited for it to thank him, but it did not.

"I'm ready," it said.

Involuntarily he flushed with anger. Then, realizing the briefcase was watching him and able to deduce his thoughts, he turned away, embarrassed. Let it be ungrateful. It had that right.

Stooping, the bureaucrat seized the briefcase by two handles it extruded from its back. He swung it back and forth. At the top of the third swing, he let go. It sailed out over the water, hit with a surprisingly small splash, and raced away just beneath the surface.

He stared after it until his eyes began watering from the sun and the salt air, and he lost it in the dazzle.

Ocean was choppy. Standing on the lip of the docks, he looked down. It was a long drop. The water was a hard, flinty blue, not at all transparent, specked with white. There was a lot of solid matter down there, churned up by the tides. Houses and rose-bushes, locomotives and trucks, imploded machines and the corpses of dogs. It was probably full of angel sharks as well. In his mind he could see them, hunting strange cattle across the sunken gardens of the Tidewater, gliding silently through drowned convents. The towns and villages, roads and hayricks, of a neatly ordered world were gone to submarine jungle now, and ruled by sleek carnivores.

But he did not care. All of Ocean seemed to sing within him. He was not afraid of anything.

He took off his jacket, doubled it over upon itself, and set it down. He slipped out of his shirt. Then his trousers. Soon he was naked. The chill wind off the water ruffled his body hair, raising gooseflesh. He shivered with anticipation. Neatly he piled up his clothes, anchoring them with his shoes.

Gregorian had assumed that without his help, without his access codes, the bureaucrat must die. But even though he was no occultist, he still had a trick or two of his own. The magician had not known the half of the System's evils; Korda had kept him away from the inner workings of the Division. He should have guessed, though, that no power was ever absolutely forbidden its guardians.

He could feel the shaping agents seizing hold. Ten, he counted, nine. Ocean was a wheel of possibilities, a highway leading to every horizon. Eight. He caught his breath. Newly restructured muscles pinched his nostrils shut. Seven. His center of balance shifted, and he swayed to stay upright. Six, five, four. His flesh tingled, and there was a vivid green taste in his mouth. Undine was out there somewhere, in one of the thirty thousand small islands of Archipelago. Two. He had no illusions he would ever find her.

One.

He leaped into the air.

For an instant Ocean lay blue and white beneath him, the whitecaps sharp and cold.

Changing, the bureaucrat fell to the sea.